AMBUSHED IN PARADISE

PARADISE SERIES

BOOK 12

DEBORAH BROWN

This book is a work of fiction. Names, characters, places and incidents are either the product of the author's imagination or used fictitiously. Any resemblance to actual persons, living or dead, or to actual events or locales is entirely coincidental. The author has represented and warranted full ownership and/or legal right to publish all materials in this book.

This book may not be reproduced, transmitted, or stored in whole or in part by any means, including graphic, electronic, or mechanical without the express written permission of the author except in the case of brief quotations embodied in critical articles and reviews.

This book is dedicated to Dr. Gwyn Richardson,
for being the best Doctor ever.

Thank you for saving my life.

AMBUSHED IN PARADISE

Chapter One

"He's dead."

The man's voice continued, "Shot in the line of duty."

"Nooo…" I heard a woman scream.

Was it me? I couldn't be sure. The world went dark.

The first time I laid eyes on Creole, he came up the driveway at The Cottages, lean and lethal, his dark hair pulled into a ponytail. Too bad he didn't stay around long enough to exchange a word of conversation.

"Creole," I murmured.

He pushed me up against the wall and kicked the front door closed. Tracing a trail with the tip of his tongue down my chin, down my neck, nibbling lightly, sending shivers through my body. Our first kiss. Taking me by surprise, he backed me against the door, pushing my hands above my head, holding them in place while devouring my lips.

I threw my hands out, struggling to ward off…what exactly?

* * *

In the early afternoon, dark clouds had rolled in,

bringing a noisy, pounding storm that covered the town of Tarpon Cove at the top of the Florida Keys in fat water drops that beat against the roofs and windows. At one point, the clouds were so low, I was certain I could reach up and touch them, just to see how full they were. Eventually, the rain rolled out over the Gulf, leaving rising temperatures and a taste of humidity hanging in the air.

I glanced sideways as Fabiana Merceau, my best friend and roommate, wiggled out of the house in a black string bikini, setting a tray of drinks at the end of the patio table.

"Stay down there." I pointed and put the finishing touches on the table settings for four.

The two of us had planned a dinner for our boyfriends—our favorite Mexican foods—and I'd picked up an assortment of beers for the guys.

"We could eat off paper plates." Fab smirked, handing me a margarita.

"And deprive me of the chance to drag out my collection of dishes? I don't think so." I'd chosen the mismatched Fiestaware in assorted beachy colors for tonight's dinner.

I had inherited the two-story Key West-style house from my aunt Elizabeth. One of my biggest projects had been turning the outdoor patio space that overlooked the pool into an entertainment area for family and friends. Any excuse to eat outside.

Fab clinked the edge of her martini glass

against mine. "To friends."

"You're up to something." I narrowed my eyes in an intense stare meant to suck the information out of her brain without having to ask.

"I hate it when you do that. Stop it." Her lips quirked, so I knew she was on the verge of laughter.

"Cherie." Didier appeared in the French doors that separated the patio from the living room.

Fab's boyfriend—Didier, just the one name—was tall, dark, and deliciously naughty. He'd charmed the entire family and was the love of Fab's life, and he felt the same way. He was also a roommate; the three of us made it work, as we often kept different hours.

Both Fab and I looked up.

He looked straight at me. "Help is coming up the driveway."

The undercover detective's name was supposedly Stephan, although Fab and I had never been able to verify that; his attitude about it was "mind your own business." The moniker of "Help" was one that Fab and I had given him.

Right on cue, the doorbell rang.

"What does that cretin want?" Fab turned up her nose.

"Fabiana," Didier chastised.

I pushed off the side of the table.

"Stop at the junk drawer and grab your Beretta," Fab called out.

I shook my head and hurried through the house, opening the door.

"You should be asking who's there before opening the door," Help grumped. He appeared disheveled and worn around the edges, as though it had been a tiring few days.

"I already knew it was you." I motioned. "Come in."

"Do you mind if we talk out here?" He led me a foot away from the entry, stopping in front of my latest acquisition, a two-tone pink hibiscus.

"I'm sorry to have to tell you this," he said with a solemn air.

I zeroed in on his face, his words filling me with dread, nausea creeping into my stomach. I couldn't bring myself to snap, "get to the point." Instead, I stared.

"Creole's dead."

* * *

"Madison Westin, open your damn eyes!" a familiar voice yelled.

I tried to jerk away from a foul odor, but to no avail; the last thing I expected to see was Fab leaning over me, waving a small bottle, her troubled eyes expecting something from me. I didn't have the energy to ask what.

It took me a moment to realize that I was lying on the daybed. *How did I get here? Was I out cold?*

Fab threw her arms around me, hugging me

tight. "Thank God."

"What happened?" I tried to shove a pillow under my head. I vaguely remembered the last thing that happened…words…dead and shot. Then understanding… Creole wasn't going to walk through the door and hold me in his lap and kiss me ever again.

I rolled onto my side, tears coursed down my cheeks. "He promised," I sobbed. "He promised."

It was early morning. Creole picked his jeans up off the floor, whispering, "I'll be back in a couple of days. You behave yourself." He leaned down and brushed my lips with his.

"And you?"

"No getting hurt," he promised.

We hooked pinkies.

He zipped up his pants, wiggling his hips, then sat on the bed and pulled me into his arms and kissed me, a kiss that was rough and sweet and possessive. A hungry kiss. It lasted longer than usual, and when his lips pulled away, I moaned.

"Where's Creole?" I wiped furiously at my face. Fab helped me to a sitting position. "I need to go to him."

Help stood on the other side of the room. He fidgeted from one foot to the other, briefly making eye contact. "The funeral's tomorrow."

"Tomorrow?" I shook my head, certain I hadn't heard correctly. "That's not possible." Water dripped off the end of my nose. "Why wasn't I called to handle the arrangements?"

"You're not his wife or a blood relative. Since Creole didn't have a next of kin, the department made the arrangements. He was cremated," Help said to the floor.

Didier crossed the room, sitting down and putting his arm around me. Fab sat on the other side, handing me a tissue.

"Where the hell is the chief?" Didier growled. "Why didn't he show up for the notification? Do you think this is the way Creole would've wanted the woman he loved to find out about his death?"

The Chief of Police in Miami was Creole's boss and a friend to both of us.

"I don't know all the details," Help said, an inscrutable expression on his face. "Three days ago, Creole's cover was blown. His partner's too. A shootout ensued, and they both died at the scene."

"Three days!" Fab shrieked.

"What took so long?" Didier asked. "I'm surprised you showed at all. You draw the short straw?"

"I volunteered." Help shot Didier a withering glare, but no one believed him. "I thought it would be better coming from someone Madison knows."

I sniffed and blew my nose, head pounding. My mind filled with thoughts of what Creole would want done. Anger seeped in. *I'd rather have heard the news from a stranger.* "Creole's

6

murderer…arrested? Dead? That would be better."

"This case is being kept under wraps, need-to-know basis, and I'm not on that list," Help said.

"Where's the funeral? The time?" I hugged myself for comfort. "I can get there early and take care of any last-minute details."

"Don't have the information on me." Help had one eye on the door, taking a step in that direction. "I'll…uh…call you."

"You get the damn information," Fab exploded. "It better be tonight."

Didier nodded in agreement.

"I loved him beyond reason," I whispered, mostly to myself. Tears filled my eyes again; I couldn't hold them back and didn't try very hard to keep them from streaming down my face. "I want the funeral information before you step foot off my property," I choked out, then gulped in some air and continued. "Screw me, and I'll make the biggest scene at Miami PD headquarters that they've ever seen. They can arrest me; I'll go to court, demand a jury trial, and invite the media."

I scooted into the space Fab had vacated and curled up in a ball as she followed Help out the door. She wouldn't let him out of her sight until she got the information. My hundred-year-old, long-haired black cat, Jazz, jumped up next to me. I laid my head on his side. "Dead." The tears came in a torrent.

Chapter Two

Mother commandeered a waterfront table at the family's favorite restaurant, The Crab Shack. I'd wanted to go home after the dreadful excuse for a funeral and sleep for a week. Questions floated through my mind, one after the other, with no answers and hardly a second to think. I was under the watchful stares of everyone in the family…waiting for me to do what, I wondered.

The day had dawned sunny and bright, the sky a brilliant blue offset by white, fluffy clouds. The extended Westin family had gathered graveside around an empty hole. It was a bleak scene, unlike the one a few rows south, which had chairs, strips of carpet, and an awning to block out the scorching heat of late morning.

Four men and two women stood off to one side of Creole's grave, not a one of them in uniform to mark the loss of one of their own. They talked quietly amongst themselves, and I didn't recognize a single face. None of them made eye contact or showed any curiosity about what our connection to Creole might be. We might have stood there all day if it hadn't been for Fab, who stormed off to get answers. She returned riding in the front of a hearse, a backhoe not far behind.

Fab got out, urn in hand, looked around, approached the mound of dirt, and set it down. She moved to stand between me and Didier and whispered, "The older lady in the office apologized but said no service had been arranged. They planned to fill in the plot later."

"This is the damndest..." Mother started sadly.

Brad stepped forward, patting Mother on the shoulder. "I can think of something nice to say." He walked over and stood next to the urn. When he cleared his throat, the small group went silent, and he related a story about his friendship with Creole.

I mentally planned a memorial service on our favorite beach. What would Creole want? He'd want drinking, laughter, and not a sad eye. I could do that.

Didier came forward, talking about his and Creole's love of the two women in their lives. He ended, "We'll all miss him."

Two of the other men stepped forward, one after the other, and mumbled a few words, nothing personal; it sounded as though neither man knew Creole. Either that or a few words of attempted tribute wasn't their area of expertise.

The server came around for drink orders. "Margarita, rocks, with salt. Bring a pitcher," I said.

Mother cleared her throat. "Just bring her one."

That's just the sort of thing a grown woman didn't appreciate: her mother telling her how much she could drink. A repeat of this morning, when I'd wanted to drive myself to the funeral and was directed to get in the back seat of my own vehicle, carpooling with Fab, Didier, and Brad. I leaned my head against the window, closing my eyes and shutting out the small talk.

Fab turned her head so no one else could hear her order. "I'll take two martinis and a margarita."

"Love you," I mouthed across the table.

When the drinks arrived, Mother frowned at the three glasses sitting in front of Fab. I downed half of mine and broached the subject that had been on my mind. "Spoon, I'd like to ask a favor."

"Anything," he responded.

Mother clutched his arm. "I'm trying to get him to wait until he hears what someone wants before just agreeing."

"I don't think you need to worry; the big guy isn't in the habit of waving his magic wand." I winked. "Besides, I'm not just any person." *This wasn't going to be easy.* I downed the rest of my margarita. "I want to know what happened to Creole." 'Shot dead' wasn't enough to put this behind me. *At least, not anytime soon.* "Would you hit up your connections, find out exactly what went down? The murderer – what happened to him?"

"That's a terrible idea," Mother said. "Creole wouldn't want you involved."

"I agree with your mother," Spoon said.

"Me too," Brad said.

I gritted my teeth, determined not to blurt out something hurtful. I looked around the table. "I'd hope that, if any of you were in my shoes, and I sincerely hope you never are, I'd be more sympathetic."

Fab nudged my leg under the table.

Didier murmured something in French. His hand covered mine and gently squeezed.

"You'll have to translate later." I eyed the second margarita and reached out, fingers hooking around the stem of the glass and dragging it across the table.

To fill the awkward silence, Brad changed the subject. "Liam called this morning. He's sorry he couldn't make it, but he had his first final and couldn't reschedule."

Liam was an unofficially adopted member of the family. His mother and Brad used to date, and when she got her big acting break, sending her to California, Liam had stayed with Mother to finish his senior year in high school, then got accepted to the University of Miami.

"We talked." Liam had made me laugh with stories of college-boy pranks, but I wasn't in the mood to share. "He's coming this weekend. I'm looking forward to him staying with me. We're going to the beach."

"A better idea would be for the two of you to stay at our house." Mother patted Spoon's arm. "We have plenty of room," she insisted.

When Liam lived with her, she'd watched him

like a hawk. She didn't share well—actually, at all—and apparently that wasn't going to change anytime soon.

I looked at Brad, whose face telegraphed, "She does the same thing to me."

I was pretty much on my way to getting sauced, having finished my second glass. I turned the glass upside down, eyeing the inside. Nothing came out.

Fab giggled.

The server had delivered menus, which I barely gave a glance. The thought of food didn't appeal. Not even taking home leftovers held interest, and I constantly took any food left on my plate to-go for breakfast the next morning.

The ringing of my phone saved me from having to order, and I fished it out of my purse. Mac Lane's smiling face popped up on the screen. If I were sober, I'd have groaned and maybe hit the ignore button. I tried to remember whether I'd ever done that – probably not. I'd inherited the property on the beach from my aunt and hired Mac shortly after; as a manager, the woman was calm under chaos.

"Yeah, what now?" I answered, a touch surly.

"Big plumbing problem… Water can shoot a decent distance into the air, did you know that?"

"Sounds messy."

"Didn't you say to get my ass on the phone when the cops are involved?" Mac blew a loud huff of air through the speaker.

I got distracted by the loud noises in the background and Mother glaring at me from the other end of the table. I turned away slightly, and Fab leaned in; damn her eavesdropping. "If *anyone* calls, you better tell them the earth is coming to an end, got it?" I told Mac.

"I just won't answer. You'll be here soon?"

I glanced up at Fab, and she nodded. "Give me ten, fifteen minutes." I hung up, wondering what plumbing had to do with the cops. I didn't care about the answer; actually, I was ecstatic at the opportunity to leave and shoved back my chair. "Sorry to break up lunch," I said, not sounding the least bit sorry. "There's an emergency at The Cottages."

"Sit back down," Mother ordered. "Mac is capable of handling anything."

"Mother, I'm the owner, the police are involved, and I need to be there."

"What's new about the cops stopping at The Cottages? You should think about selling." Mother looked exasperated.

"Or find a good management company," Brad suggested with a half-smile. "Give the weirdos the boot."

My brother needed to mind his own business.

Fab stood. "I'll drive."

"No, you won't," Didier growled. "I'll drive you two. I haven't had a drink."

I flashed Brad a payback smile. "No reason to break up lunch; you can entertain Mother and

Spoon. I'm sure they'll give you a ride, since it's on the way." I wanted to laugh at the withering glare he sent me and ignored the warning look in his eyes promising retribution.

I overheard Didier reassuring Mother that he'd get me home and call and update her.

"Race you to the door," I said to Fab as she looped her arm in mine. "Once we get out of sight, I'll kick off my shoes so I can beat you." I slowed going past the bar. "I want a margarita to go."

"I suggest you not dawdle and get your butt to the car before your mother decides to follow us."

We crossed the parking lot and climbed into my black Hummer, which was always in pristine shape, thanks to Fab. She couldn't drive an auto that had a speck of dirt on it and had some high school kid on speed dial who came with his own cleaning supplies. I crawled into the back, kicking off my sandals, and put my feet between the front seats. Although the car was legally registered to me, I rarely got to drive. Fab always had a ready excuse that my driving gave her a headache or some other health malady. Driving the speed limit never made *me* sick.

"You, young lady…" Didier turned and pointed at me before putting his foot to the gas and roaring out of the driveway. "Are you telling the truth about there being a disaster in the making or some such drama?"

"Moi?" I feigned innocence. "This is what I heard: plumbing…water everywhere…cops on the way." I rubbed my painted toenails on his sleeve. "Could you take off your shirt when we get there? You'll be such a hit with the female regulars and out-of-town guests."

Fab rubbed his arm, laughing.

Didier remained silent. The only indication he'd heard me was the shaking of his head.

"Not my fault that you're man candy," I said.

Fab and I laughed.

Chapter Three

A police car pulled away from the curb as we rounded the corner to The Cottages: ten individual cottages, all brightly painted, that sat around a u-shaped driveway and backed up to the beach. The pool and barbeque area were on the far side of the property.

Kevin blocked the entrance, arms crossed, and judging by his expression, clearly annoyed. He was decked out in wrinkled shorts and a stained t-shirt, his sweaty brown hair sticking to his face—not his usual attire: a neatly pressed sheriff's deputy uniform. No wonder he was having a minor hissy fit, shifting on his feet, being bothered on his day off. Glaring, he stepped aside.

Fab pulled into a parking space in front of the office. We all climbed out. Mac came running down the driveway and came to a screeching halt in front of Didier, her tongue nearly hanging out. She patted her overly large girls—which couldn't have moved if they wanted to in the white, button-down shirt, the buttons straining, threatening to pop off—and adjusting the black skirt of her schoolgirl uniform. She must not have been able to locate a pair of saddle shoes and had opted for orange flip-flops instead.

"What do women see in him?" Kevin asked, showing up at my side and staring at Didier.

"You need glasses." I was surprised, to put it mildly, at realizing he was referring to Didier. I tried to will Kevin to go away, but it didn't work.

"Such a big mess. No one's answering their phone, and I don't have anyone else to call," Mac said in a harried voice, directing her words to Didier.

I cleared my throat, a reminder that I was standing next to her. "Calm down and start from the beginning."

"Crum was sitting on the toilet...doing his business, and he says a snake licked his butt."

"What a bunch of..." Kevin shook head. "You have the dumbest dick tenants."

"You live here, are you in that group?" I quirked my eyebrow. We had a tenuous relationship. We'd been working on getting along, for family reasons past and currently present, due to his nephew, Liam.

Kevin's eyes narrowed.

"Crawled up out of the drain," Mac continued. "Crum grabbed his shotgun... Not sure what it was doing in the bathroom. Kaboom." She threw her arms in the air. "He blew the porcelain god to bits, hitting a water pipe, and whoosh!" she yelled. "The ceiling got a good spraying."

As hard as I tried to stop it, I laughed. It took

me a minute to recover.

"Got the water turned off at the street; can't stay like that." Mac shuddered. "We're full up. We'll have to relocate everyone to a motel."

Didier pulled his phone out of his pocket. "I'll get someone over here."

Mac practically swooned. She licked her lips. "Almost forgot, there's more than one snake. I saw a second one crawl out with my own eyes."

"Gives new meaning to snaking the toilet." I laughed. Everyone else pretty much thought I'd lost my mind. "We need to get a snake wrangler or whatever… And when they get out here, they're to check the pipes and under Crum's cottage."

"I've got this covered." Didier questioned Mac, and with her directions, headed to Crum's cottage. Fab went with him.

"We need to get the water turned back on," I called to Didier. "Crum can stay with a friend."

"He doesn't have friends." Mac snorted.

"Let's make one thing clear: Crum's not to use the bushes as a bathroom," I told Mac.

"Mac," Didier called and waved her over.

Kevin groaned. "Tell Crum, I catch him doing his business in public, he's going to jail." He stared at me. "Don't start with me. I'm a mean ass, got it? You're lucky I was here when Officer Johnson showed up. I assured him that no one had been hurt, and we laughed over a few snake references. He was happy to get out of here."

"Hiya," shrieked a female voice from behind me.

Kevin and I turned as Miss January tripped down the stairs from her cottage, a man hanging onto her arm jerking her upright.

"She needs to be committed," Kevin said in disgust. He nodded and jogged towards his cottage.

I'd inherited Miss January and Joseph along with the property. Both were terminal, according to their doctors, but the lure of cigarettes and alcohol kept them alive.

"Who are you?" I asked the man.

"This is my new beau…" She fluttered her eyelashes at him.

"Nestor Pace." He extended his hand.

I kept my hands clasped in front of me. "No offense. I don't shake hands."

"You one of them germ folks?" He rubbed his hand on the seat of his pants, inspected the palm, and declared, "It's pretty clean."

One would guess Miss January to be in her eighties, thanks to a rough life and hard living, but in actuality, she was forty. The man by her side was younger; dressed in wrinkled Dockers and a golf shirt, he made a passable first impression. I hoped he didn't have a hidden agenda. It was none of my business, but I had come to love her.

"Where did you meet?" I asked.

"Custer's on singles night," Miss January

cooed. "We're serious, you know," she said in a whisper that could be heard at the end of the driveway.

I flinched at the mention of the rat-hole bar. Hook-ups from there came with the risk of a social disease.

"We're in a hurry." Nestor pulled Miss January in the direction of the street. "We'll catch up later."

"If anything happens to her, you'll answer to me." I flashed a phony smile.

Didier came around the side of the building, complete exasperation on his face. "I've got a man on the way. He assures me he can cap the pipe for tonight and get it fixed tomorrow." He looked expectantly at me. "Fab?" I shrugged. Last I saw, she was following him. Must have wandered off somewhere. He turned to Mac and asked again.

"The office," she answered.

Didier headed in that direction, Mac hot on his heels. I grabbed her arm. "He's taken. His girlfriend will shoot you. Keep that in mind. Who's Nestor, and why haven't I heard about him?"

"You've had a few things to deal with, and I was going to avoid bothering you for another day and *then* load up on you." Mac sounded frustrated. "Some guy Miss January's banging. I don't think it's serious, but I did see him coming in with a big plastic bag and wondered if it held his worldly possessions. So that could mean he'll be around for a while."

"What else?"

"Joseph is drinking more than usual. The last I looked, he had passed out on the couch."

"Now stop drooling on Didier," I admonished.

"You know how easy I am for hot, hunky men." She gave me a slight smile.

I swayed on my feet, and Mac steadied me.

"What the hell?" she said, the concern evident in her voice.

"I'm hungover. The tequila has worn off, and my head's killing me. I didn't eat, and I want to go home," I whined.

Mac held her arms out. "I'll carry you."

"Don't be ridiculous. I'm going to go sit in the car. Probably lie down on the back seat."

Mac grabbed my arm. "Pretty dress."

"It was Creole's favorite." I looked down at the fitted top and full skirt. "Hot pink isn't funeral appropriate, but who cares. No one else's opinion seemed important today. I need a favor, but I can't ask you today; I don't want anyone to hear."

"I'll do it." Mac beamed.

"Walk naked in the middle of the street."

Mac threw her head back and laughed. "I'll need liquor to pull that off." She wiggled.

Fab came running across the driveway. "I leave you for a second, and what happens?" She practically pushed Mac aside.

"I need more tequila and a nap…or just the latter."

"I've also had enough of today. We're going home, and Didier will take care of us. You, girlie…" She glared at Mac. "You're lucky I don't black your eyes. You need a boyfriend, tell Madison's mother; she's a one-woman dating service."

I flashed Mac an "I told you so" smile.

Fab reached out and grabbed my arm. "I guess Didier's had enough; he's got the engine running."

"Where have you been?" I asked as we cut across the driveway.

"I got the latest gossip from the tourists. Recognized a couple as having been here before. They're a good source of information. You'd think they'd mind their own business, but they don't and they're bold about it."

Didier had the back door open and helped me in. He walked Fab around to the passenger side, kissing her before opening the door.

Chapter Four

I'd been awake for hours. I stayed in bed, reading, thinking if I stalled long enough, Fab and Didier might leave for the day. Eventually, desperate for coffee, I gave up and slunk downstairs. I knew the coast wasn't clear based on the voices coming from the kitchen.

"Bon morning," I said, showing off my ability to butcher the French language, and headed straight to the cupboard for a mug before retrieving my can of "ick," as Fab called my flavored coffee drink. Her coffee choice reminded me of a Turkish blend I'd tried once that made me think my hair would burn down to the roots.

"Bonjour," Didier returned patiently.

Putting my mug in the microwave, I closed the door and pointed to the island countertop. "What's my Glock doing out?"

"Happy you noticed. You're going to need it tomorrow when we go to see what Brick wants. 'Stolen gifts,' he said."

"I don't know..." I turned to the garden window, surveying the front of the house. When the microwave dinged, I retrieved my coffee and took a long swig.

Replacing the square kitchen window with a six-foot-long one with a shelf had been one of my favorite renovations. I picked a dead leaf off an African violet, tossing it in the trash. All of my projects turn out to be *the* favorite.

"Madison, I'd like you to come over here and sit next to Fab," Didier said, his face hard to read.

I turned back around and scowled at him. If he was going to get all dominant, I'd need to remind him that I wasn't his girlfriend.

"The safety rules still apply. Just because there's two of you for me to look out for, don't think I'll be a pushover." He flexed his biceps.

"See his face?" Fab pointed. "That means he's serious about our safety. You might as well get over here and listen up."

"You two are the bossiest. I'm going to need more coffee."

"I'll make it; I know how you like it," Didier offered.

Fab snorted.

I shuffled over to the island and slipped onto a stool, one eagle eye on Didier while he showed off his prowess at boiling water. It touched me that he made my coffee exactly like I would have.

He set my mug in front of me. "I would expect Creole to do the same thing, not letting Fab jump into danger with both feet. So same rules as before. There's a problem, you call or text.

Consider me backup if you need it."

It hadn't escaped my notice that those I'd called, wanting answers to my questions about Creole, couldn't be located. Fab and I needed to be really careful; we suddenly had fewer reliable allies.

"Don't roll your eyes." Didier shook his finger at me.

Damn, I didn't look down quick enough.

"I didn't spend all those hours at the shooting range doing nothing," he said. "Standing around talking, like some of them do. Turns out I'm a pretty good shot."

Fab ran around the counter, throwing herself in his arms. "Don't worry, we're going to be careful. Aren't we?"

"Okay," I mumbled.

Didier winked at me.

I stood and headed to the stairs. "I'll be ready early. Today, I've got to check on Jake's, so I'm going to get dressed. See you later. I'll be gone most of the day."

"I'll be waiting right here," Fab said.

I turned to see Fab smiling at me, the scary one that only frightened others.

"I can drive you where you want to go," she offered.

"You don't have to do that." I hopped up two steps at a time.

"I want to," she yelled.

* * *

"What are you up to?" Fab came close to screeching as I climbed into the passenger seat, pulling my jean skirt down.

When I came downstairs and no one was around, I figured I'd sneak out and apologize later. One step ahead of me, Fab was already sitting in the driver's seat, engine running and air conditioning keeping the heat at bay. No one sat in their car in Florida without it turned on unless they wanted to melt into a sweaty mess.

I shook my head. "Use your indoor voice." This must be killer-looks day. "Sounds way better than some variation of shut up." Finally laughter. That was a good sign.

"First stop?" Fab demanded. "Then spill."

"Jake's," I sighed. "I need some time to myself. I'm sure you understand." I pasted my face against the passenger window, staring out at the water.

Fab knocked me in the shoulder.

"Ouch," I whined. Knowing she'd never give up, I said, "I'm not going to ask you to keep things from Didier. I have a few things on my own agenda, and you jeopardizing your relationship by sneaking around with me isn't on the list."

"Didier and I talked last night. Neither of us was happy with your family's response to you wanting answers regarding Creole's death. We get that they want to protect you and don't want anything bad to happen or whatever, but we both agreed that we'd want the answers you're seeking. Didier will understand and keep your confidences if you ask. But he won't stand by and let you go off half-cocked. You have me for that." Her features were rigid and hard to read.

Scary girl slipped into the driver seat.

"Stop at the lighthouse. Our lawyer friend usually gets to work at the crack of dawn and sticks close to the office. Let's see what she can find out."

"Have you noticed Phil has made herself scarce of late?"

"Right after we set her up with my brother. I tried to get information out of her, like if they'd seen one another again. The first time, she told me in a friendly tone to mind my own business." I screwed up my nose. "My second attempt, she answered with a glare."

"Your mother's track record of fix-ups isn't that great. Maybe this is another fail."

"It was my idea, can't push all the blame on her, although it's okay with me if you do."

The Overseas Highway was quiet, even though it was almost midday; the tourist traffic bypassing the Cove for keys to the south was trickling through town. It made it easy for Fab to fly down the road, rolling into Jake's parking lot and slowing in front of the lighthouse that housed the Law Office of Philipa Grey. A sheet of paper was taped to the door, saying "At Jake's" with an arrow. Fab scored a parking spot next to the front door.

Jake's, a tiki-style dive bar, shared the driveway with an old 40s gas station renamed Junker's. It had been given a spit shine, and an antiques garden store had moved in, though some might say the inventory was nothing more than trash. Twinkie Princesses, a roach coach parked parallel to the curb, hadn't served a lick of food since I owned the property, which I overlooked since the rent was paid on time. The lighthouse had shown up in the middle of the night, offloaded from some mammoth hauler, I presumed, because no one saw a thing. Some deal of a deal, friend of a friend, with Fab smack in the middle. She reminded me often that she owned the building, and I reminded her I owned the land. Stalemate, as they say in chess.

Now there was a game I'd never been more than barely marginal at. Lack of interest and skill, and it didn't take long to forget the names of the pieces and how they moved.

Fab and I got out of the car. Music drifted out from inside the bar when we opened the door. I waved to the new bartender, Doodad, who replaced Phil when she passed the state bar and hung out her lawerly shingle. There had been a few complaints from women who said "that new guy isn't very nice." Since they couldn't elaborate, I ignored them. I wanted to tell them it wasn't in his job description to make every woman who walked through the door "happy."

Fab nodded to the outside deck, where Phil sat at the reserved table by herself. "I'm going to order us some lunch."

"I'm not hungry."

"You didn't eat yesterday either."

"I'll have a bottled water." I turned and headed out to the patio. "Philipa," I said and sat at the end of the table, adjusting my chair so I could see inside; if a fight broke out, I'd have a ringside seat.

She smiled back. She'd always been a straight shooter, and it didn't escape my notice that she fidgeted in her seat.

Fab hustled through the door, setting down a beer bucket filled with waters, taking out two. "Hope I didn't miss anything," she said, sitting next to me and handing me one.

"I need some information," I said to Phil. "This is a rush job, and I'll expect to pay whatever it costs."

She raised her eyebrow. "A new client?" She looked back and forth between me and Fab.

I shook my head. "I want to know everything you can find out about what happened to Creole. The how, the why, the when, and what happened to the shooter."

Phil looked down for a moment before slowly raising her head. "I've been meaning to tell you that my information guy left town. Personal problems." She smiled weakly. "I thought about replacing him with another of his ilk and decided against it. In the future, now that I have a reputation to protect, I'll be using a reputable investigation firm. Anything that approaches the grey line isn't a service I'll be offering."

"No, I suppose not," I said slowly, trying to discern if there was a word of truth in what she'd just spouted. Maybe she'd gotten into trouble using this source of hers. Heck of a way to start a law career.

"You're going to be a lawyer without a decent investigator?" Fab looked suspicious. "I take it you're not doing criminal law."

"I haven't decided on a specialty; my options are open. Thinking about contract law."

Sounds boring. "If you like that sort of thing," I said absently.

Mac blew through the doors, reminiscent of a strong hurricane. "Mind if I join you?" she asked, already dragging over a chair.

"Take my place," Phil stood. "I have an appointment to get to. Sorry I couldn't be more helpful. If I find someone, I'll let you know," she said somewhat apologetically.

Phil squeezed out of her seat, and Mac took her place and banged down a bottle of beer. Phil waved and practically ran out of the bar.

"What was that all about?" Fab asked in confusion.

"Good question." I stared after Phil's

retreating back. "For one thing, it was a very poor way to end our discussion."

"Her no-more-'shady'-business-dealings rule sure sounds like she's kicking us to the curb." Fab watched as the woman exited the bar.

"She's up to something," I said to Fab. "You need to find out what it is. I'm tired of feeling like I'm a step behind."

"I know you have a job." Fab squinted at Mac.

Mac thrust her torso forward. "I've got free food privileges. I'm also dropping hints that that hot bartender of yours can park his tennis shoes under my bed anytime."

"The Cottages? Anyone die? Arrested? You know, the usual stuff," I asked, not giving her the opportunity to reveal graphic fantasies starring her and Doodad.

"The drunks got sloshed early and crashed in their cottages. The guests are all happy — I set up a tour bus deal for them that includes a stop where the women can shop and the men can drink. Today's quiet. Tomorrow...I'll end up paying for today when all hell breaks loose. But don't worry; I've got you both on speed dial."

"You know everyone in town." I thought twice about what I was about to ask and, against my better judgment, asked away. "Know a really good hacker, one with an impeccable track record?"

Mac scratched between her breasts, a thoughtful look on her face. "Gunz – Fab's friend." She jerked her head in Fab's direction. "You know I once had a crush on him. Then I met his sisters, both of them, and got over it real quick. Hot mess is too kind."

I turned my gaze on Fab.

Fab quirked an eyebrow. "Are you forgetting that you don't like Gunz and the feeling's mutual?"

"If I can do the bygones thing, then so can he." By that point, my frustration was at a boiling point at not being able to get the information I wanted. I'd never had this kind of problem before; it had always been a phone call away.

"I'll test the waters. I'll ding his vanity by asking him for the name of someone else." Fab laughed devilishly.

Cook's son delivered our food; since we always ordered the same thing, he knew which plate went where. He'd brought a couple of extra plates, and I gladly shared my enchiladas with Mac, which brought a growl from Fab.

Chapter Five

"Hey, ladies." Doodad came outside to clear our plates, putting them on a tray and setting it aside. He took a beer bottle from under his arm, exchanging it for Mac's empty one. "Doll." He winked at her.

When Phil got ready to leave, she'd chosen the man to succeed her as bartender: Charles Wingate III, aka Doodad, a retired sea captain. Well over six feet tall, he cleaned up well; his work uniform—shorts and a shirt—beat the dirty jeans he had on when I first met him.

Fab nudged me under the table.

I watched as Doodad and Mac did a googly-eyed dance of flirtation, thinking no one would notice. I'd put money on the two having already done a horizontal tango and her being here to let him know she was ready for the next go-round.

Doodad broke the eye contact and clapped his hand down on the table in front of me. "You two women ever need backup, I'm available."

I nodded. Fab checked him over, and whatever conclusions she came to she kept to herself.

"There's a man at the bar that would like to

talk to you." Doodad pointed. "The old one on the end. I can vouch for him."

"Does he have a name?" I asked. "Why me?"

"Butch Randall – everybody calls him Corndog. Lived here most of his life. Nice guy. You apparently came recommended." Doodad flashed a slight smile.

"Corndog?" My eyebrows shot up.

"Forty years ago, he was corndog-eating champion several years in a row; the name stuck."

"How many do you have to wolf down to get the crown?" I wondered out loud.

"Don't ask." Doodad shuddered. "The story includes vomit."

"Thanks for the heads up."

"I've got a few vomity stories," Mac boasted. "Not a one of them is fun."

"For an old loner that lives in the weeds, you seem to know everyone in town," I told Doodad.

"You run a name by me, and if I don't know the person, I'll find out," he said. "Just so you know, I respect that your business is yours alone to be sharing, and I won't be disclosing anything I hear, and that includes your friend here." He eyed Fab. "I've got your backs."

"Thanks. Send Corndog over."

"See you later." Mac stood and headed into the bar behind Doodad.

An older gentleman strode over to the table. He had short gunmetal-grey hair, combed back, and wore jeans and a button-down shirt.

He looked at me directly. "Madison Westin," he said, a friendly smile on his weathered face. He introduced himself, holding out his hand.

Fab shook his hand.

"This is my partner, Fab," I introduced and motioned to a chair.

He sat, setting down a bottle of beer. "I'm an old friend of Gus Ivers. Had plenty of nice things to say about you."

"Gus is dead and has been for years." I pointed to Fab. "She was his favorite, not me." I put my hands on the arms of the chair, about to stand.

"Sit back down. Hear me out. I know the old devil's dead. But you did come recommended by his friend and neighbor, Tolbert Rich. He relayed how the two of you saved him from a drug-addled neighbor."

"You have neighbor problems?" Fab asked.

"I own a piece of property down in the dock area, the part that's under revitalization. All of it is waterfront." He took a long pull on his beer. "It's standing in the way of some grandiose plans by a local businessman. I don't think he'd kill me for it, but maybe, at the very least, try to scare me to death. He probably thinks he'll get my grandson to sell it dirt cheap at my gravesite. Thing is the little bastard isn't getting a penny to stick up his nose. I'm a little nervous about what will happen if that fact gets around."

So often when folks didn't look like they had two nickels to rub together, it turned out those looks were deceiving, and this was one of those times.

"Does this businessman have a name?" Fab asked.

"James Bordello. Heard of him?"

"I've met him," I said. "Not terribly impressed."

"He's got a reputation for doing whatever it takes to close a business deal," Fab said.

"What do you want from me?" I asked.

"I want you to find enough dirt on him to keep him away. He's threatening to put a light under some old rumors that I killed my first wife. He's spreading gossip that she was murdered."

"Did you do it?" I asked.

He leaned in and said, "No. All I know is that one day she up and disappeared."

I liked his unequivocal "No" and that he maintained eye contact.

"Maggs was a pain in the ass, but kill her? Why, when I could have divorced her, like I did my second wife? The third one died on the operating table while they were attempting to repair a heart valve. Much as I bitch and moan, I have a type—I like my women mouthy and feisty." Corndog released a bark of laughter.

"What are Bordello's plans for the property?" I asked.

"Bordello wants to level the property and

build condos and an office building to house his own mini-empire. I've got to come up with an alternate plan so that if I do disappear, mysteriously or otherwise, Bordello and his ilk will never get their hands on the property."

"I thought there were strict building codes as to how much tearing down could be done in what's considered a historical section," I said, horrified by the idea that all the old buildings would be torn down.

"Bordello laughed when I insisted a renovated area rich in history would be better for the neighborhood." He scrubbed a hand through his hair. "Just last week, someone started a grass fire across the street. Didn't do any damage; the fire department got it out before it could spread. I think it was meant as a message. Every time I go near the area, something happens; the time before that, my car disappeared. Never was found. It wasn't one of my vintage ones, but still a loss, as I only carried minimal insurance."

"In the interest of full disclosure, I should tell you my brother is friends with Bordello," I said. This had me wondering if my brother's business practices would be changing. So far, he had a good reputation. I guess I'd have to ask him. "I know he and Bordello were talking about some kind of business deal, but I'm not sure anything got signed on the dotted line. I do know Brad wouldn't be involved in hurting anyone."

"The area wasn't going to stay a rat hole for

forever," Fab interjected. "I'd heard that the plan being kicked around by the city was for loft living, trendy shops, and restaurants. A few fun amusements along the lines of Key West."

"I'm happy to hear that you're interested in what happens in the Cove," Corndog said in a sober tone. "At the last council meeting, it became apparent that Bordello has at least two board members in his pocket. He's gathering power so he can control the changes. I expect him to try changing the name of the town to Bordello Key."

"That will never happen, no matter how important he thinks he is," I said. "I'm for cleaning up the area and like that the plan is for more of a renovation than a tear-down and rebuild. There are some historical buildings down in the area that I'd hate to see go." I'd watched closely as emotions flitted across his face as he talked about the area and was convinced he loved it and wanted to be involved in any changes. "I can get a background check for you, but then what? Blackmail? That's a bad idea."

"If anything happens to me…" His voice dropped, eyes narrowed. "I want Bordello prosecuted."

"Seems to me that you're passionate about the area; why not develop it yourself?" I suggested. "That way, you can call the shots."

It was clear he liked the idea. "That's a lot to

think about."

Fab kicked me under the table; she was ready to wrap up this impromptu meeting. "What you need is a full-time bodyguard," she said. "We're not in that business, but if it's something you're interested in, I can get a man on the job tomorrow."

"I'll think about it," he said, not outright liking the idea.

"I'll get on finding out everything there is to know about Bordello." I hoped I could keep my promise, seeing as I was short one information specialist.

Chapter Six

The next morning, Fab hit all the signals right, and we arrived at Brick's luxury car lot, Famosa Motors, located in South Miami, without a minute to spare.

"There's an SUV in Brick's parking spot, so he's here; no one else would have the nerve to park there." I craned my head around. "No one who works the front has shown up yet. We caught a break and don't have to pretend to be nice to anyone but him. I think you need better backup than me. I'm not bringing my A-game – I'm not even sure what that is."

"Do you hear me complaining?" Fab asked in exasperation. "Now get out of the car."

We got out and entered through the closest door.

"The sooner we get done here, the sooner we can go home and go for a swim," Fab said.

Walking through the lobby, I challenged, "I'll race you up the stairs."

Fab hooked her arm in mine and held on. "We're not going to annoy Brick before we even sit down. I'll handle this meeting. You listen and do what you do best – come up with a plan."

We walked up the stairs to Brick's second-floor office and found him leaning back in his chair, phone to his ear. Fab took a seat in front of the desk, and for a change, I sat on the windowsill that overlooked the car lot and street below. The only thing going on was the half-dozen cars lined up for repairs.

Brick abruptly ended his call with a grunt. He sat up in his chair. "This is a delicate family matter," he said, voice low and edgy. "Distant relatives, thank goodness."

"Something about stolen gifts," Fab prompted, already eyeing the door for a quick escape.

One corner of his mouth lifted in a smile. "Two weeks ago, the Famosas put on a splashy wedding for my great-nephew. Presents stacked to the ceiling and even more cash, all handed directly to the groom, Neil, who made the colossal mistake of handing it to his mother, Rosarita, for safe-keeping. Once everyone left, she had everything hauled over to her penthouse."

"This all sounds really nice," Fab interrupted; her tone of voice said otherwise.

"Just hold on." He graced her with an indulgent smile. "Rosarita then claimed that, while the couple was on their honeymoon, a break-in happened and the gifts – including the cash, which she said she'd placed in a purse – were stolen. She didn't report it to the police, although she did report it to building security."

"What are we supposed to do?" Fab asked. "Check pawn shops?" She turned up her nose. "Do you have a list of the gifts?"

I turned my face back to the window, rolling my eyes. Nothing surprised me when it came to the Famosa family.

"Got it all planned out for you." He sounded pleased with himself. "You go over to Rosarita's place and check it out from top to bottom. The last thing I want is for Neil to get arrested for filing a false insurance claim if she's got the gifts stashed. They might both end up in jail."

I twisted on the sill. "What makes you think Rosarita would steal from her son?"

"She had access, opportunity. A hundred large in a purse…people would do almost anything."

Fab whistled. "Remind me to invite your relatives to my wedding."

"I'll guard the gifts." I laughed. "You hang onto the money."

Brick shot me a dirty look.

I wanted to boast that my family doesn't steal but refrained.

Brick scribbled on a notepad. "Here's the address." He ripped the paper off and handed it to Fab.

"Does Rosarita pack?" I asked. "You know, carry a gun."

"She's a sweet older woman," Brick grunted.

"And possible thief," I mumbled. "I don't suppose you have a door key so we don't have to bother with security guards and probably surveillance equipment."

"Rosarita's got a standing weekly appointment at The Hair Bar. It's today." Brick checked his watch. "You've got time to get to her place before she leaves."

"Forward a picture," I said, hating to mention that my neck hairs were standing on end. This meeting was going well so far; he hadn't shouted or threatened us once. "I hope you haven't left out anything that would get us shot or tossed in jail."

It hadn't escaped my notice that, in addition to ignoring me, he'd ignored most of my questions.

"Why doesn't Neil just confront his mother?" Fab asked.

"Neil's a good son. He doesn't believe she'd do such a thing. Me, on the other hand… This has got her greedy paw prints all over it."

"I'll give you a call when I get the job done." Fab stood, took a couple of steps toward the door, stopped, and shot me a "move it" look.

I slipped off the windowsill and said to Brick, "I'm trying to get ahold of Casio."

He stared back at me, as if he didn't know what I was talking about.

"Your brother," I reminded him. "Would you ask him to call me?"

"Casio's a busy man. He did mention that you've been burning up his phone. He hasn't returned your calls because he's not interested in what you've got to say." He smirked.

Struggling not to scream in his face, I took a breath and closed the short distance between Fab and I. At the door, I turned and said, "When you talk to him, let him know I have a long memory, and next time he needs a favor, he'll get zip."

Fab and I were halfway down the steps when I realized that neither Fab nor I had raided the snack bowl, a long-time tradition. Fab steered me toward the shortcut to the parking lot. I stood with my hand on passenger door handle, the sun in my face, trying to shake off the meeting. When Fab got in, I said, "Brick's behavior and his attitude of 'get the job done at any cost' is going to make it easy for me to quit this business."

Chapter Seven

"We've got two choices," I said to Fab as she got closer to Coral Gables, a suburb of South Miami. "We either stake out her condo or the beauty salon." I flicked through Fab's phone, looking at the two pictures Brick had sent. "I feel the need to remind you that this job is breaking and entering, burglary, and worse if we take firearms."

"That's why you're not going in with me." Fab laid on the horn. The guy who'd just cut in front of her almost ran off the road. "You're going to stake out the parking lot in case she returns early. Don't worry, this is in and out."

"That's a tired old line." I pressed my forehead against the glass as we passed by the old Biltmore Hotel.

Fab pulled up in front of a fifteen-story concrete building with shopping at the street level and residences above, each with their own balcony. She double-checked the address.

The first thing I noticed was there was no lot for visitor parking and signs prohibiting on-street parking. I didn't ask the obvious question: "Even if you find a place to park, how do you get in the building unnoticed?"

Fab scooted up in her seat, driving slowly around the building, scoping out the side streets – more condos and small businesses. She drove to the back, where the security gate was in the process of opening. As a sedan pulled out, Fab pulled into the underground garage. "That's her leaving," she said excitedly. "We got lucky." She double-checked the license number with the one Brick had written down.

Fab drove into Rosarita's parking space…the one marked with her unit number anyway. "It's dark down here. They could use a lot better lighting. Maybe you should sit in the car, and if she returns, you move the car and call me."

"Anything goes wrong, your backup is in the car." My voice dripped with sarcasm. "Hand over your Walther. I'll lock it up. At least you'll stand a chance of making bail."

Fab slid out of the car, pulling her firearm from the waistband of her pants and handing it over. She closed the door and headed to the elevator.

I blew out a mental sigh of relief that she'd handed her gun over – one less thing to worry about. I got out and locked both of our firearms in the special box that Creole had installed in the back. I leaned against the bumper and pulled out my phone, punching in his number and listening to his message and the automated reminder that the box was full. How many times had I done that? A lot. No one needed to know. If he'd answered, I would've said, "You'll be happy to know that I'm giving serious thought to telling Brick and his dysfunctional-ness to get screwed." Then I'd whisper, "I love you."

As we drove by the front of the building, I'd noticed that there was no large front lobby. The entrance, an unassuming set of double glass doors, opened into a small area that housed a bank of elevators. The locked door that stared back at me appeared to be the only building entrance from the garage. There was a walkway and a steel mesh door that opened to the outside. Surely tenants didn't use the garage as an exit to the sidewalk. I scoped out every inch and decided that whoever designed the cramped area didn't know what they were doing. Not wanting to attract attention by pacing back and forth, I got back in the car.

For the hundredth time, I checked the clock that illuminated the dashboard. Thirty minutes was stretching all previous records for Fab to toss a place and get the heck out. My nerves were frayed, and I couldn't take much more waiting. I texted her number, waited not very patiently for two minutes, and when I got no response, I called and got voicemail. Fab *always* answered the phone. Next call: Brick. Something had gone wrong, and he needed to make it right. That call also went to voicemail. I hit redial three times in a row and got the same damn "leave a message" recording. I texted him "911."

Finally, my phone rang. Brick's picture popped up.

"What?" he snarled.

I told him the job was taking too long and Fab wasn't answering her phone.

"Fab never listens to me when I tell her she needs a more qualified partner," he grouched, his irritation booming through the line. "Whatever the hiccup is, she'll fix it and be out in a flash. What are you going to do," he taunted, "involve the police?"

"I'm expecting you to get your big ass over here and take care of this," I seethed, unleashing my anger. "I'm telling you that this is out of character for Fab."

"Give it an hour. You still haven't heard from her then, call me back. I ride to the rescue now, that's going to create family drama I don't want to deal with. Fab's the professional; let her do her job. Stop bothering me. When this is over, have Fab call me." Brick hung up.

Pretty much without thinking, I crossed over to the plain door I presumed would let me into the building. I removed my lockpick and gained easy entry. The door opened into the mailroom, and another door took me to the elevators, where not surprisingly there was the set of double doors I'd seen earlier. I rode the elevator to the fourteenth floor. Taking a deep breath when the doors slid open, I stepped out, checking out the hallway.

Rosarita Famosa had three neighbors, two units on each side of the building. I knocked politely, not having come up with a reason for standing on her welcome mat. I'd surprise her and myself by whatever nonsense came out of my mouth.

Hearing a slight brushing noise from behind the door, I suspected someone was peering out the peephole. The door opened, and Fab graced the entry.

"What the hell?" I hissed. "You had me worried, not answering your phone. Let's go." I turned.

Fab grabbed my arm. "There's a slight problem." She pulled me inside the unit, closing the door.

The open-concept condo was decorator-magazine beautiful in shades of blue with a view of the treetops. The furniture didn't appear the least bit comfortable, every piece stiff and formal. This was a woman who didn't care to kick up her feet, or at least not comfortably.

I might've missed the woman tied up in the chair – that's how eager I was to get back on the road – if she hadn't started making a lot of unintelligible noises, thanks to the scarf tied around her mouth. Her deep-brown eyes glared daggers.

"I'm afraid to ask," I practically stuttered. "Who is that?"

"Meet Rosarita Famosa." Fab flourished her hand in the woman's direction.

"Nooo." My eyes shot to the woman. "Why aren't you getting your hair done?" I asked her.

Rosarita shook her head so hard, the chair tipped slightly.

"What… I mean… I don't know… You have to untie her." I had a million questions and no clue where to start.

"She tried to shoot me." Fab said indignantly, pointing to the gun lying on the floor.

"You better not be bleeding." I gave Fab a once-over and stepped towards Rosarita. "What about her? Is she okay?" I stood in front of her, reaching out. She flinched. "You promise not to yell?" I asked. "If you do, I'll just shove this scarf back in your mouth." She nodded, and I untied it, putting it in her lap. I unwrapped the cotton belt, which matched her dress, from around her wrists. "Don't do anything stupid. This day is still salvageable for all of us."

"Thank you," Rosarita said quietly, shaking her wrists. She stayed seated. "And to think I thought my idea of catching a criminal was such a great one."

"One of you needs to start talking. I came up here to rescue you." I glared at Fab. "It looks like you might still be in need of rescue but in a different way. Have a seat and clue me in – where do we go from here?" I settled on a straight-back fabric chair with no arms.

Fab leaned against the wall and pointed at Rosarita. "You first."

The two exchanged mean-girl stares. Fab won by an edge, but then, maybe I was biased.

Rosarita scrubbed her eyes with her hands, swiping a tear from her cheek. "Last weekend at a barbeque at Brick's, I overheard him bragging about proving I was the one who stole the wedding gifts. He said he was sending over a woman to ransack my place while I was at my hair appointment. I got a friend to drive my car to her house, telling her the garage was being repaved. If I'd told her the truth, I'm pretty sure she would've called the police."

That was good to know – she didn't want the cops involved either.

"What did you do to make Brick so mad that he'd set this up?" I asked.

"It would achieve his goal of making me persona non grata in the family. In his opinion as self-appointed head, I'm no longer family since the divorce. He doesn't want me around. According to him, I'm not a real Famosa."

"Skip to the part where you planned to shoot me," Fab said in indignation.

Rosarita rolled her eyes. "There's no bullets in the gun – it's empty."

"Do you know how to use it?" I asked.

Both women said "No" in unison.

"I suggest you take a gun safety class," I said. "At least be a responsible gun owner. Just know that shooting someone leaves a big mess, not to mention the guilt." *How to get out of this?* "Did you steal the gifts?"

Once again, both women answered at the same time. Fab said "yes" and Rosarita "no."

"I only borrowed them," Rosarita defended herself. "I really can't stand my new daughter-in-law. Tried talking some sense into my son, practically begged, but he just rolled his eyes and looked embarrassed when I told him that thinking with his lower anatomy wasn't going to end well."

"Men don't like to hear that," I said sympathetically. I knew my brother hated it when I told him the same thing.

"If there's a woman who doesn't deserve gift one, it's my new daughter-in-law," Rosarita spat. "Once I put the plan into motion and declared them stolen, it was too late to change my mind, though I wanted to. I didn't see any way out other than to stick with the lie."

"Brick mentioned something about an insurance claim and that you and your son could go to jail."

"Insurance," she snorted. "I just threw that out there because I thought it sounded official. I never actually planned to do it." She leaned her head back, closing her eyes for a moment. "The Famosas are a close-knit family, and I love them. Some of them, anyway. It never occurred to me that Brick would try to kick me out. Didn't help that I saw Brick kissing one of his other sisters-in-law. I daydreamed about holding it over his head but came to my senses on that one."

"I'm calling Brick. Let him deal with his own family problems." Fab took her phone out of her pocket. She winced when she looked at the screen. "Sorry I worried you."

"Put your phone down." I motioned. "I'm not inclined to do any favors for Brick after calling him, anxious about you, only to have him hang up on me after telling me to let you fend for yourself. He didn't give a diddly about any consequences." I raised my eyebrows at Fab, trying to communicate that there were plenty of repercussions to go around and we needed to be careful.

"Whatever Brick's paying you two, I'll double," Rosarita pleaded.

"The only money we're taking is from Brick," I told her. "Please tell me that you still have the gifts."

"Two of them are here." Fab covered her eyes with her hands. "She opened them and forgot to toss the cards. No sign of a purse full of money."

"Where's the rest?" I asked Rosarita.

"A storage unit across town."

I didn't care how she accomplished that – there must be more people involved, but that was another thing I didn't want to know anything about. "You're going to tell your son that you hired a private detective, who tracked down the gifts and is retrieving them for you. The reason you didn't involve the cops was because you didn't want the family smeared in the news." I smiled at her. "You'll be the hero."

"The cash?" Fab demanded.

"Rosarita can figure that out with her son." I returned Fab's squinty-eyed look. "All this is on the condition that the three of us keep our mouths shut." I waited on Fab and Rosarita to respond, and they finally nodded.

"I'm supposed to tell Brick that I didn't find anything?" Fab asked with some skepticism.

"If anyone can sell him on a story, it would be you," I said. "Tell him the reason it took longer than usual to get out was that the neighbor was using the elevator to move something." I turned to Rosarita. "Maybe you being the hero in this scenario will put you on a good track with your son's wife. If you get the chance, you should at least fake it for your son's sake; otherwise, you run the risk of being left out of family gatherings."

"If Brick confronts you," Fab said to Rosarita, still irked at having a gun pointed at her, "you need to keep your story straight and lie to his face. Can you handle that?"

"I'll deal with him," she said quietly. "After all, I've had years of practice. I must be getting older; the drama's not as much fun as it once was."

Fab moved to the front door.

"Figure out all the details you need to sound convincing," I told Rosarita. "Then forget any other version of what went down today, and that includes meeting us. Our story is going to be that this was an in-and-out job, nothing to find. If we ever meet up in the future, remember it's our first meeting."

"I'll hold up my end," Rosarita said.

I stood and closed the space between Fab and me, exiting the condo as she held the door open.

When the door clicked closed, Fab said, "Let's hustle." She hit the elevator button. "I was about to suggest we hit the stairs, in case she double-crosses us, but decided I'm too tired for fourteen floors. I'll feel much better when we get on the highway."

Chapter Eight

I stopped in the entryway, smoothing down my full black skirt, tucking in my sleeveless top, which buttoned up the back, and slipping into a pair of low heels. Bending down, I reached for a pair of sequined flip-flops to toss into my carry bag. I had dressed up for my midday appointment, forgoing something casual and tropical.

Didier whistled as I stepped into the kitchen. "Either of you going to tell me what's going on?" he directed to Fab and I.

Not wanting to get into a long-winded explanation, I took the easy way out and ignored him.

"Where are you going?" Fab demanded, her eyes boring through me.

"Creole's lawyer called and wants to meet at Jake's." I held up my hand. "Before you ask, he didn't say what he wanted."

"You shouldn't go by yourself, not because you're not capable but for moral support." Didier crossed his arms.

"I know that the two of you have plans," I

said, edging toward the door. "I'll be fine." I was certain if I'd been standing next to Fab, she would've kicked me.

"Sorry, hon," Fab said to Didier, making a slightly sad face, which made me want to laugh. "I'm going with Madison. Lawyer? She needs me."

"Beware of the small print." His brows knitted together. "I'll be fixing dinner, and you'll be eating." He pointed at me. "I'm not as clueless as you two think, or as forgetful. The two of you will take turns telling me in detail about yesterday's job."

"We're here, aren't we?" I said.

"Sarcasm isn't going to deter me." Didier stared at me with reproving eyes.

"I predict you're going to regret trying to keep two women out of trouble." I re-thought my quick-exit plan and crossed the kitchen to where Didier stood. Lifting up on tiptoes, I kissed his cheek. "You need anything for dinner, text one of us. I'm requesting margaritas. Come on, Mom, or I'm going to be late." I tugged on Fab's arm.

"What are we really doing?" Fab asked after she slid behind the wheel.

* * *

I was certain Fab didn't believe me until she turned into Jake's parking lot and I still hadn't given her a different address. We entered through the kitchen and walked down the hall past the bar. I slowed before getting to the deck; at the reserved table sat an older gentleman in shorts and a button-down shirt who appeared vaguely familiar.

"You're not listening in," I said.

"I might as well," Fab said with an exasperated sigh. "Saves you from repeating everything word for word. I'll remind you that your record is less than stellar in that regard."

"This is one of those times that you have you and me mixed up. You're the one who sucks at details." I avoided her stare, which appeared to be trying to ferret out something I might be withholding. "It…it might be personal."

Fab gave me a one-armed hug. "No crying." She produced a tissue out of nowhere. "Don't worry, I'll leave if the conversation gets too personal."

"Is there anything you don't think you should eavesdrop on?"

"Of course not. But I'm not eavesdropping; I've been invited."

"I want a margarita," I said. "Right now."

"You are going to do this sober. I'll be sitting right next to you. We don't want to forget a single word." She signaled the bartender. "Two waters and a dish of limes," she said, raising her voice to be heard over the customers, and pointed to the deck. "What's this man's name again?"

I pulled a piece of paper from my pocket. "Enfinger Briscoe."

"I wonder how many times he's been called 'Finger'?"

"Dare you to ask him."

Fab ignored me and headed straight for the table, challenging me to keep up. She gave the lawyer a snooty once-over. "You're a member of the bar?" she asked in a superior tone. "Don't bother to lie; I've got ways of finding out."

So much for civilized introductions.

"You must be the best friend." Mr. Briscoe stood, grinning at Fab. "Creole told me about you." His smile disappeared momentarily. "Call me Briscoe." He nodded to me. "You must be Madison. Sorry to meet you under such circumstances; didn't think it would happen in my lifetime."

"I'm not sure what I'm supposed to do," I said, my cheeks warming up.

He pulled out a chair for me. "You may remember me as one of the old-guy gamblers Madeline invites here regularly." I sat down, and he pulled out a chair for Fab before reseating himself opposite us.

Mother had turned the rental room, which had been a complete failure, into a gambling den for her friends. It stayed constantly booked by her or one of her friends eager for a friendly card game.

"Does client confidentiality apply, since I'm not actually your client?" I asked.

One of Cook's sons – he had several but had been vague on the exact number – set down our waters and another beer for Briscoe. There were certain times of the year that experienced heavy turnover, and a lot of that had to do with school schedules and when Jake's utilized more of Cook's family members.

"No worries. You're my client now, and even if you weren't, I got in the habit of keeping people's secrets and now it's second-nature." He finished off his beer and set it on the corner of the table before picking up his new one.

"Why am I here?" I asked.

"About a year ago, Creole had a will drawn up that left everything to you, assets and property. There were no other mentions. He loved you, my dear. Told me once that he knew you were the one because you were the only one to make him laugh."

"I'm not sure what to say," I said. That had been happening to me a lot lately. "I loved him in return. I'd trade everything I own to have him back, even though I know it doesn't work that way."

"The reading of the will is usually done posthaste, but I haven't been feeling up to snuff of late," he said in an apologetic tone. "I have a copy for you here in my briefcase." He patted the leather case next to him. "If you'd like, I'm happy to read every word to you now, or you can peruse it at your leisure."

I nodded at the latter. "If it's as straightforward as you say, I can do it later." The last thing I wanted to do was start crying.

"There's a slight wrinkle that I intend to check out thoroughly," he said sternly. "I'm not an old fool; wasn't a young one either."

"What kind of wrinkle?" Fab leaned in and asked, voice laced with suspicion.

Briscoe hesitated. Too long, in my opinion. I tried to brace myself for whatever was coming. He took a deep breath and blurted, "There's a woman claiming to be Creole's wife."

"A what?" I demanded, giving my head a slight shake, certain I hadn't heard him correctly.

"That's ridiculous," Fab said emphatically. "He wasn't that kind of man." She stood and scooted her chair closer to mine.

I closed my eyes and hoped that when I opened them, I'd be stretched out on the daybed at home and this could all be written off as a bad dream.

"Let me make this clear: when I met with Creole, he never mentioned this woman, a Ms. Beaumont, in any conversation, although I did meet her in passing. In fact, I asked if he had any ex-wives, and the answer was no," Briscoe said.

"Met her?" I said in shocked surprise. "How did that happen?"

"Months back..." He paused, as though recalling the event. "...Creole and I had a quick meeting scheduled at a fast food joint, which she interrupted. He not only wasn't happy to see her, he didn't introduce her — she had to do it herself. I found it odd and completely out of character for him to be so ungentlemanly. And not a word about her being his wife. The only thing that was clear was that he didn't appreciate the interruption."

"Marriages are easy to prove, and it's also easy to figure out if the paperwork is a fraud," Fab declared.

"I'm not sure what to make of Ms. Beaumont's claim, but I plan to check it out thoroughly and told her as much. I also told her she'd need solid proof, with the aforementioned paperwork a requirement, not just because I'm asking but because the court would demand it."

Florida was an easy state to get married in; a notary could take care of the forms, and as Fab and I had learned, there was always one willing to take a few bucks in exchange for breaking the law. I couldn't imagine Creole asking any woman he loved to get married in that quickie fashion, and I knew with certainty that he wouldn't tie the knot with someone he didn't love.

"I've got the supposed date from her and already assigned an assistant to go through the court records. She's dragging her feet, claiming the marriage certificate is in the possession of her lawyer. She reluctantly gave me his number, but after several attempts, he still hasn't returned my calls."

"Is the man a real lawyer or a paralegal that only files paperwork?" Fab asked, her eyes never leaving Briscoe's.

"I checked that out," Briscoe said with a grin, enjoying Fab's questions. "He's listed with the bar, and before you ask, not a single complaint has been filed against him."

I really wanted a drink or a nap. I'd settle for going home and straight to my bedroom. I was grateful that Fab had ignored all my attempts to avoid her, as I'd struggled to focus on the conversation after hearing the word "wife."

"How did this woman get in touch with you?" Fab asked.

"Ms. Beaumont showed up at my office. I wasn't in, which I rarely am, and she left a message, making it clear that she plans to contest. Since I'm mostly retired, I rent office space and share a receptionist, who fields phone calls and messages, allowing me to stop by about once a week to pick up mail and poach a cup of coffee."

A couple of men hollered, "Hey, Briscoe," from inside the bar and waved; he waved back.

"So the will isn't valid until you verify her claim?" I asked.

"If her claim is proven, by state law, she's entitled to a certain percentage. The rest would still go to you."

"If it turns out Ms. Beaumont is Creole's wife,

I'd like to meet her. I'd like to see for myself what kind of woman he picked." The pain that shot through me must've shown on my face. Briscoe flinched.

"If it turns out to be a hoax…" Fab cracked her knuckles.

I shook my head and glared down at her hands.

"I'll beat the holy hell out of her." She flashed Briscoe her scary-girl smile.

Fab had me almost smiling. *There's nothing better than a best friend.*

Chapter Nine

The bed dipped slightly, and I rolled over and rubbed my hand across my eyes, blinking away the haze of sleep. Fab held out a mug of my favorite brew. "What time is it?" My eyes were adjusting to the sun that shone directly through the window, so I knew it wasn't early.

"Almost noon." Fab brushed my hair over my shoulder. "I have a favor to ask. And please say yes. It's an easy one."

"Please, don't ask. I don't feel good." I closed my eyes and pulled the sheet up under my chin.

"You've been sleeping too much and not eating." Fab's tone was slightly lecturing. She swung her legs up and sat cross-legged on the bed. "Brick has summoned me. All you have to do is ride along. I'll handle everything, and if it's a job, I'll put it off until tomorrow."

"Do I have to get dressed?" I had no desire to get out of my pajama shorts and top.

"You have to shower." She shook her finger at me. "While you're doing that, I'll surprise you and pick out something super comfortable."

"Tomorrow would be better." I closed my eyes again.

She removed the cup from my hand and set it on the bedside table. "Has to be today." She tossed back the sheet. "On the way, we'll stop at The Bakery Café; I had them set two pecan rolls aside for you." She pulled me into a sitting position, moving my legs over the side in one swift move. "No crying," she said sternly.

"You're being so sweet."

"I know. But I've about run out of sweetness; it's hard on a person when they haven't had any practice. So if you don't get your ass in the shower, I'm going to drag you."

"I still don't want to go."

"Tough totems." She grinned. "Heard a kid say that at the beach and thought it sounded cool; didn't think I'd ever get to use it." She tugged me to a standing position. "You've lost weight. Bony's not attractive. I read somewhere that it's better to pack on a few extra pounds; that way, if you get sick, you won't waste away."

I looked down. "My boobs are still big."

"Bigger than mine is what you're saying. I'm well aware. Now go shower."

Before closing the door, I said, "Remember – comfortable."

Eventually, on the verge of running out of hot water, I dragged myself out, wrapping myself in a big towel. I wondered if this what was roadkill felt like; the image in the mirror told me I looked the part. Fab hadn't banged on the door; maybe she'd rescheduled for tomorrow. Zero chance, my inner self whispered.

I opened the door, peeking out.

Fab's blue eyes stared back. She'd made the bed and sat down in the chair. "I'm not going to complain about how long that took. Or how patiently I waited. My foot would disagree since I tapped it the whole time." Her foot engaged in a little show.

I eyed the bed. Laid out on it were a black jean skirt, a short-sleeved off-the-shoulder top, and a pair of ballerina flats. "You did a good job."

"Five minutes." Fab tapped her watch. She stood and crossed to the door. "Don't think, if you even attempt to dally, that I won't be back."

I hurried into my clothes and pulled my hair back into a ponytail. To show my appreciation, I wore the flats instead of flip-flops.

Fab sat at the bottom of the stairs, our purses at her feet. I wasn't sure if she'd thought I would try to sneak past her or not.

"Look at you. And a whole ten seconds to spare," Fab said with a laugh. "You can leave your Glock behind."

I raised my eyebrows.

"More reassurance that this isn't a work day. On the off chance a gun is needed, I'll do the shooting." She held the front door open.

I bent down and picked up a pair of flip-flops from the tray, shoving them in my purse before following Fab. "Any clue what Brick wants?"

She shook her head. "He was in a testy mood,

so I didn't hit him with questions. Instead, I lied about a previous appointment, thinking you couldn't possibly sleep all day. Wrong about that one."

"Try not to scare me with your driving," I said, climbing in and readjusting the seat.

"You haven't complained lately, so that's a good sign."

"For today, no personal talk. Just girl stuff. Whistle at hot men in traffic, things like that."

"No hanging your head out the window," Fab admonished.

* * *

The prime front spots at Famosa Motors were taken. If I were driving, I'd opt to drive under the roll-up doors and park inside the showroom, but I didn't voice the thought, knowing I'd be vetoed. Fab pulled into customer parking.

"I hope this doesn't take long," I said.

Two salesmen who'd worked for Brick for years stood talking a distance away; they both waved.

"Brick asked that we be nice to Everly," Fab said before getting out the car.

"You hopped at that opportunity?" I slowly slid out, joining Fab, who waited as though I'd make a run for it.

"I believe I responded with something non-committal," she said, flicking her hair in an impatient gesture. "Leaving him to believe that there might be a chance."

We crossed under the doors, stepping inside the showroom, and were about to skate past Everly's desk when the six-foot, florescent-haired redhead jumped to her feet. Her hand flew up in the air. "Stop right there," she commanded. "I'll announce you."

We both turned, Fab shooting daggers and me pasting on an insincere smile. To say we ever had any rapport with the woman would be an understatement. It had to do with guns and who pointed one at who first.

"Go ahead," Fab barked and looped her arm in my mine, ushering me towards the stairs.

"That 'nice' business lasted…what? A second and a half?" I asked.

"Time I'll never get back."

I laid my head on her shoulder and giggled. "If looks could kill, our favorite funeral directors would be planning a double send-off."

"Triple!"

"Let's make this quick," I said as we bounded up the steps.

"Ladies," Brick said as we entered his office. He pointed to the leather chairs in front of his desk.

I claimed the one closest to the door, figuring Fab would sit next to me since she was lead on this meeting. Instead, she took her favorite seat on the edge of the windowsill.

"I have a few questions about how the Rosarita job could get so screwed up." Brick raked a folder on his desk over in front of him, removing a piece of paper.

I couldn't read his scratch from my vantage point. It took a bit of work, but I mustered up a bland face, determined not to react to anything he said, one way or the other.

"I already told you everything that happened," Fab said, crossing her arms. *Wanna fight?* was written on her face. *Bring it on.*

"How does Rosarita manage to come out the hero?" he demanded, his voice growing louder. "Imagine, she found the gifts!" His tone dripped with sarcasm. "She's a hero, and me, I'm the horse's ass for even suggesting she's a miserable thief." He banged his open palm on the desk. "I know she was running a con. Who steals wedding gifts? Her! What she planned to do with the stuff, I don't give a damn; I wanted her caught red-handed." He shot a flinty glare at the two of us. "Did you two go all soft and give her a free pass?"

I wanted to laugh at the shear frustration riddling his body. Instead, I glanced down to hide my smile.

"Somehow, this one is involved." Brick pointed to me. "Calling all hysterical about you taking longer than usual. Did she screw everything up and you're covering for her?"

Fab pushed off the ledge, standing in front of

him in indignation, and told him, "Even if Madison had gone in with me, there was nothing to screw up, and I told you that. No gifts. No money."

I briefly considered barfing to bring this meeting to a halt. But I'd never been sick on command, and today probably wasn't a good day to trot out a new and untried skill.

"Investigate the storage place." He pushed a piece of paper in Fab's direction. "This is where the gifts were supposedly found, still covered in wrapping paper." He snorted. "Find out what really happened."

"Then what?" Fab demanded. "Have you thought this through? Even if you prove your theory, then what? You drag her in front of the family, humiliating her? After all that, the family will still think you're the bastard."

Lolling my head to the side, I eased out a snore that came out louder than I expected. Trying to time the next one with a mental count of three, I was startled by a pounding noise. I jumped, my eyes flying open.

"What in the hell...?" Brick leaned over his desk. "Did you go to sleep?" he yelled.

I rubbed my ears. Where was a mirror when a girl needed one? I wanted to pull a contrite face but had no clue where to start.

"You're her partner." His eyes narrowed in on me as his voice hardened. "You've got one job here, and that's to listen to what I've got to say."

I nodded, putting my hand over my mouth and yawning. "Got it."

He pointed to the door. "Get out," he thundered. "And I mean all the way out of the building."

"Have a nice day," I said sweetly, turning slightly to wink at Fab, who was having a hard time controlling the laughter about ready to fly from her lips.

If my skirt had had more room, I'd have ridden the banister to the bottom. But showing my panty-clad bottom wasn't happening today. I cut across the lot to the SUV and climbed in. It didn't take as long as I expected for Fab to reappear.

"Nice job." She clapped. "I'm happy you got us out of there."

"How did it go after I was tossed?"

"The job was rescinded. He didn't use the word 'fired,' so I imagine he'll call again if he can't find someone else. You need to give Rosarita a heads up that she better shore up her end."

"Might I suggest a new line of work? I know I've mentioned it before, but this time I'm more serious. You joke about us herding cats, but the chances of one of *them* shooting us is nil. They could only scratch us or get hair on our clothes."

"Are you finished?"

"What would've happened if Brick found out the truth about our part in the cover-up?"

Fab shuddered and shook it off. "I thought the same thing. My guess is it would get damn ugly."

Chapter Ten

Fab pulled into the driveway and let the engine idle. "There's a family meeting tonight."

I shifted in my seat and scanned the street, not seeing any familiar vehicles. "My family is about to descend on the house?"

"Not that bad." She scrunched up her face. "It's just the three of us. We're forming a secret group. I thought that would appeal to you. Didier has some information he wants to share."

"That doesn't sound so bad." I opened the door, lowering one foot to the ground.

"I'm warning you now," she scolded. "You need to eat, or Didier will have a fit. He's worried about you and so am I. So make us both a little happy."

"Yes, ma'am."

"Get out already. We need a swim."

* * *

"This has been fun," I said, pushing my plate away, trying to think of a way to sneak off unnoticed and go upstairs to read.

As soon as we walked in the front door, I escaped to

my bedroom. Soon after, Fab came barreling into the room in her bikini, wrap tied around her waist, and reminded me of my promise to go for a swim, which sounded more like a declaration that that was what we were going to do. She rummaged through the armoire and tossed my hot-pink tankini at me.

After a few laps, we dragged out the floaters, mindlessly drifting along in the water until Didier arrived home and dumped grocery bags on the kitchen counter. It didn't take long before he was standing on the patio in bathing trunks, holding a tray with glasses and a pitcher of flavored water, which he set on the table. Didier served the drinks and then dove into the water, swimming laps while Fab and I sat on the steps.

He eventually joined us and asked about our day, wanting to know about the new job and in the next breath reminding us that he had yet to hear about the previous job. It was clear Fab hadn't prepared an answer and she wasn't about to tell the whole truth if it could be avoided. Some things never changed.

I jumped in. "Brick wanted us to get involved in his family melodrama, and when we couldn't produce the dirt he was looking for, he called us back a second time. It didn't take us long to decide we're not taking any more of those kinds of jobs. After what I did, there's probably a slim chance he'd even ask."

Fab mimicked my snore and went on to relate that part of the story.

"You're making that up." Didier laughed.

"I could tell Fab was unenthusiastic about the job, and not feeling the same loyalty to him that she does, I

thought a little prank would change the conversation to him unloading on me, and it worked. He ordered me out. Not sure if he's going to put up with any more of the daring duo. Don't worry, I won't let Fab go out on a job without backup."

Fab sighed heavily. "This will probably shock the both of you, but I'm tired of most of these jobs. Been thinking lately that I have a lot to lose and that I could ultimately pay a high price."

Didier swam over to her, hooked her legs around his middle, and laid a long kiss on her. The two of them then got out to prepare dinner. Didier told Fab to stay in the water, but she wanted to help.

When the smells drifted over from the barbeque, I got out of the pool, pulling a cover-up over my head. I sat at the table and picked the dead flowers out of the centerpiece that I'd put together a few days ago. Tropical blooms didn't last long in water, or on the vine for that matter.

"Don't think you're going to bed," Didier cut into my reverie. "I'll block the French doors if I have to." He gave me a half-smile. "It wouldn't be much of a family meeting with one of us missing."

"You didn't eat much." Fab glared first at the skewer of vegetables, of which I'd only managed to eat two pieces, then the fish that had gone largely ignored. "All you did was push your food around."

I pulled the napkin off my lap and, with a fork, scraped the food into it, wadding it up. "Oh look, I cleaned my plate. Proud of me?"

Fab glared at Didier's laugh. "Is this some trick you learned as a child?"

I nodded. "Brad and I got rid of a lot of vegetables using the napkin trick followed by a trip to the trash. The key is disposal of the evidence — don't leave it on the top." I smiled at them both. "I just have a little stomach ache."

Didier stood and pointed his finger at me. "Don't move. I have a present for you." He left the table with an armful of plates.

Fab and I finished cleaning off the rest of the table. Didier came back through the patio doors, plain shopping bag in hand, and set it in front of me. "This is from Fab and me."

I peered over the edge of the bag, then reached in and pulled out an old-fashioned Key West sand bucket.

"I love this." I jumped up and pulled them into a group hug.

"It's for you to fill with seashells," Didier said.

Fab groaned.

"I haven't done that in a really long time. Maybe Fab will come with me. She can help me fill it to the top so we get home faster."

"Okay, it's not my favorite activity," Fab said. "But I do think they look good scattered around the base of the plants. Tired of the plain dirt already."

The last hurricane had blown the shells to who knows where. I'd thought several times about stopping at my favorite shell store and picking up a couple of bags, but decided that wasn't as much fun.

"Is that a compliment?" I asked.

"Possibly," Fab hedged.

Didier had also come back with a bottle of wine and three glasses. I indicated that I wanted less than half.

"To friends," Didier toasted. We clinked glasses. "I'll go first," he said.

"You need to call the meeting to order," Fab instructed, amusement in her eyes. "Not sure what happens after that."

"Since we're an informal group, I suggest we suspend the rules," he said. When we didn't object, he continued, "Fab came home the other night and told me about your meeting with Phil and how evasive she was. She planned to follow the woman, but I asked her to hold off until I talked to Brad." He paused, looking at me. "I walked in on Brad and Phil about to have…well, they were in a…romantic clinch. I learned my lesson about knocking, even with the door half open. Surprised them and me. Needless to say, Brad will be locking his office door in the future."

"Have they been doing it since Mother fixed them up?" I asked.

Mother would be happy that they got together but not about being the last to know. On the other hand, maybe I was the last one to know. I wasn't sure since I hadn't seen much of her lately.

Didier frowned.

Fab patted his arm. "At least she didn't say 'banging.'"

Didier shook his head. "I was surprised myself and asked why all the sneaking around, and apparently your brother and Phil want to keep their hook-up a secret."

"So I take it Mother doesn't know?" I asked.

"He told her they had coffee a couple of times and that's it," Didier said. "Brad asked me to keep their secret, and I reluctantly agreed, making it clear I wasn't going to lie if asked directly. We both agreed that no one would probably ask." Didier shrugged. "Given recent events, I think Madison deserves to know."

A silence descended around the table, all of us lost in thought.

"Do you know if Brad told Phil to cut us off as clients?" I asked.

"I think so," Didier said. "Though he didn't say so directly. I demanded an explanation after she broke your agreement and didn't get one. I may be the only one other than you two who thinks you deserve to know the details of what happened to Creole. To be honest, I'd like to know. He was my best friend."

"Phil handled the whole situation so poorly — lying, not being straightforward — that I don't trust her anymore," I said.

"What happens when you have to look at her across the table at family dinners?" Fab asked.

"It'll be fine. If I can put up with Kevin, I can put up with her. Besides, that depends on Brad and whether he continues the charade. If he doesn't invite her, then he doesn't care about her very much."

"I did give Brad a heads up," Didier said. "He knows that you're about to find out they're dating. He wasn't happy when I told him I wasn't going to keep the secret any longer and, since Fab was ready to investigate, it was only a matter of time before it came out anyway. I told him I'd been lucky to stall Fab on checking out Phil but I'd never be able to put her off indefinitely. If I didn't tell her first, when she did find out, it would hurt our relationship. I can't harp on trust and not give it back."

The front door banged. Didier jumped up, but before he left the table, Brad and Phil appeared in the doorway. Brad nodded to everyone.

"Didn't know you two were stopping by," Didier said. "Grab yourselves a drink."

"It's not every day that I find out I'm about to be followed," Phil said, full of indignation. "And for what? Because other people can't mind their own business."

"Don't get so high and mighty," I said. "A little truth-telling would've averted the whole situation. This wasn't a big deal until you made it one by lying. Why not just say Brad didn't want you looking into Creole's case?"

Brad reached into the refrigerator, grabbed

two bottled waters, and returned, pulling out a chair for Phil. "I just want to make it clear that my personal business is just that – personal. No more background checks. I can do my own and figure out for myself if the woman is a nutcase."

"Is that what you're mad at? That I figured out the last one was certifiable before you did? Sorry I didn't let her ruin your life like she did a couple other men's. Is that what you want me to say? Visit her in prison yet?" I asked.

"She entered into a plea bargain," Brad said.

"That's a happy ending."

"Another thing: I'll be the one to tell Mother."

"It's good to know we won't all have to lie for you. That must make you feel special," I said to Phil.

"The only reason we kept our relationship under wraps was because it's still in the early stages," Phil said.

"Can you refer me to an information procurer since you're out of the business?" I asked.

"I realize that it's hard to lose the man you love, but Creole was an undercover detective and knew that danger was part of the job," Phil said.

So? That doesn't mean I don't have a right to know what happened. I forced myself back to the conversation.

Phil was still talking. "You don't know what Creole was investigating. It could bring big trouble to your family's doorsteps. I'm sure you don't want to be responsible for any of them getting hurt…or worse."

Brad cleared his throat. "Sis, I love you and the last thing I want is for anything to happen to you."

"I'll stop looking for answers. Happy now?" I looked away and managed to hold myself together and not scream.

"There's another thing," Phil said. "I'll be moving out of the lighthouse."

That's old news, I wanted to tell her. I'd already heard from Doodad that she'd moved out. My plan was to turn it back into a place for tourists to take pictures.

"We're making space for her at the condos. She's a good choice to handle our legal affairs," Brad said.

Didier raised an eyebrow, this clearly was the first he'd heard of it.

Fab held up the wine bottle. I shook my head. She finished off the bottle between her and Didier.

"So we're agreed," Brad said.

About what? I wondered. I didn't ask. There wasn't a happy or satisfied face at the table. I nodded, sad that Brad had more secrets than who he was banging and I was the last person he felt like he could share with.

Fab asked about a referral for a private investigator, but Phil didn't have one of those either. The uncomfortable conversation came to an end. Brad brought up a bike ride, which was once a passion for the guys, but neither seemed terribly excited.

Fab made a face at me when she thought no one was looking. It made me smile.

"Heard Liam cancelled his weekend plans to come down to the Cove," Brad said.

"Mother's meddling probably had something to do with that. We'll reschedule," I said.

Now that Liam was out from under her eagle eye and enjoying his freedom, I suspected he'd come for a visit soon and simply not tell anyone he was in town.

"Just don't take him out on any jobs." Brad leveled a stare at me.

I tapped Fab's hand. "Can you remind me if I forget?"

"You know what I mean." Brad stood. "We've both got early appointments." He extended his hand, helping Phil to her feet.

I waved in an off-hand manner. "I suppose once you tell Mother, there will be a family dinner. See you then."

"That was weird and uncomfortable," Fab said after they left.

"You okay?" Didier asked me.

"I don't blame Brad for not wanting his sister and mother meddling in his love life. In the future, I'll have to keep my opinions to myself."

"Was I the only one seeing a different side of Philipa?" Fab asked.

"Noticed that, did you?" I said.

"New lawyer?" Didier shook his head. "You'd think as a partner, I'd be consulted. Wonder when I was going to be told—when I walked in and found her sitting behind a desk? Who knows, it might've even been mine since we don't have an extra one."

Fab growled. "I'd be happy to beat the hell out the two of them."

Didier cupped her face in his hands. "That's what I love about you – fiercely loyal." He brushed a kiss across her lips.

"No more office space rental for the lighthouse." I smirked at Fab. "It's going back to being a tourist attraction. We'll drag the benches and potted flowers back out. Maybe I'll hire a teenager to take pics on the weekend."

"This will shock you," Fab said. "Love the idea."

Chapter Eleven

"No!" I yelled. "I'm not going." I tried to dig my toes into the tile floor of the kitchen, gaining no traction as I attempted to slow Fab's progress. She had me in a headlock and was dragging me toward the front door. "Didier!" I yelled again, this time at the top of my lungs.

His deep laughter sounded from the kitchen.

The door opened and slammed shut. Fab spun me away and barred the entry, arms crossed.

"How dare you?" I growled, attempting to straighten my hair and clothes at same time, giving up with a hiss.

"Go ahead, run. The side gate is locked, and you'd suck at climbing over it." She swung her arm around. "There's always the street. Run up and down it all you like. I'll follow you, and when you tire yourself out, you'll be happy I'm there so you can climb in the car and get out of the heat."

"I don't want to go on a dead-people job," I whined, stomping my foot and annoying even myself. "Are you sure the deceased is really dead this time?"

"'Deader than a doornail,' Raul assured me. His humor makes me laugh."

"Of course it does," I said in exasperation. "But I tell a funeral joke and you go all snooty, rich schoolgirl on me, like I've offended your sensibilities."

Fab turned to the garden window and blew exaggerated kisses, complete with hand motions. Didier grinned like an idiot and blew one back.

I stuck out my tongue, pretending not to notice that it only made Didier laugh harder. I crossed my arms and watched as Fab wiggled her way to the SUV, climbing in behind the wheel. A few seconds later, she gunned the engine several times.

Damn her! Here I was, dressed in a colorful short-sleeved sundress for what I'd thought was a shopping trip, and instead we were headed to Tropical Slumber. Something about a misplaced corpse; hopefully, this one wouldn't sit up and wave.

I walked as slow as humanly possible. Pausing, my hand on the handle, I waited until Fab turned towards me before opening the door and sliding into the passenger seat. "I promise that I will get you back."

Fab waited until the seatbelt clicked in place, then flew out of the driveway. "No, you won't. You're the nice one that doesn't hold grudges. Me, on the other hand, I'm neither of those things."

Traffic was light, Fab knew all the shortcuts, and we arrived at the funeral home in record time. I'd never wondered before, or maybe I had and forgot, but today it popped into my mind to wonder who'd thought it was a good idea to turn a drive-thru hot dog stand into a funeral home. Several owners later, the original building still stood, blending into the add-ons.

I'd met Dickie at my aunt's funeral and referred him to a lawyer for help getting out of a legal predicament. From that, we'd become friends. His partner, Raul, and Fab became fast pals when she hid out at their house, which was attached to the rear of the property. No one had thought to look for the sexy French woman at the local funeral home.

Fab parked under the portico at the front door, straddling the red carpet. How they kept it clean and star-ready was another question I'd never asked. There must be some action planned for today—the hearse was parked two feet in front of us, the sun gleaming off its sides. I couldn't spot the top of a casket through the back window and surmised the dearly departed hadn't been loaded yet.

"Put on your party manners." Fab closed the door before I could make a rude gesture.

Raul blocked the entry, looking a shade or two paler than his usual dark-haired, dark-eyed, bodybuilder self. His normally smiling face was lined with worry. He hugged Fab, holding on longer than usual. I waved politely and, once inside, claimed the plastic-slipcovered chair at the door.

Astro and Necco, the Dobermans, barked hello and skidded to a stop at my feet. I held out my hands. "No food." I frowned at there being no leftover funeral nibbles in sight and scratched both their ears. They took it well and sat by my side.

Dickie's tall, thin frame was hunched over as he paced back and forth on the far side of the entry, barely acknowledging our arrival. He finally looked up. "Thank you for coming," he said solemnly and ran his thin, bony fingers through his short-shaved hair in a nervous gesture.

"We seemed to have misplaced a body," Raul said to Fab, who was in the middle of her usual ritual of going from one visiting room to the next, checking out the dead.

"We certainly did not," Dickie screeched, an ear-splitting noise. "That body was stolen right out from under our noses, and now we're being blackmailed."

"I think there could be other charges in addition to the blackmail," Raul said with deceptive calmness, his fists flexing at his sides.

Dickie crossed the room in several long strides, stopping in front of me. Pulling a piece of paper from his pocket, he thrust it out. "We got this."

I smoothed out the note and read, "20K for the return of Robert Dunce or he'll be left on the bus stop in the middle of town and you can explain to his family." It included a crudely drawn smiley face.

"Found a second note taped to the back door this morning." Dickie handed me the second one.

I read out loud, "Tonight, 9pm, leave the cash in a brown bag, Avenue K dock trash can. Don't bring anyone with you. This is a one-time offer – don't screw it up. I'll call within one hour with directions where to pick up Dunce." Written in crayon, same demented happy face. I handed them both to Fab, who was reading over my shoulder.

"This is an easy one. We'll stake it out and catch the weasel," Fab said.

I groaned at *easy*. "Is the body in a casket?"

Raul shook his head. "Body bag."

"I'm telling you now, not in my car." I gave the two men a frosty look.

Dickie smiled, which didn't happen often. "Agree with you there. Once you get the body, call us, and we'll go wherever you tell us."

"You got a plan?" Fab asked.

"That's your area of expertise."

"Stakeout. I suggest we get there early. Pee first, might be a long wait."

"You said pee. I'm telling Didier." Fab didn't hide her annoyance at my inappropriateness. "While you're at it, tell him we may need his backup services. He's always offering; time to put out."

Raul raised his hand. "I volunteer."

"This idiot—" I nodded to the notes Fab held. "—might recognize you. I don't think whoever it is is very smart. You haven't said – how did this person get the opportunity to make off with a body? Was he sitting outside or what?"

Dickie winced. "Mr. Dunce arrived last night, right before we left for a party. We had him stored to be prepared today…" He choked up.

"Party?" I tried not to squirm. Funeral directors? I didn't need to know. All eyes turned to me, and I added, "That sounds fun." It appeared Dickie and Raul bought my sincerity; Fab rolled her eyes.

"While we were gone, this person broke in— smashed a window and climbed in. Made a big mess. We don't keep valuables around. Not sure why they took a body."

"Were any of the other bodies disturbed?" Fab asked.

I hung my head, not sure where she was going.

"We keep the viewing room doors locked when we're not here."

"I think one of us should go along. We'll stay close by and out of the way," Dickie suggested.

"We've got this covered. Don't we?" Fab turned to me.

"We need to drive by the area. From what I

remember, it's a rundown, rat-infested area with several apartment buildings that need to be red-tagged and the residents relocated. I'm thinking this person must be a local."

"The fewer people that are involved, the better the chance that we won't be seen," Fab said to Dickie and Raul. "I do promise that we'll call as soon as we have something to report."

Chapter Twelve

I flipped down the visor so I could make faces at Didier, who scowled from the back seat. "If you're going to sulk, you shouldn't have offered your backup services."

"In this case," Didier ground out, "what exactly does 'backup' do?"

"Carry the dead body," I said in all seriousness. "It's in a body bag, so you won't have to throw your clothes out afterwards."

Fab laughed. "Honey," she said to Didier, whose eyebrows had shot into his hairline. "The funeral guys are on standby for pickup. If they're a no-show, which I doubt," she added in response to his deepening frown, "I'll take one end and Madison the other."

"I wouldn't count on that," I said, loud and clear.

Fab had driven to the drop-off point earlier, and as suspected, there was nowhere to hide out. The designated trashcan was in the parking lot of a boat launch ramp that got used by locals. The sign clearly stated, "No parking unless towing a trailer." Street parking was minimal and only on one side, and the SUV would stick out amongst the beater cars and trucks. I was adamant about not setting my car up to be picked off.

"I say we rent a driveway to park the SUV in, and I'll sit and keep watch. The key is to stay hunched down; no one can see in unless they smooch their face against the glass." I didn't feel the least bit bad about wanting to weasel out of the job. "You and pretty boy go find a place to make out or something," I said to Fab, catching Didier's reaction out of the corner of my eye; he wasn't amused. "Might I also suggest that you not shoot this person unless they've got a gun pointed at you and you've got witnesses? A shoot-out in the street isn't good for real estate values." Once again, I eyed the run-down building across the street. Day or night, this wasn't a good place to hang out.

"What are you going to tell the driveway owner?" Didier asked in a way that made it obvious he didn't think I could pull it off.

"Something truthful." I hesitated before continuing, "That doesn't include any mention of a body and ransom."

Fab giggled. "How about staking out a cheating spouse?"

"Perhaps something more heartfelt, like a missing dog." Both Fab and Didier groaned. "There's always the incentive of extra money for not asking any questions. Maybe I'll luck out and it will be an old man, and I can send Fab in for the negotiations."

"Call Mac," Fab blurted. "She probably knows someone over here."

I fished my phone out of my pocket and punched in her number. "You know anyone who lives on Avenue K, the closer to the boat ramp the better?" I asked after exchanging hellos and clicking on speakerphone.

"What are you two up to?" she asked.

I told her.

"Ick. But if the body's in a bag…I could still put that on my resume. You need my help?"

"Not this time," I said, wishing I'd thought of her sooner and persuaded Fab to take her along instead. "You better not be out looking for a new job."

"Not going anywhere. No other job on the beach can offer up the entertainment." She laughed. "Got it! Old man Cain. Lives next to the alley, one lot over. He'll be good and drunk by this time, and even if he weren't, he'd take the money and not care what you do."

"We'll bring you in on the next job. We've got Didier, and my guess is he won't volunteer again." I promised to call if we needed anything. "Now what about you two?" I asked after I hung up.

"That's Cain's place." Fab pointed. "You park in the driveway. We'll hide in the row of hedges on the opposite side. The trashcan is close enough that we can see it all go down."

"Take a flashlight," I said with a big smile to

Didier. "Careful where you sit."

"Fifty dollars this goes down fast," Fab said.

"No thanks," I said. "Nothing about this screams easy."

Fab made an unintelligible noise.

"And you —" I pointed behind me. " — do what Fab tells you. She's boss."

"You just wait," Didier half-threatened. "I'll be extracting my revenge."

I smiled to myself, knowing that he'd never follow through on that threat. He might grumble throughout the job, but if we needed him, he'd help us out again.

Fab backed into Mr. Cain's driveway. I got money out of my purse and shoved it in my pocket, then jumped out and headed for the front door. I could hear a television blasting inside – from the sounds of it, a police chase in progress. I rang the doorbell. Not getting an answer, I peeked in the window and saw an older man stretched out in his easy chair, fast asleep or…I refused to contemplate that. I'd send Mac over tomorrow to check on him.

Fab and Didier had disappeared by the time I got back to the car. I sat in the driver's seat, reclining it, and powered down the window. I too had a bird's eye view of the trash. With an hour to kill and dusk turning to dark, I'd have to be careful or I'd soon nod off.

The street was quiet. Across the way, a Great Dane walked a man and woman, who had little say in the direction the dog took; they disappeared down the block and didn't come back. A couple of cars turned out of the alleyway and parked in their assigned spots in the parking lot in front of the apartment building across the street. For an area with such a bad reputation, it was quiet tonight.

A couple of important details Fab and I hadn't discussed were the payoff and the handling of the recovered body. I hoped Fab had a plan. I'd follow her lead, and if necessary, we'd improvise. We excelled at that.

Raul pulled up in the nondescript enclosed van that they used for body pickups. After idling in front of the trashcan, he got out and scoped out the area before dropping the paper bag in. He looked around again, got in, and drove slowly out of the parking lot.

Movement across the street caught my eye. A man slunk out from the far side of the building. Stepping behind the dumpster, he craned his head and watched Raul's van drive out of sight. He leaned against the building. Partially outlined by a weak bulb overhead, he extracted a cigarette from his pocket and began patting himself down, I presumed for a light. Not finding one, he crumpled the cigarette between his fingers and tossed it on the ground.

As impatient as his actions made him out to be, he continued to stand there, practicing fake boxing moves, seemingly on high alert.

Eventually, he pushed away from the building and started up the street, heading away from the boat launch, keeping one eye over his shoulder. To the casual observer, he was just another person out for an evening walk. A few houses up, he suddenly turned around, walked straight to the trashcan, and retrieved the bag.

Instead of bee-lining back across the street, he checked out my SUV and headed to where I was parked. I was already leaned back out of view; there was no room to crunch down without sitting under the steering wheel, and I wasn't sure it was physically possible. I watched as he stepped around the broken-down, waist-high fence.

"Some people are so stupid," he said to himself, one hand reaching inside the open window, the hand with the bag resting on the sill.

I reached for the bag, and his eyes locked on mine. Somehow, I managed to get my hand on it and toss it over my shoulder.

He jerked open the door. "Give me that back!" he yelled.

Fab ran up the driveway. The crunch of gravel diverting his attention, his interest shifted to the approaching woman, me and the bag forgotten. He stepped around the driver's side door, shoving it wide open in Fab's face, and hightailed it to the back of Mr. Cain's property.

"Grab him," I squealed.

Fab had already whirled around, running around the opposite side of the car in hot pursuit. Didier, right behind Fab, took off after her. Before jumping out, I retrieved the bag that had landed on the console and tossed it in the back, locking up the SUV and shoving the keys in my pocket. I went and stood by the street, one eye on the driveway and the other on the road.

The runner reappeared one house over, emerging from the trees. That told me that there was probably a seldom-used path there and he was a local. The man and I made eye contact, and he turned and hightailed it up the street. If it weren't for needing that body, I'd have voted to let him go. Fab reappeared the same way she went and bent over, gripping her knees and panting.

"That way!" I yelled and pointed. No point in me pursuing the man; I'd never catch up.

Didier came into view, crawling out of the overgrowth. He hadn't been far behind our man on the run. He spotted Fab a half-block up and took off in pursuit. He'd be passing her up in a few seconds; all those grueling runs were about to pay off.

I ran back to the SUV, jumped behind the wheel, and followed, beams on high. The foot chase veered off the road, and the men disappeared between two commercial buildings.

I stopped for Fab. "Now what?"

"Drive." She waved me on, jumping in. "Cut

through the gas station."

I rounded the corner in time to see Didier put a foot to the runner's behind, sending him sprawling on the pavement. It didn't appear that Didier bothered with introductions. Flipping the squirming man over, he leaned down and said something, and the man stopped moving. Didier jerked the man up by the front of his t-shirt and mostly dragged him over to the SUV. Fab hopped out, twirling a pair of handcuffs.

"I've informed our friend here that he has options. Jail and a prison sentence or give us back the damn body and he'll get a few bucks." Didier shook the man until he flailed, trying to get away. "What's it going to be?"

Watching Didier play the tough guy was impressive. His biceps bulged with the tight hold he had on the man, who didn't have a prayer of escaping.

"I hid him in the haunted house, next street over," he whimpered.

People are stupid.

The "Haunted House" had been owned by an old woman in failing health. Not having the energy or the ready cash to take care of the place, she let the weeds run wild, and soon after, she passed away. With no relatives to fight over the land, it had become more rundown, a hurricane relieving it of part of its roof. Since it was no longer a quick fix but a gut job to repair the ravages of the intrusion of water, investors shied away. The rundown condition had earned it its nickname.

Fab called over her shoulder, "Call Raul."

"I don't want *him* in my car." I pointed a finger at the man as though no one knew who I meant.

"We need to get out of here before we start attracting more attention." Fab jerked her head to where we'd attracted a crowd of two people that stood and stared.

I groaned at the sight of their cell phones, and that was the only reason I relented.

"He doesn't smell too bad." Didier grinned at me. He pushed the man into the back seat. Fab waited on the opposite side, handcuffing the man to the sissy bar.

"I thought you said no police," he yelped as she snapped them on.

"Calm down," Didier ordered, letting the man know who was in charge. "You keep your end of the bargain, I'll keep mine."

On my way around to the passenger side, in addition to calling Raul to give him directions to the new location, I took a moment to close my eyes and calm my nerves. Raul assured me he'd step on it, and I warned him not to get a ticket. Climbing in, I noticed that Didier barely had a hair out of place and Fab, always calm under pressure, appeared irked. If I had to guess, I'd say it was because she hadn't been the one to put her foot up the man's butt.

Once everyone was settled in their seats with Fab headed to the haunted house, Didier barked, "Start talking. What's your name?"

The man jumped. "J...Johnny M...Mason," he stuttered.

"What the hell were you thinking?" Didier snapped out his question. "A dead body for ransom!"

Johnny flinched. "I need money," he whined. "I saw the two men leaving the funeral place and figured it would be good place to find a few bucks."

"How did Mr. Dunce figure into your plan?" Fab asked in a no-nonsense tone that matched Didier's.

"Who? You mean the dead guy?" He looked at Didier and shrugged. "I searched all the usual places people keep valuables and couldn't find anything. Then I spotted the bag. Thought maybe I'd get lucky, so I unzipped it and checked for jewelry or a wallet, but nothing," he said in all candor, not appearing the least bit embarrassed by his behavior.

"Did you think up this bright idea all by yourself?" I asked.

"I got it off the news," he said proudly. "Although that was the funeral home owner blackmailing the family. Seemed like my idea was better. I wouldn't pay extra for one of *my* relatives."

There needed to be a disclaimer at the bottom

of the television screen: "Don't try this at home."

Fab parked in front of the rundown house, cutting the lights. Nothing was discernible in the dark except the point of the roof sticking up above the trees. The windows of the houses on either side showed no signs of anyone being at home; most likely, the owners had gone to bed.

Minutes later, Raul pulled up and backed into the driveway. Dickie got out of the passenger side.

"Dude's in the kitchen," Johnny said after Didier jerked him out of the back none too gently.

I stayed behind, the window down. Fab could handle anything that came up, and Didier had proven himself to be calm under chaos. Fab and Didier returned within a few minutes. Raul turned the van's lights on and drove out of the driveway, turning in the direction of the funeral home.

"Where's the criminal?" I asked when Fab got behind the wheel.

"Johnny's with Raul and Dickie," Fab said in disgust. "They're interested in his sob story."

I powered up the window as Fab followed the van, though not for long, as she soon passed them and they became a dim shape in her rearview mirror. "I hope you gave Johnny the 'stay out of the neighborhood' speech," I said.

"After thinking about it, I didn't want to stick to my end of the bargain," Didier said, "but it didn't matter. Fab told me the guys didn't want the man arrested. They're afraid of negative publicity. I made it clear to the funeral duo that if they get swindled by that guy again, they're not to call either of you."

"I love it when you leave out pertinent details," I said to Fab. "When Dickie comes around, crocodile tears on his cheeks, I'm directing him to you."

Chapter Thirteen

I choose a white sundress with rope straps and a matching belt and slipped into some tan leather flip-flops. I knew Fab and Didier had a romantic lunch planned at their favorite restaurant in South Beach and would be gone all day. So would I. Knowing my family, as soon as Fab and Didier hit the highway, they'd start stopping by to check on me. I didn't think I could stand a minute of that, let alone a whole day.

I grabbed my hot-pink purse and headed down the hall. When I got to the top of the stairs, Didier let out a wolfish whistle.

I curtsied. "Merci."

Fab eyed me up and down. "I like that dress. Where are you going?" She looked hot in her short, sleeveless black dress with a flared skirt, paired with stilettos.

"Fabiana," Didier mildly chastised.

"What? You want to know too. If I try to nice it out of her, it will take all day." Fab's hands went to her hips. "Well?"

I sat down on the edge of the daybed, Fab and Didier across from me. "Later, I'm hitting up my favorite seashell stores," I lied. It sounded good and like something I would do. "But first, I'll be going to Jake's because you're getting on your phone right now and telling Gunz to get his ass over there." Didier shaking his head wasn't lost on me. "I'm going to mend fences. Looking cute and showing a little leg should help my cause."

"Maybe you should wait until I can be with you." Fab shook her head in doubt.

"No," I said adamantly. "If I can't get a working relationship pieced together with the man, then it's time to move on to someone else." I cut off her next objection. "After a little lunch, I'll stop by The Cottages." Throwing in food was a seller, I mentally patted myself. I definitely had plans for a strawberry lemonade but was otherwise uninterested in getting something to eat, but I kept that part to myself.

Fab engaged me in a stare-down, but since I was used to her tactics, I didn't flinch.

"Madeline mentioned she might stop by; she'll be disappointed to have missed you," Didier said.

I knew it. "She should've called or something, not have you make me feel guilty about having plans to get me to change them." Time to turn the tables. "Aren't you happy that I'm getting out for a day of sunshine?"

"Of course," Didier said.

Fab didn't comment, just continued to stare, as though I was under her own personal microscope.

"Will you call Gunz?" I asked again. "I want to get over to Jake's right away. I called Phil to track down the furniture that was in front of the lighthouse and found out that she gave it to Junker. I plan on having it moved back."

Fab went out to the patio to make the call. I wasn't sure why I couldn't listen in, but now wasn't the time to nitpick.

"You could come with us," Didier offered.

"Absolutely not. You need to romance that woman of yours." Changing the subject, I gave him a once-over. "You look pretty darn good yourself." He was rocking a pair of black pants, a button-down, and his signature leather loafers.

"Fab picked it out." He smiled. "You will call if you need anything?"

"Of course. Now go have fun or I'll be mad at you."

Fab came back through the French doors. "Gunz is on his way. I didn't give him a clue as to what you wanted, so that piqued his interest. Don't take any of his…well, nonsense. Make it clear that you're no pushover."

"I'll be fine."

We left together. Didier opened the driver's door of Fab's seldom-driven Porsche, and she slipped behind the wheel. It didn't tweak his masculinity that she drove. He once told me that it made her happy and it wasn't an issue.

I realized that I had no clue what had happened to Creole's testosterone truck, as I'd dubbed his Ford 650, and hadn't thought to ask anyone. Now that I had more questions than ever, starting with his "wife," I planned to get answers. I was tired of being put off as though I had no right to know.

The only thing on the list that I'd rattled off to Fab and Didier that was truthful was going to Jake's. I rolled down the windows and let the air whip through crosswise, which never failed to perk me up.

As I pulled into the driveway and parked in front of Junker's, I sighed at the "Closed" sign. I walked around the perimeter without locating my furniture, walked back to the car, and reached into the cup holder. Removing my phone, I called the man himself.

"Where's my furniture?" I asked when he answered with a gruff, "Huh?"

"Who's this?" He let out a rusty laugh, amused with himself, and continued, "Sold it. Had to recoup my money."

"What money? I paid for it." I stamped my foot, which left me wincing.

"The lawyer wanted cash. She dissed it as crap, I believe she called it. I gave her five cents on the dollar."

"She told me that she gave it to you; I guess in a way she did," I huffed. Knowing it wasn't his fault, I added, "Happy you got a good deal." I wasn't, but I'd definitely use it as an opportunity to get my own discount.

He grunted. To say he was a man of few words was an understatement.

"Here's the deal. A couple of your pieces already caught my eye, and I wondered what I'd do with them; now I know. I'm tagging them with a sticky note, which means do not sell to someone else. I want a deal, not the ten-thousand-percent markup you give the public."

"You want it cleaned up?" he asked.

"You know a little rust on my wrought iron doesn't bother me. I'm also in the market for a few good metal containers to plant flowers in."

"Sold those too. Sorry."

"One more thing. The lighthouse is going to be open on the weekends for pictures and so tourists can stick their heads in the door, so please have your store open."

"I'll have Grandma man it; she's been wanting a job."

"You have a grandmother?" I asked, a bit shocked since I guessed him to be seventy.

"Don't be a smartass."

"Yes, sir." I almost laughed. "I won't even ask how old she is."

"Good thing. You get your picks tagged, I'll drag them across the parking lot. No extra charge. Anything else?" He hung up without waiting for an answer.

"Thank you," I said to dead air.

When a motorcycle roared into the driveway, I didn't need to turn around to know it belonged to Gunz. He rolled up in front of the lighthouse, turned off the engine, and looked around the parking lot. Pulling off his gloves and helmet and fastening them to the handlebar, he heaved his considerable bulk off the immaculate black Harley, shot his eyes in my direction, and sauntered over. At least six foot and several inches and bald, he presented an intimidating picture. He usually favored painted-on hair, goo in a can; today, he'd gone au natural, and I thought it a huge improvement.

I waved as I crossed the parking lot, meeting him halfway. Having decided direct was best, I said, "I know I'm not your favorite person, but we don't have to be bosom pals to do business. As long as we both score, we're happy." I arched my eyebrow, hoping that he would agree.

"You're a nervy chick." He stared but didn't look the least bit irritated, which surprised me and made me hopeful. "Let's lay out our cards. What do you want?"

"Information." I went on to tell him that Phil was out of business, along with her source, and that Fab and I needed someone who would deal with us directly.

He looked thoughtful. "Used to like Phil, maybe a little too much. Once suggested we do some business together, and she flipped. I can't quite put my finger on it, but I don't trust her anymore. Here's a freebie – that 'source' she used is not out of business. You know how I know?

Because he's a good friend."

"I suspected he wasn't. And that was before I found out that my brother told her to cut off the connection."

"Heard they were doing it." He laughed at my surprise. "I know everything. I boast about it all the time, and no one believes me."

"Freebie for you – you should keep that 'know everything' piece of information under your hat, lest it be used against you."

"I've been told that more than once. Guess I should listen. Speaking of me, what do I get?"

"What do you want? Cash? Free food at Jake's?"

"No offense, but Jake's isn't my kind of crowd. Got plenty of cash. What I want is to use the lighthouse for meetings when I have a legit client and need to look like an upstanding pillar."

I told him about my weekend plans for the lighthouse.

"That will work for me. Any business I conduct will be done during regular business hours on weekdays, and that won't be every day, just when I need it. I'm using a business rental office now and don't like it. Too many people wanting to snoop into my affairs."

"You'll have to supply your own furniture. Phil took it when she left." I didn't mention the faint odor that came back when it didn't get regularly aired out.

"I'm telling you now, I'll be the ideal tenant.

I've smoothed a few of my rough edges, and once word gets out that I'm moving my business into the neighborhood, any and all dirtballs won't set foot on this block." He gave me a wolfish smile.

I wanted to step back but held my ground. His reputation preceded him. This wasn't a man you screwed, and if anyone who hadn't gotten the memo challenged him, he quickly brought them up to speed. "One other thing, Junker and his wife are friends; they won't bother you and vice versa. Agreed?"

"Junk and I are simpatico, no problems there."

"I'll have the locks changed and leave a key at the bar," I said.

"I'll do it. I want something that can't be opened by anyone who happens to have a lockpick." He pulled his phone out and snapped pictures of the exterior. Turning back, he said, "Let me check with my friend. I'm sure there won't be a problem, but I can't give out his number without a heads up. If for some reason he says no, I'll get you the name of someone equally talented."

"Thanks, and I mean it." I smiled at him. "Also happy you didn't make me grovel."

He nodded. "The boyfriend. That sucked. Sorry."

"Careful, we just might become friends."

* * *

I left Jake's and suddenly feeling hungry I stopped to grab a grilled shrimp pizza before hitting the Overseas Highway again, heading south. I laughed at my paranoia, but that didn't stop me from keeping an eye on the rearview mirror, deliberately missing my turn off and making a u-turn several exits later to double back. I pulled into the driveway of what Creole and I had referred to as the Beach House. It sat at the end of the road, one way in and out, in a remote section of the Keys, the nearest neighbor a half-mile away. It saddened me that I couldn't remember the last time I was here or what we'd done together. I also didn't want to think about another woman coming here—this was our hideaway.

A fence surrounded the property, accessed by a security pad. I entered the house through the kitchen, putting the pizza on the counter. I looked around the open space—nothing was out of place. The first thing I did was cut across the living room to open the sliding doors that ran the entire length of the wall, allowing the salty Gulf breeze to air out the room.

Creole had bought the property for a song from an investor wanting to dump it when he had no takers for the secluded property, which was several exits outside of Tarpon Cove. He'd ripped out the walls of the two small bedrooms and turned it into one open, airy space, the only bedroom behind a pair of bamboo screens. The bathroom was a woman's dream, with a sunken tub that overlooked the water and a walk-in shower with numerous jets.

I stood next to the king-size bed and undressed, mimicking Creole by tossing my clothes in a pile on the floor. I crossed to the closet and took out one of his dress shirts, wrapping myself in his scent. Then I curled up on the couch and reveled in the quiet, thankful to not have to smile, or think of something pleasant to say, or do anything I didn't want to. No one to monitor my every move. I turned on the television, hitting the mute button, and closed my eyes.

Chapter Fourteen

It wouldn't have surprised me if I looked in the rearview mirror and saw "crappy friend" tattooed on my forehead. When I woke up at Creole's, it was dark outside. I flew off the couch and fished my phone out of the bottom of my purse. Between the missed calls and texts, I'm surprised my phone hadn't melted down.

I immediately texted Fab that I was fine and would see her in the morning. And for her not to worry. To my surprise, I got "fine" as a response. I wrapped myself in a sheet and went out to the patio, lying in a chaise and counting stars until I dozed, eventually making my way back to the couch, ignoring the big comfortable bed.

The next morning, when I turned the corner to my house, the first thing I noticed was that Didier had left for the day. I sighed in relief. I'd have to face him later, but the two of them at the same time could be overwhelming. I pulled in and parked next to Fab's Porsche. As I came through the front door, my phone rang. I glanced at the screen and, not recognizing the number, answered anyway.

"Hello." I dropped my purse in the entry, crossing to the island and sliding onto a stool across from Fab.

"This is Gunz's connection. I'm willing to work for you with a few stipulations." He laughed. "You can call me GC."

It took me a minute to get the joke, which I thought was lame. But I knew he was the best at getting information, so he was welcome to his eccentricities.

"Can I put you on speaker? My partner, Fab, is here. Saves me time repeating everything to her, which she complains I'm bad at, but I disagree."

"Whatever." He snorted. "Here's the deal, the number on your screen is assigned to you. Don't give it to anyone else. You do, and the number gets disconnected. Payment in cash; leave it in an envelope at Gunz's office. Capiche?"

"Yes, got it." I ordered a background check on Bordello, feeling bad I hadn't gotten back to Corndog in a timelier manner. I told GC about Creole and the so-called wife, the questions I had, and to get me whatever information he could.

"You'll be hearing from me." He hung up.

"That's one less problem," I said with a smile and laid my phone down. "It will be more expedient not to have to go through a middle man."

"I've got a job for one of my clients today," Fab said in an unusually polite tone. "A delivery.

No cloak and dagger. But we need to be dressed in business attire."

That explained the black suit and six-inch heels. "You need me to come along on a delivery job?"

"I'm not interested in driving to Miami by myself. I'd like company."

"How much time do I have?" I walked out of the kitchen, stopping at the couch to scratch Jazz and Snow.

Fab opened the case on her diamond watch. "Half-hour."

I nodded and ran up the stairs.

* * *

"I should warn you," Fab said. "I called Madeline last night when you didn't answer your phone. She felt certain that you would show up by morning. Her unconcerned response surprised me, but just to let you know, she's exasperated with you and Brad."

"I'll call her," I sighed.

"No hurry. I texted her you were back." Fab's annoyance was coming out. "Actually, I did it last night after getting your text. Expect a lecture about worrying those that love you and hiding your whereabouts."

"I never had any intention of staying away so long. It was my plan to take a short nap, not fall into a deep, dreamless sleep, but that's what happened the second I closed my eyes. When I woke up and realized it was dark outside, I didn't want to drive home."

"Didier figured you probably went to Creole's. As your best friend, I should've been the one to figure it out," Fab grumbled. "I want the address. He's dead, so there's no longer a promise to break."

I flinched at the finality of her words.

As an undercover detective, he'd kept his home address a secret, not wanting unwelcome visitors or the arrival of disgruntled persons he'd arrested who wanted revenge. I had it on good authority from the man himself that he and I were the only two who knew where it was located; without precise instructions, it was easy to miss the turn off the feeder road.

For someone who said she wanted company, Fab didn't say anything else the rest of the drive. Finally, she exited the Interstate in the heart of Miami.

"What's this job about?" I lifted the hem of my black dress. "I remembered my Glock." I'd strapped the handgun to my inner thigh.

"Straight delivery job. Mr. Frank has a sterling reputation; this should go smoothly. I'm picking up a package at his office and delivering it to a financial advisor in Brickell, the neighboring area."

"Just read in an article that Brickell is one of the hottest areas in Miami. What will I be doing?

Besides looking pretty?"

"I'm not expecting trouble, but we don't have a good track record of jobs going off without a glitch."

"Yes…glitch…that's an understatement when describing most of our cases."

Fab pulled to the curb in front of an all-glass tower. Depending on the location of the office, the occupant would have a view of Biscayne Bay on one side or the bustling commercial area on the other.

"Our only other option is the building parking lot. It would be faster if you cruised around the block and picked me up." Fab opened the door.

I slid out and circled around the front of the SUV.

"I'll call you when I get back out front." Fab shoved her phone in her pocket.

I settled behind the wheel and watched as the delivery truck in front of me pulled out. I took his spot — better a yellow area than a red. I powered down the window and left the engine idling, figuring that when I got a glimpse of meter enforcement, I'd be on my way.

Fab came back in a few minutes, a small shopping bag from an upscale jewelry store and a business envelope in her hands.

"This was a score." She nodded approvingly at the parking space.

"Where to now?" I asked as I climbed out, skirted around her, and went back to my assigned seat.

"A few blocks up." Fab handed me a slip of paper. "Victoria Linus, Financial Advisor."

"What do you suppose is in the bag?" I asked.

"I'm guessing a necklace based on the shape of the box. I thought about taking a peek but worried I might not get the beautiful bow back on just right." She sighed, glancing at the bag.

"Spoken from experience?"

Fab blushed. "This time, we're using the parking garage," she said, leaning out the window to grab a ticket from the machine. "We'll play it up, make it look like it takes two to guard the delivery. Mr. Frank does require a signature."

We rode the elevator to the fifth floor. Linus and Associates ran the length of the front side of the building. We entered the reception area through the glass doors.

Fab explained the delivery to the bored brunette at the desk, adding that if it wasn't convenient, we could wait or come back.

I leaned toward Fab and whispered, "We getting paid by the hour?"

The brunette relayed the information over the phone. When she hung up, she said, "Have a seat. Ms. Linus's assistant will be right out."

A few minutes after we sat down, a leggy blonde came down the hall, a smile pasted on her face. "Ms. Linus will see you." She motioned for us to follow.

Victoria Linus sat behind a mammoth u-shaped desk. Another blonde, with her long hair fashioned into a bun at the nape of her neck, fortyish and screaming "professional" in her designer power suit, she zeroed in on the bag and held out her hand. "A delivery?"

Fab handed it over. "I'll need a signature." She shoved the envelope across the desk.

I hoped this wasn't going to take long. I refrained from sitting, since Ms. Linus hadn't offered and Fab still stood.

The woman glared at the box as she withdrew it from the bag, a brittle smile on her face. She shoved the ribbon off and snapped open the lid, turning it around and showing it off.

"Beautiful," I said in awe.

Nestled inside was a thick snake-chain gold necklace, an impressively large diamond in the center. To my untrained eye, it looked to be in the three to four carat range.

"You think so?" Ms. Linus took it out and twirled it on the end of her finger. "It's my 'your services are no longer needed' parting gift."

I felt flushed, embarrassed for her, and I didn't want to witness whatever was about to unfold. I glanced at Fab out of the corner of my eye, but she was showing no reaction. It took me a millisecond to realize that she'd delivered "see you" presents before.

"If you'll just sign, we'll be on our way," Fab said.

Victoria picked up the envelope, tore it open,

and extracted a piece of letterhead, which she ripped to shreds, dumping the pieces in front of Fab. "The bastard had me convinced I was the one, until…well… I just wasn't." She tossed the necklace box onto a console table. "The upscale bag was a giveaway. Pretty good idea what was inside. A very expensive bauble," she sneered.

Fab brushed the paper pieces into her hand, stuffing them in her pocket.

"We'll get out of your way," I said. If there was a better way to announce our departure, it didn't come to mind.

"You're professionals?" Victoria quirked an eyebrow.

Fab straightened, giving her the "don't screw with me" smile.

"I have a job for you. Name your price." She opened her desk drawer and produced a pearl-handled pistol, the make not one I recognized at first glance. "Kill Bill Frank."

"We're not murderers." I tried for a laugh, but it came out as a strangled noise.

"Put the gun down," Fab ordered. "No man is worth spending the rest of your life in prison."

Victoria casually shifted the gun from one hand to the other and then steadied it. My problem was it was pointed directly at me. I was relieved to see that her finger wasn't on the trigger, but my body went on high alert anyway.

"Sure, old Bill would be dead," Fab said in a conciliatory tone, "but the satisfaction would be short-lived. Life as you know it would crumble at your feet."

The silence was more than my nerves could bear, and I gauged the distance to the door, trying to decide whether to turn tail and run or draw my own gun. Once again, I followed Fab's lead; her handgun was still under her skirt and her hands in clear view.

"Just kidding." Victoria laughed, sounding a bit unhinged. "Hope I didn't scare you." She made brief eye contact before tossing the gun in the drawer, slamming it shut. "I'd like to reassure you that it wasn't loaded."

I itched to draw my Glock and inform her, "Guess what, hon? Mine's loaded. How do you like it pointed at your face?" Instead, I left her office without a word. The sound of Fab's voice followed me out the door, but I couldn't make out the words.

I hustled to the elevator and was jabbing my finger at the button when Fab appeared at my side. The doors opened, and when they closed, I said, "Reassure us," and shuddered. "Killing the messenger took on new meaning today."

"When we get to the car, I'll call Mr. Frank and suggest he hire an extra bodyguard."

"I need a shower. That is the slimiest job we've ever been on."

Chapter Fifteen

Late the next afternoon, Fab pulled up in front of Jake's, shutting off the engine. I'd gotten a call from Doodad that a woman wanted to speak to me concerning Creole. She wouldn't leave a number and instead insisted on calling back to confirm that I'd meet with her.

I'd also received a call from the lawyer, Mr. Briscoe, who informed me that Cheryl Beaumont, Creole's "wife," was demanding a meeting. He admitted to being reluctant to meet until after he'd fully checked out her story and frustrated by her foot-dragging about handing over the paperwork he'd requested. When he questioned Cheryl, she snapped, "Call my lawyer." He'd done just that, but none of his calls had yet been returned. It also worried him that she seemed to know too much about me, and he wondered where she was getting her information.

"Don't get out," I said on an exasperated sigh. "I may have been less than forthcoming when I told you we were coming to grab paperwork."

Her eyebrows shot up in surprise. "You lied to

me? Your best friend? How could you?"

"Stop the melodrama. And I never used the word 'lie.' That's your interpretation."

Fab shook her head. "I'm listening."

"I have a meeting inside…" I said, checking the dashboard clock, "…in ten minutes." I told her about the calls from Doodad and Briscoe. "My gut tells me we're about to come face to face with the other woman." I managed a half-smile, and just as quickly, it disappeared. *It might turn out that I'm the other woman.*

"So if I hadn't kept an eye on your slippery self, you'd have met with her alone?" She ignored my eye-roll. "Bad idea."

"I realize that, and I feel a tad guilty, which is why I'm fessing up."

"You sound like me, and I'm not sure that's a good thing."

I launched myself across the console, and she flinched as I threw my arms around her. "I'm so happy you're here."

"Let's get inside so we can be ready for…what's her name again?"

"Cheryl Beaumont." It was a name I'd never forget.

Fab slid out, and I joined her. When we walked inside, I looked over at Doodad, who shook his head. Ms. Beaumont hadn't arrived yet. It was busy for a weekday afternoon, the regulars lined up at the bar and more than half the tables filled.

"Pitcher of margaritas," I yelled.

"No, you don't; you'll have water." Fab signaled Doodad.

We cut across the floor to the outside deck. Fab tossed aside the "Do not sit here" sign.

"Sit on this side." She motioned to the far side of the table. "That way, we have a ringside seat for what's going on inside, including her arrival. Any idea what she looks like?"

I shook my head. "How did she find out about me? Where is she getting her information?"

"Good questions we'll get answers to."

I wasn't confident about how the meeting would go and wished I'd never heard the woman's name. It threw mud on my memories of Creole; staying open-minded was taking a toll.

"We should be thankful she didn't show up at the house." Fab's expression hardened. "This whole meeting stinks to me." Her eyes narrowed, focused on the inside. "Don't react. A woman I've never seen before just walked in… She went straight to the bar."

Doodad came through the doors, setting down one of the new paper coasters I'd designed and a bottled water.

"There's a woman at the bar, and it might be Madison's appointment," Fab told Doodad.

"I'll send her right over." He went back inside, headed straight to the woman, and after a brief exchange, pointed her in our direction.

"Here she comes," Fab said. "She's blond but

not naturally so, judging by the black roots."

I looked up and locked eyes with the woman in question. She had a purpose in her step, and she didn't take her eyes off me either.

The woman was curvy and buxom under her loose-flowing tropical dress, with colorful bracelets lining her arms and large hoop earrings. She gave off an air of being able to handle herself, no matter what life served up, hardened around the edges. Creole certainly didn't have a type; the two of us couldn't be more different, looks-wise. What caught my eye was the small child holding her hand. As she got closer, I couldn't tear my eyes away from the boy, checking him out. He appeared to be about four or five.

"Madison?" She zeroed in on me, dismissing Fab.

Interesting. She knew what I looked like. I gripped the bottle of water tightly in my hand, giving me an excuse not to extend it, the whole "don't touch me" thing having gotten worse since Creole's death. "I'm Madison. This is my friend, Fab."

She ignored the introduction. "Madison, how nice to meet you," she said, her tone insincere. "I've been wanting to meet the other woman for some time. I'm Cheryl, Cheryl Beaumont, Creole's wife." Ignoring my reticence, she stuck her hand out. I flinched back.

Fab waved her hand in front of me, knocking

over a water bottle while shooting me a slight wink. Who knew Fab could do mother hen? Lately, she'd been getting a lot of practice. She'd successfully sidetracked Cheryl, mopping up water with a napkin while the woman dragged a chair out from under the table and sat down, picking up the boy and plunking him in her lap.

"Mommy, I'm hungry."

"We serve hamburgers," I said inanely and turned to Fab, who had already flagged down Cook's son, who was working the busy shift. "Order me a tequila, straight up, lime," I whispered to Fab.

"I can't pay," Cheryl said flatly.

"It's on the house," Fab said and asked the boy what he wanted on his hamburger. He buried his face in his mother's chest. Fab placed the order, asking that everything be put on the side. "You can build your own hamburger," she said to the boy, who peeked out at her. "And of course, you order whatever you'd like," Fab said to Cheryl in a dismissive tone.

Doodad reappeared and took drink orders. Cheryl ordered a bottled beer, a common brand. Apparently she didn't share Creole's love of the European selections that we carried.

How are you? seemed phony, and I knew that neither of us cared about the answer. Straightforward had always worked for me in the past. "What is it you want?"

"I'm sorry we have to meet under such

circumstances," Cheryl said smoothly. Which rang hollow to my ears. "I'm here to get what rightfully belongs to Creole's son, what Creole would've wanted him to have." She glanced down at the boy. "And for you to do the right thing without a court battle."

The air sucked itself out of my body. I felt lightheaded. "You're telling me that's Creole's son." I nodded at the boy.

Fab smiled down at the boy. "What's your name?"

"Milton," he squeaked out, smiling shyly.

"A family name?" Fab questioned Cheryl.

"You don't know?" Her eyes swept over Fab to me. "He's named after Creole's grandfather, a decorated general."

Another thing I hadn't known, assuming it was even true. He'd rarely talked about his past and very little about his childhood, growing up with an abusive father.

"And what is it that you're claiming on your son's behalf?" I asked.

"I know you were named beneficiary on the life insurance policy Creole had through the department, and it's not right. Once the will is filed, I'll know more. I'm fighting for every last dime for our son," she said, her eyes sparking.

How did she know all these details? This was the first I'd heard of a life insurance policy. Nothing she was claiming about Creole's character added up to the man I knew. He'd never fail to provide for a wife and son.

"Do you have proof, as in a marriage license and birth certificate?" Fab stared at her, sounding incredulous.

"I've got a lawyer, and all the necessary documents are in his possession, which neither of you are entitled to," she said, angrily and on the defensive.

"I've also got a lawyer, and I think we should let the two of them sort out the details." I just couldn't deal with her. "Did Creole know that he had a son?"

"Of course he did," she practically spit, taking another swig of beer.

Doodad was back, setting down a plate in front of the boy, along with a glass of milk and more bottled water.

"Your hamburger was top priority." Fab patted the boy on the head. "You can choose any of these items over here…" She pointed. "…to put on your bun. Or none at all – your choice."

Girl wonder never ceased to amaze me. But the lack of tequila annoyed me greatly.

I watched as Milton separated the bun from the meat, discarding the bun, and that had me smiling. My guess was he was more closely relate to Fab, as he sorted through his sides, sniffing a pickle, which he tossed to the other side of the plate, and then tearing off a piece of the meat, sticking it in his mouth. He smiled, a mouth full of food on display. My heart squeezed. I'd lost my father in my teens, which was life altering, but three or four years old…he'd never know his father.

"How old are you?" I asked.

He held up four fingers.

"You can stop staring," Cheryl whispered to me. "My son isn't a lab rat."

"I was looking for similarities to what Creole might have looked like as a young boy." I gave her a tired smile. It was hard to believe that either Creole or she had sired the little boy, as he didn't resemble either of them. He was a pale blond with green eyes, both of his supposed parents dark-haired and blue-eyed. Being a decent judge of people, I figured every minute of this woman's appearance and performance had been pre-planned.

"So you're telling us that Creole knew he was a father," Fab said.

Cheryl bristled.

"It's hard to believe that we're talking about the same man," I said. "The Creole I knew wouldn't have lead a double life, and he certainly wouldn't have left a wife and child unprotected." But how could I know for absolute certain? The reality was he had a whole other life as an undercover police officer that I knew nothing about.

"But he did have a wife and child, and here we are in the flesh," Cheryl countered. "How many nights did he spend away from you when you had no idea where he was? Or who he was with? I can assure you, he was with me and has been for years."

I downed the rest of my water and capped the bottle, which did nothing to calm my nerves. I was at the end of what I could stand of this conversation. I didn't have any answers for her smug self-assuredness.

"You've accomplished your goal." Fab forced a smile. "Madison knows about you. You want money from the estate, but she has no control over that and you know it. That's a matter for Creole's lawyer, Mr. Briscoe."

"I need a loan, or my son and I are going to end up homeless. I can pay you back when Creole's affairs are settled."

"You come here and tell her that her boyfriend was unfaithful, had a second life and family, and you want money?" Fab wasn't faking her shock. "Take it up with your lawyer. You're not bleeding her heart strings for cash."

I'd faded out of the conversation. I didn't want to hear another word. I had a hard time wrapping my mind around all the deceit. A wife? A son? We'd just started talking about marriage, starting a family of our own. He'd had an ambitious goal—twenty-five children. I joked that we might want to think about cutting back. He laughed that deep growly laugh that I loved and kissed me, the kind of kiss that makes you lose your train of thought.

"I'm not feeling well." I stood up. "I'm going home." I turned to Fab and mouthed *car*. "Mr. Briscoe is my attorney," I told Cheryl, even though I knew she already had that information. "Talk to him."

Fab passed me the keys. "I'll take care of everything here," she reassured me.

"When will I hear from you again? There's Milton to consider," Cheryl said. Her eyes shot sparks.

"In the future," Fab said, ignoring the woman's anger, "any meetings will take place at Mr. Briscoe's office."

"It was nice meeting you." I patted Milton's head, not making eye contact with anyone else. "Parlez-vous français?" I asked on a whim.

He flashed a two-tooth smile, concentrating on his burger, which he had eaten from the middle to almost the outer edge.

"What?" Cheryl demanded, her anger unabated.

"Just wondered if Creole had taught Milton a few words of French yet?"

Judging by the look on her face, the question took her completely by surprise and the answer was no.

"How strange," I said, "he even taught me a few words." I didn't know what else to say to Cheryl. Fab signaled with her eyes for me to leave. "Good luck."

"That luck is dependent on you, now isn't it?"

Cheryl huffed. "I hope you'll make Milton a high priority."

I nodded and stepped into the bar, forcing myself to maintain a steady pace as I headed straight for the front door, happy to see my SUV parked one space over. I slid in on the passenger side and reclined the seat as far as it would go, lying back and closing my eyes.

Nothing that had happened made any sense. Was it as simple as that he'd liked living a double life and wasn't willing to give either one up? That made the headlines every now and then; of course, the man usually ended up in jail for bigamy.

Fab knocked on the driver's side window. I hit the button to let her in.

"Cheryl is a money grubber," Fab declared as she slid behind the wheel. "I gave her some money and told her to call her lawyer when she ran out."

"I owe you. I appreciate your letting me dump it all in your lap so I could get out of there."

Fab nodded, starting the engine and pulling out.

I took a deep breath. "You think it's all a scam? She has to know it won't work unless she can prove her claims." Was it too much to hope that this was an elaborate ruse? The other option...all the memories I had of the man I loved would be ruined. As it stood now, Cheryl had pretty much accomplished that end. If

Creole were sitting beside me instead of Fab, I'd be tempted to shoot him.

"And in the meantime, she squeezes as much money as she can out of you. I don't think so." Fab pulled into the driveway a short time later. I didn't bother with shoes but climbed out, walking barefoot into the house and dumping them in the boot tray.

Didier was standing at the island in bathing trunks, chopping something. He flashed me a smile, and that started a flood of tears that ran down my face.

"I'm going to bed," I choked out and headed for the stairs.

"Cherie." Didier dropped his knife, which clanged against the counter, and rushed toward me.

"I can't." I shook my head. "You tell him." I ran up the stairs and banged the door shut behind me. I didn't bother with the lock, knowing that wouldn't keep Fab or Didier out. Not long ago, she'd whispered conspiratorially that she'd taught him the fine art of lock picking and was quite proud of her star pupil. It was to be a secret, as he didn't want anyone to know that he had a criminal trick up his sleeve.

Chapter Sixteen

"I don't want to go anywhere," I said, burying my face in my arms, my head on the island. I didn't dare mention I wanted to take a nap when I'd just woken up not long ago.

"You need a new pair of shoes," Fab pronounced, pleased with herself.

"If I get any more shoes, I'll have to wear them mismatched to get them all worn."

"That's a horrible problem to have." She looked thoroughly amused.

My phone rang, Doodad's picture popping up on the screen. I flashed the screen at Fab. "He never calls, so this might be trouble."

"Hey boss," he said when I answered. "Thought you might want to know — Corndog had the snot beat of out him last night, and he's in Tarpon Cove Hospital."

"Is he going to live?" I asked, squeezing my eyes closed.

Fab had turned her back to me, staring out the garden window. She whipped around. "Who?" she mouthed.

I hit the speaker button.

"Yeah, but he'll be in the hospital for a day or two." Doodad paused to speak to what sounded like one of the delivery guys.

"Corndog," I mouthed to Fab.

"Odd thing…" Doodad said, back on the line, "…he was found down in the dock area near some property he owns. A local cop friend, who I bought off with a couple of beers, thinks the beat-down happened somewhere else and he was dumped there."

Why go to all that trouble? Another message to sell?

"Put those kinds of expenses on a tab labeled 'money well spent.'"

"When the cops got to the scene, there were no signs of a fight. And they can't figure out how he got down there; his car was still parked in the driveway of his house. The hospital has kept him sedated, so they haven't been able to question him."

"I'll go check on Corndog." I looked at Fab, who shook her head, a militant look on her face. "I have a nurse friend who works there, and I know she'll keep an eye on him." I felt like I had let Corndog down, not following up on his request. I'd get back in the game now; this was just what I needed to keep my mind off my own problems. "What do you know about James Bordello?"

Doodad whistled. "He wouldn't beat someone up, but he'd pay to have it done. Thinks he's big league. Those designer suits aren't the sign of the gentleman he likes people to mistake him for; they just show he can afford expensive clothing. He's not to be trusted, and that goes for his smarmy brothers too."

"You hear anything, call me."

As soon as I disconnected, I flipped through my contacts and called Gunz's connection, GC.

"Yeah," he answered.

Another one with impeccable phone manners. "Hey GC, don't want to be bugsome, but you got anything on the Bordellos? A friend's in the hospital, sipping through a straw, and this might have their fingerprints all over it." I told him what Doodad had relayed.

His interest level rose a notch. "What's your friend have that Bordello wants?"

I gave him the backstory and the previous incidents involving Corndog.

"I'll get on it. Pricks like that bunch always have something to hide; I'll find something to keep them at bay. If need be, I can put together a parade of unwashed laundry—real or not, doesn't matter these days."

"You're the best."

"Don't tell anyone," he grouched.

* * *

I had run upstairs to change my clothes and now stood at the top of the stairs, hoisted my leg over the banister, and rode it to the living room. "Let's go," I said to Fab, who was stretched out on the couch.

"I don't like hospitals." Her nose crinkled.

"You know I don't know how to drive. And that would be your fault, which you can remedy by driving."

She snorted and stuck her face back in the pages of her book.

"Where's my phone?" I asked myself. One eye on Fab, I pulled it out of the pocket of my skirt. "Didier at the office?"

"Why?" She slammed the book closed.

"A little favor." I cast her a brief glance. "Thought he could talk to you about your unhelpful attitude."

"You've got a lot of damn nerve!" she yelled, sitting up.

Snow jumped up and leapt off the couch.

"You're scaring the cat." I frowned.

Fab shoved her feet into a pair of sandals under the table. "I'm not going inside."

"I've got your purse." I lifted mine and hers off the entry bench, smiling all the way to the car.

Fab stalked out of the house, sliding behind the wheel and slamming the door shut. She squealed out of the driveway.

I screamed, and she skidded to a stop. "Get out," I told her. "You're in good enough shape— you can walk back home." I opened the door to climb out and go around to the driver's side.

She stepped on the gas. "I'm going."

Thankful I had a bottle of water in my purse, I took a long drink to calm my nerves. "How old are we?"

"Old enough to not act like this." She hit the accelerator, rocketing through a yellow light.

* * *

As quietly as I could, I opened the door to Corndog's hospital room, Fab hot on my heels. When we arrived, she'd gotten out of the car without a word and followed me inside. Reclined in his hospital bed, he turned his head—only one eye open—halfway anyway. The other was a blackened mess. He nodded with a grunt.

I crossed to the bed. "You look like crap." He looked like he'd been hit by a bus and lived to tell about it.

Fab stood at the door, flicking at the blinds to peer into the hall.

He tsked. "Is that any way for a young lady to talk?"

"You haven't lost your sense of humor. That's a good sign," I said. "Can I get you anything?"

"Out of here," he grunted. "The doc is reluctant to release me since I don't have anyone at home."

"I might have the answer to your dilemma. That's if you're open to a change of scenery?" It was the least I could do.

"I'm not going to no freakin' convalescent home," he said adamantly.

"Calm your shorts."

He attempted a laugh, winced, and closed his eye.

"I own a property of beach-front cottages, and you can move into one temporarily. I'll get the tenants to come annoy you on a regular basis. A few days of that, and you'll be happy to get home."

"Why?" he asked, his voice laced with suspicion.

"I feel like I let you down. I was supposed to be helping you with your Bordello problem, and should've kept you informed. I lost my Information Procurement Specialist, but I've just filled the opening with someone equally talented. It's being worked on as we speak."

"This was inevitable. When a man who's used to snapping his fingers and getting what he wants hits an obstacle, he makes it disappear." He reached for his cup of water. I handed it to him and held on until it was stable in his hand.

"That's not what's going to happen to you. If you're fretting about it, you can stop now."

He nodded.

"What happened?" I asked.

"Got a call that one of my buildings, the abandoned apartments, got broken into. Man said he was from the city, rattled off his name, but I didn't write it down. Probably phony.

Halfway to my car, I walked into a fist. I'd like to say I gave as good as I got and the other guy ended up in the emergency room, but that'd be a lie. I didn't land a punch."

"You know how you got down to the docks?"

His shook his head and winced. "Vaguely remember a bumpy ride in the back of a pickup."

"Got a description of your attacker?"

"Not a good one. Taller than me, stick-thin, and younger. No one I recognized. Fists like steel."

There was a knock at the door and it opened. Fab stepped back as the doctor walked in.

"It's settled. You're moving into The Cottages." I waved and left.

"Now what?" Fab asked.

I shook my head. "Who beats up an old man for property?"

"Someone who wants it pretty badly and is willing to do whatever it takes to get it. Where does this stop? Let's hope it's not when Corndog is dead." Fab grimaced. "It was nice of you to offer up The Cottages, but my advice is to tell no one. Why ask for trouble?"

"Buy me a lemonade."

* * *

Fab got the last parking space at the farthest end of the sidewalk that ran in front of The Bakery Café.

"Look over there." She pointed. "Your brother and the devil of the hour seem to be having a good time, laughing it up, each thinking they're funnier than the other."

I followed her finger to where James Bordello and Brad sat, front and center. "Shall we join them?"

"Let's observe for a while."

"I don't want to suggest that Brad is stupid, but why doesn't he think it's good to know as much as he can about a potential partner before going into business? Or does he know and not care?" I asked in exasperation. "He and Didier already work well together, a proven team, and he wants to walk away for…" I shrugged, at a loss for an answer.

"Did you ask Brad what the heck is up?" Fab asked. "What was the response?"

"Brad brushed it off as business as usual." The conversation hadn't gone well, but I kept that to myself. He'd thought I was meddling. "He pointed out that he'd been upfront about leaving the option open to branch out, potentially partner with someone else."

"Didier's fine with whatever Brad wants to do. I suggested that if a great deal came his way, he should jump on it. I probably shouldn't have shared," Fab said.

"Our talks are private, and that privacy extends to Didier."

"They're leaving." Fab nodded, scrunching

down a little. "I'd follow them if your SUV wasn't so recognizable."

"We could use your Porsche once in a while, but it also sticks out like the expensive custom auto it is. If we had to actually get out and run down a perp, we'd get back, and poof…gone." I made all the appropriate sound effects, hoping to annoy her, and it surprised me when she laughed.

"You think the Porsche would go for parts? Or be black-marketed with a counterfeit title?"

"Black market." I shuddered at the thought of the beautiful auto being dismantled for parts. I leaned forward, watching Brad's Escalade head down the road. "Follow them anyway. Hang back."

Two signals later, Fab said, "They're headed back to the office." She veered left and headed home.

"They're no fun."

Chapter Seventeen

When I woke up the next morning at Creole's, the sun streaming in the window warned me that I was in big trouble. There'd be no sneaking into my house past the guard. No matter where Fab was on the property, she'd appear out of nowhere and bark out more than a few questions.

I jumped out of bed and paid too much attention to the details of making it. Trying to hide the fact I'd spent the night. *From whom?* I wondered. Intellectually, I knew that dealing with the loss of Creole might not be so gut-wrenching if I stopped seeking out his bed. The truth was that being nestled under his sheets felt like a big hug and I slept better.

Traffic was light heading back toward the Cove. I pulled into the coffee drive-thru and ordered a latte. I licked the whipped cream off the top before snapping the lid back on and heading home.

Fab had pushed aside a plant and shoved her head in the garden window. I looked around as I drove in, wondering if something had gone on in the neighborhood to attract her attention and I'd missed it. I cut the engine and waved. In response, she disappeared and the front door cracked open.

"Sorry, I overslept." I threw my bag down and entered the kitchen, slugging down the last of my coffee and dumping the cup in the trash.

When she didn't answer, I stopped myself from sitting and turned. "I'm going to shower. When you want to talk, let me know."

"I wish you'd stop sneaking out at night," she said quietly.

I sighed, not wanting to hurt her feelings. "People grieve in their own way and time and shouldn't be made to feel guilty. I'm not out running the streets; I just need a bit of alone time."

"Dinner at Madeline's tonight has been cancelled. Spoon is sick. So whatever excuse you planned to use to skip out, run down by a speeding car perhaps, you can save for next time."

"Sarcasm doesn't become you." I frowned.

"Whoever said that is a big liar. You can tell them I said so," she said, hands on her hips.

"I wonder if Mother managed to rope Brad into coming."

Mother had hovered of late, and I was feeling smothered. The last thing I wanted was for her to learn about Creole's double life. How would I explain it when I didn't understand myself and had purposefully forced myself not to think about the "wife" and Milton?

"Spoon volunteered to do the arm twisting."

"They don't even like one another. Well, sort of, but you wouldn't consider them bosomy."

Brad was protective of Mother and had made it clear that he wanted to see her hook up with an older gentleman—a banker or lawyer or some such thing. He had mostly adjusted to her younger, motorcycle-riding, "come looking for a fight and I'll break your face" choice for a husband.

"What you do to the English language." Fab shuddered.

"Some might see it as a sign of intelligence."

Fab laughed. "Who?"

"I'm spending the afternoon by the pool."

* * *

I was lying face down on a chaise by the pool under an umbrella when my phone rang. I reached out and pulled it across the towel towards me. The letters GC popped up on the screen.

"Got an update," he blurted. "No one's talking about your friend Creole. That case has an added layer of security. Not to worry, still working on it. The harder it is to get the information, the more I get motivated."

"Several people gave me the 'no one's talking' speech, but I figured it was not-so-subtle code for 'mind your own business.'"

"Apparently not, since I'm getting the same thing. Bordello is clean. As are all the brothers. Comes from a very well-connected family. Back in the day, his old man had mob ties, but Bordello's gone a long way to shine up his reputation and make people think he's on the straight and narrow. Sure he is," GC said with a snort. "Now the old man cleans up the messes of his clients – who are generally part of the top one percent. The only ones that can afford his prices."

"Clean? The whole family?"

"Let me rephrase that – James doesn't get his hands dirty. None of them do. But with the number of rumors floating around, it's hard to believe that all of them are lies."

I heard a voice in the background, and GC asked me to hold on. I peered over my shoulder and saw Fab standing in the doorway. I motioned her over. She sat on the end of the chaise.

"It's GC. Update on Creole, which turns out to be no one's talking. He promises not to stop snooping."

"What if your new friend—" She tapped the phone. " —can't find out anything?" she asked, worry in her eyes.

"As much as I'd hate to do it, I'll have to give it up," I lied, hoping that one day soon, I'd get answers to my questions. If GC turned out to be a dead end, I wouldn't stop; I'd find someone who could get me the information.

GC came back on the line. "James is rapidly buying up property down by the docks. His grandiose plans hit a snag when some of the old timers refused to sell to him. Several business owners sold out at the first offer, which to his credit was generous. The businesses that didn't jump immediately said they were threatened. The man himself wasn't part of the negotiations—instead sent some sleazy real estate agent and a beefy bodyguard."

"Please tell me that the developer wasn't my brother." I held my breath, waiting for the answer. I didn't think the answer would be yes, but I'd been surprised before.

"No, but they're fast friends. Both belong to a group of a-holes that meet once a week for dinner and cigars and think they're better than everyone else."

"The only thing I care about regarding Bordello is that he leaves Corndog alone, but I'm happy to know my brother isn't involved in this business deal. Brad's asked me stay out of his life, and I think it's about time I acted on the promise I already gave him." I sighed. "Sometimes being a little sister is thankless work."

GC laughed. "I hear anything, I'll let you know. You'd be surprised what I hear."

I wondered if he actually talked to people face-to-face or listened in on some device. I had an image of him in a techno-cave with all the latest gadgets in reach.

"What do I owe you? I'll drop your money at the Lighthouse."

"About that…" GC hesitated.

Fab smacked my arm, her eyebrows going up.

I shrugged. No clue what he was about to say. I hoped it didn't bode badly for me.

"How would you like to move to the top of my list of favored clients?"

I tried not to groan, but it slipped out anyway. That was the last thing I'd expected him to say. "I'll need details before you get an answer."

"I've got a friend. Yes, just one." He laughed at his joke. "His ex-girlfriend took off with his Lamborghini and is now holding it hostage behind a locked fence. Oh yeah, and there's at least one dog."

"Is she crazy? Besides car theft."

"Aw…yep!"

Fab shook her head furiously.

"I won't ask why he doesn't call the cops."

"Love," GC said dramatically. "Where's the romance if the po-po shows up?"

"Here's my counteroffer. You give me the address, and my partner and I will check out the place, but you stipulate now that we can say no with no hard feelings. And if we do the job, you owe us." I glanced at Fab for her reaction and she nodded.

"Deal. You do this and you'll move to the star

list," GC responded quickly. "Ignition key is on the desk at the lighthouse. Don't hurt the dog. Love my friend like a brother, but if I have to listen to much more of his sniveling like a whiny baby, I might shoot him."

I jerked a post-it pad from the drawer and wrote down the address. "You'll hear from me later."

"No need. Just do the job."

I hung up and said to Fab. "GC hadn't even finished talking before I ran out of fingers, listing off how this job could go wrong."

Fab grabbed the notepad. "We can make a plan after checking out the place. Might as well do it now." She looked down at me. "Put some clothes on."

Chapter Eighteen

The farther we drove down the Overseas, the more Fab complained about the remoteness. For once, even she didn't have a good feeling about a job.

"Turn the car around, and I'll partner with someone else." I turned my face to the side window, fairly certain she wouldn't take me up on the offer. And if she did?

"Who else are you going to get?" she demanded, brows knit together.

"You're annoying today." I gave her an exaggerated frown. "You know that coming through for GC and fetching this car is in our best business interest; access to information without having to wait is huge."

Fab veered off at the next exit. "At least the road is paved."

With only one option, she turned onto a mile-long street dotted with fairly new houses on acreage, plus a few decrepit ones that a strong wind would easily topple, sending the pieces airborne.

"According to your annoying friend—" I pointed to the GPS. "—we're in the right place."

The voice inside the box could best be described as condescending. "Oh great, not everyone out here has a mailbox or marker of any kind."

We'd passed through the development about a half-mile back and were now in a wide-open space of trees and foot-high weeds on both sides of the road. A road-ending sign caught my attention, along with a barely visible building surrounded by chain link. The closest neighbor was a dilapidated wood shack with no windows and posted "keep out" signs.

"This has to be the property; it's the worst one on the block." I looked around. "Since we left the new construction behind, these are the only two houses we've seen. Of course there aren't any address signs. If we find a Lambo parked in the weeds, that would be confirmation we've got the right address. Then what? You get behind the wheel, rev the engine, and jump it over the fence?" I grinned, making engine noises.

"Stop that." Fab rolled her eyes. "You see a gate bell?" she asked in all sincerity.

I laughed. *Gate bell!* And laughed again.

Fab pulled up in front of the gate and slid out of the car, opening the back door and pulling out bug spray from the bag that we kept on the floor. Dressed in jeans, she sprayed her arms. "If this is the place, we're going to have fun getting the car out. Bolt cutters won't make a dent in that chain. Make a note—we may need a blowtorch."

Blowtorch? I'd turn down the job first. Starting

a fire out here could be catastrophic.

"You're not going by yourself," I said. "There's supposedly a dog."

"You stay in the car," she ordered. "I'm not going over the fence; I'm going to check out the perimeter. Take pictures." She took her camera out of her pocket, snapping a few of the weeds.

I eyed the fence, guessing it to be four to five feet tall. I knew she could easily scale it. I didn't voice the thought for fear she'd see it as a challenge.

"In case someone lives in this jumbled mess, I need a cover story."

Knowing stories came under my purview, I threw out, "You've got a buyer for the property."

"Good one." She shoved the door closed with her foot.

Fab scoped out the gate, which crossed over a worn strip of broken concrete that served as a driveway. It appeared to have been ravaged by neglect and weather. She took pictures of the lock, then shoved her hand through and took a couple more. She followed the fence line and snapped more photos of the thick overgrowth of weeds and trees.

The last thing I expected was for her to come back to the front, grab the gates, and shake them for all they were worth, yelling, "Hello?"

Two Pitbull mixes and a Doberman came charging out of the trees, barking and snarling a return greeting. She took a foil-wrapped package of dog treats from her pocket, ripping them open and tossing them to the three, who snatched them between their fangs mid-air. She stood her ground, continuing to intermittently yell out, "Hello?" The dogs lined up facing the fence and continued to bark, but they were slightly less ferocious than when they burst on the scene and they'd stopped throwing themselves against the fence.

Something on the other side of the fence caught Fab's attention. She stopped, stared, backed up, and did that several times, then cupped her hands to the sides of her mouth and yelled, each time setting the dogs off, their barking drowning out her yells. Her hands shot over her head, and she waved them back and forth.

A petite woman slunk out of the weeds, barely five feet tall with butt-length brown hair. She was wearing a white, ankle-length sundress that knotted under her arms and molded to her ample figure and a pair of designer sandals I'd seen recently in a store window in town.

"What the hell do you want?" She whistled at the dogs, who romped to her side, skidded to a stop, and sat in response to a snap of her fingers. "You're upsetting my animals."

"Fiona Moreau." Fab extended her hand through the corner of the fence. "I have a client that wants property out here real bad, loves the area. Would you be interested in selling? I know we could come up with a mutually beneficial deal."

I smiled when it dawned on me that she remembered the phony name I'd made up for her that we'd used on a couple of jobs. The one she came up with for me wasn't worth remembering.

The woman shook her head, neither returning the handshake nor offering her name. "I'm not interested. I like the privacy to do what I please with no one to complain about it."

"What about the neighboring properties on either side? Do you know anything about them?" Fab asked.

"This back quarter section of the street belongs to me. And none of it is for sale."

"Thank you." Fab sounded reluctant.

"I'm saying this in the nicest of ways." The woman's thin-lipped almost-sneer belied those words. "Don't come back, you or your client. I'm not selling – ever."

"Well, thank you for your time." Fab returned to the car. She rolled up the windows and headed down the street before saying anything. "Beautiful woman, but hard eyes and the meanest mouth. I wanted out of there pronto. She catches us on her property and the end won't be pretty."

"Did you see anything?"

"Lambo's there. The trees and weeds are a cover for a large cement pad that could hold three cars across and three deep, minus one for the Range Rover, which must be her ride. There's a two-story pink house with an attached two-car garage, neither in the best shape but not visibly ready to fall off the foundation."

"I'll call GC and tell him no thanks." I pulled my phone out of the cup holder.

Fab shook her head, batting at my hand. "We're going to do it. But it's no freebie. Bump up the rate a bit and make it clear that the amount doubles if there are bullets."

"Are you forgetting Didier? He hears 'guns,' and he'll put his foot down."

"That's why we'll leave that part out. I'll sell it as a legal car-recovery job." She looked proud of her off-the-cuff story.

"Hate to be the killjoy here…"

"No you don't," Fab said in annoyance.

"The car isn't our personal property, nor do we have the required paperwork to pick it up. So therefore, there's no defense for stealing it back, and even if there were, I'm not certain that would reduce our jail time."

"So we won't get caught," Fab said, as though it were a given. "Got the job planned out. Write down—" She flicked her finger. "—dog treats with a mild sedative, just enough to slow them down, and high-quality bolt cutters. The thick chain is impressive, but the lock is cheap. She probably thinks the dogs are enough security."

"When are we available?" I didn't want to

admit it, but I could use an adrenaline rush. My new motto was "keep busy, less time to think."

"As soon as GC okays the new arrangement. My guess is he won't quibble. If he or someone else can afford a Lambo, they sure as heck can pay us to get it back."

Chapter Nineteen

Coming downstairs, I almost tripped on the last step but caught myself, safely ending up in the kitchen. "I need coffee," I groaned.

"Have a seat." Didier pointed to the island. "I have a few questions for the two of you."

I slid onto a stool next to Fab and squirmed, recognizing his tone as "you're in trouble, but how much remains to be seen."

"I've got a busy day, helping a man who's getting out of the hospital." I wished I'd just run out the door…except I wasn't dressed for running errands. I looked down at my crop pants and t-shirt—gardening maybe.

Without a word, Didier put a mug of pre-made coffee in the microwave. "I want a straight story on this car-appropriation job. Isn't that what you called it?" His icy blue eyes turned on Fab.

"I don't remember my exact words," she mumbled.

That earned her a glare.

"In simple terms," I said, "we're going to rescue a car that was stolen and give it back to the rightful owner. You know, female Robin

Hoods. Except this man isn't poor." I wanted to pat myself on the back for that piece of creativity. Probably not, since Didier rolled his eyes.

"Isn't that called grand theft auto, which also happens to be illegal?" he asked, not quite out of patience but close.

"Someone would have to call the cops." I reached my foot across, kicking Fab lightly. "GC agreed to our terms."

"What the heck kind of name is that?" Didier set the mug down in front of me with a bit of force; surprisingly, the contents didn't spill over the sides.

"You, with only one name, criticize initials?" I said in mock shock, sniffing my coffee to make sure I got the right kind.

"I was a superstar," he said sternly, then grinned.

"You still are." Fab jumped off her stool, running to Didier's side and enveloping him in a hug.

I squeezed my eyes closed. "I think I'm going to be sick. Too early for lovey dovey."

Didier hugged Fab to his side. "You're telling me that this is a safe job?"

"None of them are without risk," I hedged.

"Just pay for his services," Didier said in exasperation. "Let him *appropriate* the car himself."

"You call GC and tell him we flaked," I told Fab. "I've got to get to The Cottages." I raced out of the kitchen and upstairs.

* * *

Somehow, I got lucky and was able to sneak out of the house without having to explain myself. Or argue over how dangerous the latest job was going to be. On that, I agreed with Didier, even though I hadn't protested at the time. It would make things easier if Didier would just accept that all the jobs came with a certain amount of danger. He and Fab had almost split up over the issue once before, and I hoped it didn't come to that again.

Having learned from my mentor, I took every shortcut—including an alley and an empty field—to end up parked in front of the office at The Cottages one second before Mac's truck pulled into the driveway, parking in front of the cottage across from Joseph's.

I'd arranged for Mac to handle the whole Corndog-relocation plan. She'd visited him in the hospital and explained that the offer of a cottage to stay in while he recuperated came with a parade of people checking on him, whether he liked it or not. She tipped him off about the divergent personalities living on this corner lot, just in case he expected them all to be on the normal side.

When I saw Mac help Corndog out of the truck, handing him a cane, I walked down the driveway to join them. From close up, it appeared he had healed some, one eye no longer swollen shut. He slowly climbed the three steps to the door that Mac had standing open. Grabbing his elbow, she helped steer him inside.

Coming up behind, I waited in the doorway while Mac settled him on the couch, pointing out the doors to the bedroom and bathroom.

"Happy to see that you're up and about," I said.

"I'd never have gotten out of the hospital without your help. I appreciate all you're doing for me." He leaned his head back against the cushions.

"The only thing I ask in return is that you tell no one that you're here. I don't want any problems. That'll also be good for you, since you don't know who did this and they're still out there. Whether they're looking for an encore or not... Let's hope not."

"Agreed."

"I don't think my brother will show up, since he hasn't been back since he moved out," I said to Mac, "but don't answer any questions about anything happening on the property. I'll have a talk with Kevin so he can keep an eye out. Either of you see anyone lurking about, don't go all hero and confront them. Call the police."

"I don't want to cause you any trouble," Corndog said, appearing flustered, as though he wasn't sure how he got into this situation.

Mac snorted. "There's always something going on around here. As perfect as I am, even I've been known to stir things up."

"Anything you want, Mac can make it happen," I informed him. "Where's your phone?"

"He lost it while having the you-know-what beat out of him," Mac answered for him. "I got him a burner." She pulled a phone from her pocket. "Mine and Madison's numbers are programmed in."

"Corndog can probably speak for himself," I said.

"Not likely. He's asleep." Mac nodded in his direction.

"Just got my eyes closed." Corndog popped one open. "I'm trying to decide if I'm going to nap on the couch or in the bedroom."

"I'll get him settled before I go get his prescriptions filled." Mac held out her arm for support when he stood.

Satisfied that he was well taken care of, I decided to leave. "I'm off to check on the rest of the inmates."

I stopped on the porch. Noticing Crum's bathroom window was open, I headed across the driveway and paused a foot away, yelling, "Anyone home?"

The door flew open, and his bushy white head appeared. "You sure know how to scare the pants off a man."

"You don't wear pants, so you can't blame me."

The professor had on his usual tighty-whities and nothing else. I kept my eyes focused above his shoulders. There was a standing rule that if he ventured outside, he needed to cover up. Oftentimes, he chose a skirt with an elastic waistband that barely covered his backside. There were no rules regarding shoes, but he had a preference for sturdy rubber boots.

"Come in." Crum motioned.

It never failed to surprise me that, despite Crum being a known trash-picker, the inside of his cottage was neat as a pin. I sat on the couch next to Harlot, stroking her back. She let out a small meow in appreciation and went back to sleep.

"I need a favor. Will you check on Corndog while he's here, make sure he's okay, getting what he needs? Whatever you do, don't gossip about him and let it out that he's staying here."

"Mac already talked to me about the old coot. I'll go over tomorrow and give him the lay of the land. And which of the women in the neighborhood are complete nut-jobs." He flashed a toothy smile.

"You've got some nerve. Old coot and nut-job."

"Yeah, well, I dare anyone to say it to my face. I'll break their nose." He shadowboxed. "Since we're talking favors, I need one. I'd like to set up a few chairs and give gardening classes."

That sounded so normal, I couldn't believe I was getting all the facts. "Are you qualified?"

"Look what I've done for this place." He gave me a haughty stare.

Crum had gotten the gardener job by default. The last one had left town, and that left only lawn mowers. And since we only had a small strip that ran along the street side of the property, they weren't interested. The only glitch thus far with Crum had been that when a plant died, he wanted to dig up a neighbor's as replacement. I got that stopped before the police got involved.

"What's the catch?" I asked.

"You wouldn't begrudge a man staying active in his retirement years, would you?"

I did my best not to roll my eyes as I waited for the punchline. I couldn't begin to list the side jobs, some would say scams, he'd run since I met him.

"I need the money." He stated it more as a question, as though throwing it out there, testing the water.

"Truth be told, you could afford to buy this place. I'm going to trust you." I narrowed my eyes. "Go ahead, have your classes. Anything goes south and I'm kicking you out."

"Fine," he said with the confidence of a man who knew I didn't mean the latter.

I stood and crossed to the door, giving him the

same warning I gave Mac and Corndog. "You see anyone prowling around, call the police."

"Don't worry. I patrol the place at night. The only late action we get is people who don't live here wanting to use the pool."

I nodded and shut the door behind me. I probably should've cautioned him not to shoot anyone back when Mac informed me he *patrolled* with a holster strapped around his underwear. I'd make it Mac's job to find out if he had the required licensing and ask to see it. I moved into the middle of the driveway, taking a quick inventory of each cottage. Joseph's was locked up. The only one sitting outside was Miss January, who was leaning sideways in her chair, passed out, judging from the angle. One tourist guest was peeking through the blinds.

I whistled for Mac, who had about reached the office, and pointed her to Miss January's cottage, following her over there.

"I can't hoist her up and get her inside by myself. You get on one side, and I'll get on the other," I said, gently poking Miss January's shoulder.

The glass storm door flew open. "If you stand back, I'll carry her in." The man's eyes bored into me.

"Nestor, isn't it?" I asked. "What are you doing here?"

"I live here," he said in a superior tone. "Miss January is now my responsibility." He nudged me aside and picked up the snoring woman. Holding the door open with his foot, he went inside, then turned, looking out the door. "I'll be back as soon as I get her settled." He disappeared from view, which wasn't hard since the bedroom was a quick right inside the tiny unit.

"Since when?" I asked, looking at Mac, who shrugged.

It didn't take long before Nestor reappeared, leaving the door cracked open behind him.

"When did you move in?" I asked.

"Not long ago." His annoyance flared. "Is there a problem?"

"That would be in violation of her lease," I said. He didn't need to know that I'd never required a lease.

"When she wakes up, I'll tell her that we've been kicked to the curb."

Well played. "That won't be necessary. But if this relationship is anything other than a love match, I'll make sure you're kicked to the street and bounced down the block head-first."

His smirk made my hand itch to slap him. There was that elusive something about him, but it wasn't reason enough to barge into Miss January's personal life.

"It's good to know Miss January has such a good friend," he said, with an underlying tone of insincerity.

I turned and walked down the stairs to our vehicles.

"Nice seeing you again," Nestor called out.

I didn't have to turn to see his smirk; I could hear it in his voice. "What the heck?" I whispered to Mac.

"I've seen him around a couple of times and asked Miss January. She mumbled something about love, and I wrote it off to her being drunker than usual. I had no clue he'd actually moved in."

"My gut says to keep an eye on him. He's maybe thirty and sober, hard to understand what he sees in Miss January. I don't want any harm to come to her – mental or physical. You need help, call me." I stared back at Miss January's cottage, but Nestor had gone inside and closed the door.

"Don't worry. I've got everything under control. Maybe not always..." Mac chuckled. "Anything I find out about the loving couple, you'll be the first to know." She waved and got in her truck, backing out of the driveway.

I took one last look around the property and followed her out.

Chapter Twenty

"Let's get this done," Fab whispered after we tiptoed out of the house, closing the front door with a faint click.

"I'm telling you now, I'm not driving the Lamborghini."

"You're not. I am."

Not paying attention, I proceeded to the SUV. I stopped and did a double take when I realized Fab was about to get into the Porsche. "You never allow me to touch your car, let alone drive it."

"Get in," Fab said. "Your SUV is too easily recognizable." She ducked down and slid behind the wheel.

And the Porsche isn't? "Nice," I said, getting in and running my hand down the side of the leather seat. "Feels and smells expensive."

"That's because it was."

I turned in my seat. "You have tools?"

She nodded and coasted out of the driveway. "Perfect night. Look at the stars." She dipped her head and looked up into the sky. "And Didier went to bed early."

"You better hope that he doesn't wake up. No man likes his woman sneaking out in the middle of the night, especially to do something he told us not to do."

"I was being considerate, not wanting to wake him."

I snorted. "Sure."

"Besides, we talked and he relented…sort of…after I promised to be careful and reminded him it wasn't my first recovery job."

I bet he got half the truth.

Fab pulled out on the main highway and headed south. Used to driving in the SUV, I felt odd sitting in the Porsche; it felt low to the ground, as if my butt was about to scrape along the road. The traffic was practically non-existent, a stray car here and there buzzing by.

Just before we got to the turn off, I asked, "What's the plan?"

"Go in, get behind the wheel, and drive out."

"That sounds too easy."

"You won't be getting out of the car; you'll be parked just outside the gate. If I come out on foot, I'll head straight for the passenger side. You be prepared to haul ass. If, by some chance, I don't reappear in a timely fashion or you hear sirens, take off and pick me up on the highway."

My stomach twisted in a knot and tugged hard. "And if you do get the car—once you pull out, I get behind you and try to keep up?" A nervous laugh bubbled in my throat, knowing that keeping up would never happen; I'd be lucky to track her taillights.

Fab exited. At night, the road had a creepy vibe. Streetlights ran only halfway down; the rest of the way, the headlights were the only illumination. She hung a u-turn and came to a stop. "Parking here makes it an easy, straight shot to the passenger door. A lot quicker than running around to the driver's side."

"Be damn careful." That shot of adrenaline I felt when we first checked out the job had evaporated, and now all I wanted to do was go home.

On Fab's orders, I'd dressed in black in the same type of clothing as her: jeans, long-sleeved t-shirt, and tennis shoes. She unzipped her tote bag, which rested on the back seat, pulling out dog treats, tearing them open, and stuffing them in her pocket. She grabbed her bag and headed to the gate.

I'd gotten out and was ready to jump in the driver's seat before she crossed to the driveway. I watched out the open window, and if I hadn't been so close, I doubt I would've seen a thing. Seconds later, maybe a minute, the dogs came out of the weeds, barking, immediately jumping up against the fence. I hoped they didn't have some way to clear that fence that we'd missed. Fab was ready for the dogs, treats in hand, and distracted them easily. When they were done gobbling them down, they sat and watched Fab as though her reaching into her bag and pulling out bolt cutters wasn't out of the ordinary. After some research, she'd bought ones that would cut the lock off with minimal effort.

I couldn't hear what Fab said to the dogs, but she got them to move to the side of the driveway and lie down, heads on their paws. The lock snapped off. She unwrapped the chain, dumping it in a pile of weeds outside the fence, picked up her bag, and disappeared from view. My cue to start the engine.

One eye on the dogs, the other on the makeshift driveway, I had to remind myself to breathe.

A scream rang out.

Followed by a gunshot.

The rev of an engine. A silver sports car that I recognized from the photo Fab had asked GC to send shot through the thick foliage, hitting the street with a dip.

Grinding the gears, which I was happy Fab couldn't hear, I hit the gas. The sports car jumping forward startled me. I backed off the accelerator, catching a glimpse of a woman in a white chemise in the rearview mirror. A loud pop ricocheted inside the car, and the back window shattered. I slammed on the gas, fishtailing away, struggling to get control. A ping sounded somewhere inside the car. I gripped the wheel with all the strength I could muster. Before I got to the Overseas, I remembered the headlights and weaved, right on track to sideswipe a pole, before getting them on. Another fishtail and I made it to the highway.

A mile later, not seeing any lights behind me, I slowed the Porsche, not releasing my white-knuckle grip, my heart still pounding at a frantic pace. Respecting the speed limit, I breathed a sigh at the city sign and took the first exit to cut over to the dock area. We'd decided ahead of time that the only safe place we had to park the sports car and not have it stolen again immediately was the condos. I'd already told GC that he needed to retrieve the damn thing ASAP, as we couldn't guarantee its safety. We didn't want to accept the responsibility was more the truth. After what happened tonight, I was happy — no, relieved was more like it — that we'd made those arrangements in advance.

Just as I expected, Fab had parked the Lambo in the underground garage in a space barely visible from the street. She stood on the curb, arms crossed and tapping her foot, clearly communicating, "Where have you been?" Wait until she got her first good look at the window and the small pebbles of shattered glass inside the car. On the drive over, I'd decided not to mention that in addition I'd almost totaled her car.

I pulled up to the curb and cut the engine, slid out, and sucked in fresh air. Big mistake. I ran to the gutter and threw up. Lifting my head slightly, I waved her away and got sick again.

After several minutes, I pulled myself together, rose up from my crouch, and sat down. "I'm happy this night's over. Well, almost." I brushed away a tear.

"Hey." Fab patted my back. "What happened?" she asked in a soft voice.

"As my grandmother would say, 'the woman is a piss-poor shot,' and thank goodness."

Fab circled her beloved car – twice. She marched back over; if anyone could spit fire, she'd be doing it. "Give me your phone." She held out her hand. "When Didier sees this, he's going to flip. No way to pretty-spin this one." She scrolled through my phone and made a call.

"Hey, bastard," Fab said. "Crazy woman shot out the back window of my Porsche 911, almost killing my friend. You're damn lucky she wasn't so much as nicked. You're ponying up the cost of repairs, and not one bitchy word out of you."

"Blah, blah," she said in response. "Got a pen?" She rattled off the address of the condos and the code to the gate. "I'll leave the key at the lighthouse." She ended the call. "That GC moron had the nerve to complain that I woke him up."

"I wanna go home," I whined.

"Best friend favor."

"Nooo. Not in the middle of the night."

"I know," she said supportively, putting her arm across my shoulders. "Listen up. I'll help you into the passenger side and adjust the seat, and you can close your eyes. This is our only chance to maybe find out who the client is—or who GC is. We'll wait and see who shows up."

"We could mind our own business," I said, knowing the suggestion had zero chance of success.

"It could snow in Key West too."

"What if they don't show up until morning?"

"Fat chance. Did you forget that car is worth a cool 200K? If that were mine, I'd be retrieving it – now." Fab smiled down at me. "My guess is they'll be along shortly. I don't want to wait by myself."

"I'd never let you do that." Especially not since her eyes glimmered with excitement, matching the tone of her voice.

"You going to get sick again?" She looked me over.

"Thankfully, I'm over that. I'm thinking it was a combination of nerves, fear, and adrenaline."

She extended her hand, helping me to my feet. "Hop in," she ordered while scanning the street. "We'll park underground—better lighting. Might get lucky and get some video."

"You better back into a space; the less attention we draw the better." I closed my eyes. I didn't open them while she got the car situated in the parking lot, and I must have fallen asleep because the next thing I knew, she was shaking my shoulder.

"Wake up. It's opening." A rattling noise

accompanied the sliding back of the two large gates.

Opening my eyes, I peered over the dashboard. It took me a minute to remember where I was and that everything hadn't been a dream. A man walked down the slant of the driveway into the garage, stopping under a light that illuminated his face. As it turned out, the light wasn't needed.

I didn't know whether to laugh or not at the dismay on Fab's face at the identity of the car's owner. Remembering past stories and rumors, it made sense to me. Word was, one of his past girlfriends had darn near bitten his nose off, knocking out a tooth in the process, and he'd ended up in the emergency room.

"Be right back." Fab shoved the door open and jumped out. "Gunz!" she bellowed, the shout echoing off the walls, "You pull a gun and I'll put a bullet in your big behind."

"I'm not going to miss a word of this; I'm sure it'll be good," I said to myself, getting out slowly, not wanting to trigger any sickness. "Can't wait to hear this story."

Gunz was hunched over the hood of the Lambo. "You're going to give me a heart attack." He ran his hand across the front end of the car.

"Another girlfriend you can't handle?" Fab practically shrieked.

"Keep it down, you two. This isn't the kind of building where you can scream in the garage and not expect the cops to show up," I said.

"Look." Fab lowered her voice, advancing on the man. "At my Porsche, you dumbass, not me." She pointed, then poked her finger at his chest. The two engaged in a staredown. "You will get it fixed. You're the one with the connections for first-class repairs by people who won't ask questions or call the law."

The burly man scowled down at the petite French woman. "No cops. Gunzy will have your baby returned to you in better condition than before," he said in a wounded tone.

"Gunzy" made me flinch. I stood in silence, not wanting to attract attention or bring the drama to an early end.

"It was new," Fab seethed.

He reached out to touch her, and she stepped back. "It's all taken care of. I'll have it picked up first thing."

I was certain I hadn't moved, but he turned and zeroed in on me. "What are *you* doing here?" he asked.

"I'm the one who got shot at. Don't start with your snottiness; we've put that behind us. Besides, we did this job for you."

"Bullets!" Gunz pierced the air with a high-pitched scream. "My little cupcake, she's okay?" He clasped his chest. "I love her."

"Where do you find these women?" Fab demanded in disgust. "You cheated on her," she accused. "I know you did."

"Sweet Isla caught me in bed with the Tillmore sisters." He sighed, hanging his head, the picture of a man in anguish. "I told her it was just sex and that it didn't affect our relationship in any way. She ran out before I could get my pants on and took off in the Lambo. I texted her a dozen times before she answered, 'Thanks for the car. If I'd brought the right equipment, I'd also have your penis.'" He winced.

I also winced. "Has she called you in the last hour?"

He shook his head.

"That should really worry you," I said. "Isla knows the car's been stolen back. If you're capable, I suggest you grow more than one pair of eyes. Hiring a bodyguard wouldn't be a bad idea. Unless you're certain she won't retaliate with those special cutters of hers."

He shivered slightly. "Isla loves a good game of get even. I never thought she'd turn on me. Two girls is a man's dream; how could say I say no?"

I groaned inwardly and prayed that Isla never linked Fab or I back to tonight.

Fab took Gunz aside for a few words. I would remind her later that eavesdropping worked both ways. She patted him on the shoulder and walked toward me, waving to Gunz. "Don't forget. If Isla gets her hands on your car again, don't call us. Once is enough. As much as you loathe the police, I suggest you call them."

As soon as the car door slammed, I said, "I hope we don't get another job from him."

"How did you enjoy driving the masterpiece?" Fab patted the steering wheel.

"I'll never ask to drive it again."

Fab looked at me in disbelief. "You need a driving course. I'm not guaranteeing you'd get to my level, but we can get you past the old lady stage."

"So humble of you." I turned to the window, noticing a crack in it. "Just get us home in one piece."

* * *

"You think Didier slept the whole night?" I asked as we backed into the driveway, having decided that would call less attention to the Porsche from street traffic. The nightlight in the kitchen glowed through the garden window.

Fab shook her head. "Doubt it."

"I'm suggesting, if we get caught like teenagers sneaking back into the house, that you do all the talking, and I suggest the truth. Don't put me in the position of backing up some wild story."

"I've had a lot of time to think." Fab slid out and headed to the house.

"Ten minutes? That's about all it took us to drive across town since we were the only ones on the street."

We got back into the house as quietly as we'd left.

"Don't sneak in on my behalf," Didier said, flipping on the light next to the daybed. He stretched back out. "It's great for a man's ego to wake up in the middle of the night and find that his girlfriend ditched him without a kiss or a *damn* word." His voice rose at the end.

Fab ran to him, throwing herself into his arms and giving him a lip-smacking kiss. "I love you," she said when she broke contact.

"See you in the morning," I said, one foot on the bottom step.

"Stop right there, turn around, and take a seat. Tell me why you're so pale — you look as though you've had a good scare or are sick. And Beautiful here all calm and collected, like she hasn't been out boosting a car." He ended with a glare.

I sank onto the couch, grabbing a pillow and clutching it to my middle.

"We retrieved the Lambo. It's back with its rightful owner, and look, not a scratch." Fab held out her arms.

While Didier had his full attention on Fab, I stretched out and closed my eyes. I knew better than to sell it with a snore, since it sometimes came out sounding like cats mating. Knowing the gentleman that he was, even if he suspected I was faking, he wouldn't kick my foot or make some other rude gesture to get my attention.

"What about Madison?" Didier asked. "She appears to be asleep. Or is that another trick concocted by you two?"

"Innocent," Fab declared. "I've been under your watchful eye since I walked in, and I rather like it."

I wanted to yell, "Don't go overboard," but from the sounds of kissing, he'd bought the "innocent" bit.

Chapter Twenty-One

"What the devil?" Didier roared from the kitchen.

My ruse of pretending to sleep had backfired, and I'd fallen asleep for real. I'd woken up at one point but was too lazy to climb the stairs, so I rolled onto my side, closed my eyes, and went back to sleep.

Now what? Not able to follow the rumblings of the irate Frenchman, I resettled Jazz next to Snow at the end of the couch. They both meowed at being woken up. I flipped my legs over the side of the couch and found Didier with his head in the garden window. I peered around him and then at the clock – seven am.

"That's a plus in Gunz's favor. He said not to worry, he'd take care of everything, and he is." I watched as the Porsche completed its trip, hauled up the ramp onto the flatbed.

"The Porsche? Gunz? Any more details you left out?" Didier glared down at me.

"I don't remember you asking me any questions." His glare intensified, and I backed up. "I need coffee," I whined. To my relief, Fab glided into the kitchen and straight to Didier, wrapping her arms around his middle. Her hair was full-blown sexy, and there was a slight blush to her cheeks. I knew, even without a mirror, that my hair was standing on end.

Now would be a good time to go lock myself in my room, but not without my coffee. I kept my eyes averted and got two kinds of coffee from the refrigerator, filling the coffee maker with water and a ground roast, lining up the mugs.

"Look," Fab squealed. "Gunz brought me a loaner car."

Didier cut short Fab's getaway, hauling her to his side. "No way you're going outside in a robe."

Waiting on the microwave, I snuck a peek out the window. "What is it? Looks like a batmobile," was my closest guess as another black sports car replaced Fab's old one.

Fab turned on me, disgust on her face. "*That* is a Carrera GT."

"I'm impressed." I shrugged and flashed a phony smile. "Let's hope it's not stolen."

"That's not helpful. You know Gunz turned over a new leaf… He's in the process, anyway."

The doorbell rang.

"I'll get it," Didier snapped and strode to the door. The conversation was short, and he soon came back, key in hand, depositing it on the counter. "Gunz will be in touch later. Thoughtful guy." He pointed his finger at the stools. "You two sit down and go over the dozen or so details you left out last night. Don't even think about making a getaway."

Both cats appeared from around the corner, expecting breakfast pronto, which I accommodated, giving me the opportunity to let Fab take the lead. But she didn't say a word the entire time.

"You first," I told Fab. When she shook her head, I wanted to pull her off the stool and dump her on the floor. I mixed my coffee into one of the mugs and took a long drink before asking, "What did you want to know?"

Didier crossed his arms, his expression closed-off.

"Everything went down like Fab reported last night." I downed almost half the mug. "It all went according to plan until the Lamborghini cleared the driveway." I gave him the bare facts, removing all emotion. After a silent exchange with Fab, I told him that we'd met up with Gunz and how that had happened. "He offered to fix the car without a bunch of pesky questions, so that Spoon — and then Mother — wouldn't find out. Calling Brick was out of the question, as he'd hold it over our heads as a bargaining tool on other jobs."

"Anything else you two failed to mention?" Didier was still upset, but not as angry as before.

We both shook our heads.

"I understand why a woman involved with Gunz would want to shoot him," Didier said.

"But why take blind shots when she didn't know who was behind the wheel?"

"Gunz has a type," I said, remembering the one who'd tried to run me over. "They tend to be emotionally unstable, and then he pushes their buttons, giving them several good reasons to go off on his big ass. They don't care who gets caught in the crossfire."

Fab planted herself next to Didier. I thought she'd climb up his side any minute. "I feel bad about what happened last night," she told me. "The last thing I'd ever want is for you to get hurt. I'd rather it be me."

"I'd rather it be neither of us." I bent down and patted both cats as they left the kitchen. Heading to the patio door, where the sun streamed in, they curled up and went to sleep.

"Been thinking... I like your suggestion of opening my own investigation business, telling other people what to do," Fab said.

To say Didier and I were surprised would be an understatement.

"I'll help in any way I can," I offered. "Except being one of those employees that you order around."

Didier laid a big kiss on Fab.

"Maybe we'll both start new ventures," I said. "All the real estate talk in the family... I'd like to put my own deal together, and what interests me is the dock renovation. This is my town, and I'm not going anywhere. I was thinking I'd enjoy putting my stamp on something down there."

"We should talk," Didier suggested, clearly interested in the idea. "Your biggest competition in getting property is Brad's new friend, Bordello."

"Maybe it's time for all of us to move in new directions," Fab said.

Chapter Twenty-Two

"You never call late," I said to Mac as I got out of the SUV. "If you'd turned down the music, you could've told me what went wrong over the phone."

From the sound of it, a band had been set up by the pool. Ready to party, Mac was dressed in a blue, ankle-length tropical skirt, a faded denim-color t-shirt announcing "Smell the Tequila," and glow-in-the-dark flip-flops.

When the screen on my phone lit up, I'd known a call from Mac could only mean trouble. I was more than a little annoyed that Fab and Didier had gone off for an evening of fun in South Beach, making the idea of dragging one or both along with me not an option.

"We're hosting a wake," Mac announced with a cheek-splitting grin.

It took a minute to sink in. "Who died?"

"Spum Lancaster." Mac laid her hand over her heart. "Heart attack. Probably something to do with the twenty-something that called 911, hysterical over the dead customer in her bed." She ended on a sigh, arms waving dramatically.

I thought her performance deserved a round of applause but decided against it; she'd just continue her antics. "You're telling me that an old drunk, pushing one hundred, died in a hooker's bed?" Odds were he passed a happy man. "That will make for an interesting obit."

"Ninety-three." Mac snorted and handed me twenty dollars. "It's for the cover charge to join the party."

I had turned toward the pool but now came to a halt. "You're selling tickets to a wake!" Just when I thought nothing could surprise me. Somewhat leery, I asked, "Is there an actual dead body over there?"

Mac turned her head from side to side, as though expecting someone to appear, before answering. "The body is the crowning touch. Don't you think?" When I didn't answer — truthfully, I didn't have an answer — she continued, "Without it, how could we charge people to take pictures with the corpse?"

"Great idea." I felt like banging my head on something, but there was nothing close that wouldn't hurt. "Speak slowly and tell me what the hell is going on," I sputtered in frustration.

"I'm telling you now." Mac thrust out her chest. "You can skip the part where I'm fired, because you and I know the only one who'd be beating the door down for the job is Crum."

Crum had "managed" a trailer park before he was dumped on my doorstep, and it didn't have any tenants because he'd run them all off.

"Mac," a man hollered, waving as he rode erratically down the street on his bicycle.

Mac yelled back.

I was surprised he didn't stop, but didn't voice the sentiment for fear it would be construed as an invitation.

"Speaking of Crum...he's the host of this extravaganza," Mac said. "You'd be proud of him since this is all for a good cause."

"Have you been drinking?"

"Yes." She blew in her hand and sniffed it, then frowned at me.

"You know how I like it when people get to the point," I said, testily. "This would be one of those times."

"Yeesh," she huffed. "Spum croaked dirt poor. Meaning no cash for a burial."

I tapped my foot impatiently.

"Crum, being his friend, came up with the idea of charging for the wake, all money going to burial expenses. He even got Bongo to play for tips."

As far as I knew, the five stoners that made up that band couldn't get a gig, often playing on the beach for handouts from drunk tourists. Getting them to work for tips was hardly a coup.

"Crum's selling kisses for any donation over one dollar."

"Always the entrepreneur."

Mac ignored my sarcasm. "Crum put up

flyers, and so far, we've got twenty-five wake attendees."

We?

"I thought it was a good cause, so I offered my help. Besides, I didn't want to see the man tossed out somewhere."

"First off, bodies are never *discarded*. If the deceased or the family can't afford a burial, the county steps up and buries them. Second, how did Crum get his hands on the body when he's not the next of kin? The answer better not be he 'borrowed' it." Did I really want to know? No! But I had to ask.

"Crum is such a great friend, he talked the funeral guys into letting him take the body. They agreed to do a burial for whatever money he was able to raise and took care of all the details. Dickie and Raul were excited, as they wanted to check out a tropical-themed funeral before offering it as one of their services."

Test funerals! "Hate to break it to you," I said.

"Probably not," Mac blustered. "You've been a grouch since you got here. You always want to be the first to know... Well, here you are."

First? Sounded to me like I was twenty-sixth or twenty-seventh. "Spum was a retired engineer and had plenty of money. The beach house he lived in, where he claimed to only rent a room, he actually owned, along with the Land Cruiser I saw him driving around town. He had 'poor mouth' down to a tee."

189

"Well, hon," Mac drawled. "It's a nice thing, what everyone is doing. I certainly hope that you're not going to send everyone home." She scowled at me. "The money raised tonight can be used to help someone else."

"Stop looking at me like I'm the least fun person on the block. Far be it from me to break up a pay-to-attend funeral."

"Come on." She tugged on my arm. "At least check it out."

"You can party until the cops show up, and they will," I warned. "Some nosey neighbor will call one minute after ten. No one walks or drives home drunk. Arrange rides—I don't want anyone getting arrested."

It didn't seem right to me that even walking drunk could get you a ride in the back of a cop car, especially if you were headed home and not stirring up trouble along the way.

We rounded the corner to the pool, and I saw that the entire area was lit up in a seventies disco theme. Lights twinkled and crisscrossed the tiki bar, where the band had set up, a rag-tag group of men in bathing trunks and tees that advertised one brand of liquor or another. Multicolored strobe lights had been placed around the pool area, the pool itself full of floating lights. The stools under the bar had been removed, and Spum was propped up inside a coffin, the handful of plastic leis around his neck obscuring part of his face.

A few of the faces in the conga line were recognizable. Some waved as they danced around the pool, and others were drinking from a flamingo beer bong being passed from person to person down the line. Most were dressed in brightly colored clothing, some in beach attire that left little to the imagination. A few wore odd hats reminiscent of Carnival or a Key West parade. No one would ever guess a dead body lay a few feet away.

"Don't worry, I got a lifeguard," Mac reassured me, pointing to an older gentleman seated in a chair at the deep end. "I got him free after impressing upon him the need to do his civic duty."

I needed a drink, but then I'd be stuck having to spend the night.

Crum guarded the gate in form-fitting hot-pink tighty-whities. Not sure what store sold them, but the color was most likely courtesy of a cheap box of dye. He had a colorful towel skirt within arm's reach and leis around his neck, covering his bare chest.

Mac plucked the twenty from my fingers, handing it over.

"Crum." I gave him a stern look. "Don't let anything get out of control."

"You can count on me, missy." He stood a little straighter.

"You need to stick around for the eulogy," Mac whispered in my ear. "Everyone's getting up to say a few words. Told the ones that didn't know him or felt shy to say something they'd want to hear at their own funeral."

I smiled squeamishly. "Great idea." What would people say about me? *Madison was just as crazy as the kooks she rented to? Couldn't seem to help herself? Finishing off with "Bless her heart."* Translation: simple-minded person.

I scanned the crowd, not expecting to see Miss January, as most days, she passed out drunk in the early evening hours. My eyes shot to a chaise in the corner, where Joseph and a woman I hadn't seen before were wrapped in each other's arms, foreheads pressed together. Joseph laid a fumbly kiss on her lips that had me averting my eyes.

Kevin and I engaged in a staredown from opposite sides of the pool, where he sat sans uniform. Less colorful than the rest in a pair of khaki shorts and a single lei, he raised his beer bottle in a salute. I groaned inwardly.

I made my way around the pool, sat down next to him, and dipped my feet in the pool. "Hello, officer. Here to arrest someone?"

"Just stopped by to see what the racket was all about. Brought my own beer, though I did mooch a hot dog." He nodded in the direction of the barbeque. "Didn't have the heart to tell Crum that I talked to Spum's daughter; she was happy to hear about the sendoff party and that she didn't have to pay. Richer than her father in her own right. I tipped off the funeral guys to make sure they charged her full boat."

"You're an imposter. Where's the real Kevin?" I asked, looking around.

He unleashed a gravelly laugh. "Don't ruin my rep by telling anyone."

The band had gone on break and gathered around the barbecue. Someone flipped on a radio, and steel band music wafted through the speakers.

"As usual," I half-laughed, "I'm the last to know. But as long as it's all legal, I'm happy."

"So far, so good."

"I'm getting out of here before they start the farewell wishes. I don't want to hear them, and I really don't want to get roped into saying something insincere."

"Mac has a way of getting people to do things that they wouldn't do for anyone else."

I lifted my legs out of the pool, stood, and found her standing next to Spum, posing for a picture with a man that looked familiar. I motioned her over.

"I'm going. Have fun, or whatever one is supposed to say."

I skirted around the people milling about. The partygoers had doubled in number, and we were about to reach our occupancy limit. When that happened, Kevin could be the bad guy.

Chapter Twenty-Three

I lay out by the pool, book in hand, which I ignored, moody and irritable that my second-best friend, coffee, had let me down this morning. Now that it was almost noon, I thought about upping my caffeine dosage with a shot of espresso. I'd gotten home from the wake and gone to sleep as soon as my head hit the pillow, only to wake two hours later and find that sleep eluded me for the rest of the night. I contemplated running away from home, as though that would solve anything.

Fab and Didier came out on the patio holding hands and sat down on the chaise next to me. They'd left a note that they'd gone to a beachfront hotel in Marathon for breakfast.

"You could've come along instead of pretending to sleep." Didier ruffled my hair.

I pushed his hand away. "It took a lot of effort to get this hairstyle just right."

He eyed the messy bun falling out of the clips and laughed. "You look séduisante – hot."

"That is a big fib, but I love the French talk." I smiled at him.

"Nice funeral?" Fab asked.

How did she find out? "You checking up on me?"

"It's not like that. I have my sources to keep me up on the latest in the neighborhood." She smiled slyly.

"Cherie, a funeral?" Didier said in surprise.

"How could I pass up a tropical wake?" Thinking about the previous night had me shaking my head. I described the event in full color, embellishing where I could.

"Sorry we missed it," Didier said, not bothering to hide the insincerity of his words. "Water?" He stood, receiving nods from Fab and me, and headed into the house. He returned immediately. "Madeline is here. Pink bakery box in hand."

I groaned inwardly, wondering what she was up to, stopping by without warning. She'd been doing a lot of that lately, even though most times no one was home. "Hurry," I said to Didier, "take off your shirt. You know she loves to stare."

Didier blushed. "Behave yourself," he growled, although the amusement in his eyes told a different story.

Fab went to answer the door. As she crossed the threshold, I said, "If she asks, we have a job."

Didier's eyebrows shot up.

"If Mother has treats, we should move this party into the house." I stood and headed to the kitchen, Didier putting one hand on my elbow as though I might bolt.

I pasted a smile on my face and slipped onto a stool as Fab opened the door and Mother swept in, stopping to kiss Fab. Didier crossed the kitchen, taking the box from Mother and setting it on the counter. Mother came around the island and threw her arms around me in an awkward hug.

"You look tired." She patted my cheek.

I ignored her comment, turning away to grab plates from the cupboard.

Didier took drink orders and made a fresh pot of coffee, placing mugs in front of Mother and Fab. He handed me a bottle of water.

"The bakery put in a cookie bar," Mother said, opening the box. "I got a little of everything."

I peered in the box, and they all looked yummy. I'd have a hard time choosing.

"Heard you had a confrontation with a woman at Jake's. What was that about?" Mother turned an unrelenting stare on me.

Fab, who was standing behind Mother, threw up her hands, letting me know it wasn't her that blabbed.

In the process of reaching for a cookie, I withdrew my hand, no longer interested. It was unsettling to know that someone had reported on my activities to Mother. Was it just in passing, or did Mother have someone checking on me? The thought of the latter set my teeth on edge. I took a calming breath, having stalled long enough trying to figure out what she knew before completely narcing on myself. She couldn't know about Creole's wife or the drama would have hit the roof the moment she set foot in the house.

"I'm not sure who you're talking about. It's the nature of the business—an occasional disgruntled customer—I deal with it all the time," I said, managing to pass it off as no big deal. Watching Mother's body language, I was certain she didn't know anything or she would've blurted it out by now.

"Can't Charles take over for you for now and handle any problems? Give you a bit of a break?" Mother asked.

It took me a minute to figure out who she was talking about. "Doodad?"

Mother nodded.

"Although he's turned out to be a great hire, Jake's is my business, and I like to keep an eye on it."

Mother fidgeted, looking down and then back at me. "I've made an appointment for you to see a therapist this afternoon." She reached in her pocket and withdrew a business card, putting it down in front of me. "Don't tell me you're busy; I know you're not." She glanced at Fab, making it clear where she got the information.

I hadn't had time to brace myself for that bit of news, leaving me at a complete loss for words.

"When Madeline called, she didn't mention one word about an appointment with a psychiatrist," Fab said, shifting on her stool. "Did you?" she demanded, putting Mother on the spot, which she sidestepped by ignoring it.

Didier looked damn uncomfortable, glancing from one woman to the other, which had me wondering if he planned on escaping the kitchen.

"This is nice of you," I lied and shoved the card back. "If I need a shrink, I can make my own appointment."

"Just know that I'm worried about you." Mother smiled that special smile designed to induce guilt. "You keep disappearing at odd hours. No one knows where you go."

"I don't need hand-holding to walk on the beach or fill up a bucket with seashells, which happens to be therapeutic for me," I said in frustration. It showed. What I left unsaid was that it was the only time I got a moment to myself to think.

A banging on the front door brought the uncomfortable conversation to a halt. Didier couldn't wait to get to the door. My guess was he would like it if it were some kind of trouble that would send Mother home.

Fab jumped off her seat, leaning over the sink and craning her head out the garden window. "It's Brad."

They were ganging up on me.

"Business meeting?" I nodded at Brad as he came inside, taking in his immaculate black suit, even his tie tied in a respectable knot.

He scowled and flashed me a "behave" look, which I ignored. I wasn't a girlfriend but a little sister who could annoy the hell out of him if I so chose. I also wanted to suggest, the next time he visited, giving the uptight vibe a rest and coming in shorts. I liked that persona much better. It didn't feel like he had my back as much these days.

Mother confirmed it immediately. "I was just telling Madison about her doctor's appointment." She patted my hand. "I'm offering to drive you. After, we can have a girl lunch."

The smile on her face almost made me scream, except that would be like handing her proof I was unstable. I jerked my hand back, glaring at her and Brad. "I. Am. Not. Going."

"You need to move on, and this will help you," Mother said, her voice soft and sympathetic.

"That's so offensive, I'm not responding." Tears built up in my eyes. I'd be damned if I'd cry. "I'll grieve in my *own time* and my *own way*, and I'm not interested in a stranger's suggestions."

"I know that grieving is a process, and I'm not suggesting you do it in the next five minutes. I just think talking with an unbiased person would be helpful."

"Creole was murdered. It's not like he had an illness and I knew the end was coming. I didn't get to say good-bye, and no one wants me to know what happened. Barely a well-wish from anyone, and now 'get over it.'"

"I'm not suggesting any such thing." Mother patted my hand again.

"Knowing what happened isn't going to bring Creole back," Brad said, a frustrated look on his face. "Digging around in a police investigation might bring trouble to your door, and by association, your family. Creole wouldn't want that."

"I never planned to investigate anything on my own. The one person who could've got the information discreetly—you know, your girlfriend—you forbid to help me," I said, fairly calmly, I thought. Getting the referral to GC had gone a long way to letting go of my hurt feelings.

"That's because I don't want Phil doing something that might get her hurt," Brad ground out.

"It's a beautiful day out," Didier said. "Why don't we go out by the pool?"

I flashed a hint of a smile at him for his attempt to ratchet down the drama. No one responded to his suggestion.

"Anyone need a refill?" Fab asked.

Only Brad responded. "I'll take a water." He reached around her, opening the refrigerator and getting his own, moving next to me.

"I need a nap," I said, when what I wanted to say was I'd had enough. "I didn't sleep well last night."

"That's another thing the doctor could help you with. Maybe she can prescribe something," Mother said.

"I don't take unnecessary medication—you know that. Especially something that has the potential for addiction."

"You can be annoyed all you want," Brad said, softening his tone. "But we're your family and we worry about you." He laid his arm across my shoulders, giving me a light squeeze.

"What I need is for everyone to stop hovering and scrutinizing my every move."

Mother's gaze swept over me from head to toe. "How much weight have you lost? Are you eating?"

"About the same." I was close to losing the battle to keep my annoyance under control. I turned to Brad. "Did you stop by just to say hello?" And irritate the hell out of me. I did manage a small smile.

"Mother and I had a long talk, and I agree with all her suggestions. If you keep an open mind, I'm sure you'll see that the proposals are in your best interest. In that vein, I'm offering to temporarily take over your business interests, or at the least deal with any problems that come up until you're feeling better," Brad said in a tone that suggested I get on board. "I'll clean out the riff-raff." He half-smiled.

"That's rich," I huffed. "Two of the tenants that you deem 'riff-raff' were snuck in by you when my back was turned. Or did you forget that?"

Brad appeared chagrinned to be called out for his past shenanigans.

Mother and Brad started to speak at the same time, both wanting to convince me that they knew what was best for me and that I should lose my uncooperative attitude.

I cut them off. "Both of you, thank you, but I can handle my own affairs. Besides, it gives me something to focus on. Now, before I say something I'll regret, I'm going upstairs." I practically leapt off my stool and cut through the living room, leaving them to drown in an awkward silence.

"Patience," I whispered as I closed and locked my bedroom door. Quietly, though I wanted to slam it. Mother never gave up when she had a "plan" and had convinced herself she knew what was best. What I needed to do was think like her. She wouldn't hang out in the kitchen until appointment time—instead, she'd be back at the last minute, in ambush mode, and do her best to guilt me into the car.

Knowing I had a small window for escape, I pulled an overnight bag from the top shelf of the closet, throwing in a few necessities, electronics, and chargers. I'd give it some time before cracking the door open to monitor the voices downstairs, and when all was quiet, make my getaway.

A tapping sounded at the bottom of the bedroom door. *Fab!* I wondered briefly why she hadn't used a lockpick or made it sound like the door was about to be kicked in. I rolled off the bed and unlocked the door, sticking my head out. Seeing all was clear, I held it open.

"Madeline left," Fab stated as she entered, making herself comfortable on the edge of the bed.

"But she'll be back."

Fab nodded. "I was sworn to secrecy." She shifted her focus to my travel bag. "Where are you going?"

"I'm going away for a few days of rest and sunshine and some reading. I'll have my phone on, and *you* can check on me all you want, as long as you pretend that's not what you're doing." I sat down next to her. "I'll sneak out so you can claim ignorance."

"I'll have to tell Didier. Just know he might be calling. He'll want to check on you for himself. I'll tell him to pretend also; he can start out with a cat question."

"Just a few days. I need time to adjust to Creole having a wife and child."

"You don't know it's true."

"I feel like I have to believe it is. If I don't, and it turns out to be true, it'll hurt even more later."

"I wish that bastard was here; he wouldn't be having any more children by the time I was done with him," Fab said with disgust.

"You're the best." I hugged her.

"I don't feel like it. If I were doing my friend duty, you wouldn't need to go anywhere."

"You remember when you and Didier broke up, how annoying you were, wanting time to yourself?" I laughed at her wrinkled-up nose.

"That's why I'm staying mostly calm." Fab nudged my shoulder. "I know where you're going."

"You're not going to follow me, are you?"

"No, because I know there's no need to worry. But you'd better stay in touch."

"If anything comes up that you don't want to handle, call me and I'll come back to town. Under *no* circumstances are you to shoot anyone, and that includes tenants, customers—"

"You take the fun out of everything." Fab pouted, pulling her imaginary gun and getting off a couple of shots before blowing on the muzzle.

"I know." I sighed unsympathetically. "It's just a small downside in our friendship."

"Go now. While Didier's in the shower." She reached down and grabbed my bag, putting it in my hand. "And before your mother gets back."

Chapter Twenty-Four

It had been two days. I stared out at the water, sitting on the beach and sifting white sand through my fingers as the sun rapidly vanished. I had started to relax, no longer feeling like I was under a microscope, having to monitor my every move for fear of worrying someone.

As expected, Mother flipped when she arrived at the house and I wasn't dressed and ready to go to the therapy that I told her I didn't want. I made the mistake of answering her first text, and she took that as a sign to blow up my phone with more messages, which I ignored. Later, the phone vibrated and Didier's picture popped up.

"It's me," Fab whispered into the phone.

"You okay?"

"I'm paranoid that your Mother has somehow snuck back and is lurking out of sight. She's certain I had something to do with your taking flight, and she fired one question after another at me, demanding to know how someone could sneak out under my nose. Damn, I'm exhausted."

"Sorry." I chuckled. *"How did you answer her?"*

"In most cases, I didn't; in others, my answers were quite vague and deliberately misleading. She was so unrelenting, she didn't notice." She laughed. *"It's*

205

only funny now."

"Why are you using Didier's phone?"

"I don't trust your Mother not to snap up my phone when I'm not looking and check my call log."

"You must frustrate the heck out of her, always one step ahead. How did you leave it?"

"You're not going to like this part." She sighed. "Madeline stormed out, threatening to find you. So heads up."

"I have a few more books to read, and then I'll be home. I'm missing you, Didier, and the children."

"The children are upstairs, sleeping on your bed."

We ended the call with me promising to continue to answer all her calls and messages. I'd turned my phone off and rummaged through Creole's desk until I found another phone, which I plugged in, texting Didier the number.

I stood and grabbed my shell bucket, which I'd ignored on this evening's walk on the beach, and headed back to the house. I took the stairs two at a time, thinking running away from home was about to come to an end. I liked being around people, and even if I spaced out on occasion, I'd come to the conclusion that socialization would be good for me.

I indulged in a long shower and curled up in bed, intent on reading until I fell asleep. While lying there contemplating what to read, I fell asleep.

* * *

"I'm a selfish bastard, but I need you to wake up. I've waited long enough."

The familiar voice filtered slowly through my sleep-fogged brain. A second later, there was a dip in the mattress and I found myself hugged to a hard chest. Awake now — well, sort of — I slowly peeled open first one eyelid and then the other. My eyes focused on familiar male clothing in a pile on the floor. I hadn't done that, or maybe I had. I closed my eyes, not caring about the answer.

"Finally." The return of the male voice brought my head up with a snap. I slowly relaxed, certain I was dreaming, as I had been earlier, bringing a smile to my face. There was no way I could be awake and locking eyes with the man that lay by my side. It wasn't possible. A ghost? I didn't believe in ghosts... Except once, I saw my father walking across the back lawn after he died. I never told anyone, keeping it to myself; the last thing I wanted even back then was pitying glances. But I could become a believer if it brought the man I loved back to me. If this was the way to connect with him, I'd sleep here every night.

Here he was, lying beside me, just like when I had last seen him. He still had everything in all the right places.

"I've missed you," the apparition said in that low, seductive voice, the one that had always curled my toes and still did.

I watched in fascination as his lips moved.

I didn't feel like worrying about my sanity just then—all I wanted to do was bask in the dream that he was here. After all, the man had been dead for a couple of months and I'd missed him every day.

I'd enjoy this moment—another one to keep to myself and not even share with my best friend. If Mother found out I was entertaining ghosts, she might have me committed involuntarily. In my opinion, the process in this state made that all too easy.

"You're so lifelike – I would've thought ghosts would have a more ethereal appearance," I said, running my finger down his chest, his rock-hard abs. The mattress dipped slightly as he shifted. "I don't know anything about ghosts… I can learn."

"Ghost?" He laughed.

"I've missed you so much. I'll sleep here every night if you promise to come back."

"You're not dreaming, and I'm no damn ghost. It's really me. I'm here, and not going anywhere." The ghost ran his finger across my lips. "Still think I'm a ghost?" he said, slightly bemused. He lowered his face to mine, and his lips connected with mine in a hard kiss that left me groaning.

This was one crazy dream, but there was nothing to worry about because all that would happen in the end was I'd simply wake up. I didn't want to…at least not right now.

He kissed me again, and I melted against the... Ghost? I shrieked and tried to launch myself backward, which turned into an awkward roll off the bed. A long arm caught me a centimeter from the floor.

"Babe. It's me." He lowered me to the floor. Slinging one leg over the bed, he scooped me into his arms, sitting on the side.

"You're not a ghost?" I asked in a pitiful tone. I started to cry and gently ran a hand along the scruff of his beard, which made me cry harder.

He held and comforted me, wiping my tears with the corner of the sheet. "You feel so good."

"You're dead. You know how I know? I went to that pitiful excuse for a funeral." Tears welled up again. "Is this some big joke? I've been grieving for you." The anger erupted from me, and I slapped at his chest, pushing him back. "Get out." I pointed to the door.

"This is my house."

"Not anymore. You left it to me in your will."

"Except I didn't die." He tightened his hold, not allowing me to wiggle away. "We need to talk," he pleaded.

"Your wife here?" I demanded and glanced around.

"What the hell are you talking about?" His volume went up to match mine. "I'm not married and never have been, and if I were, it would be to you."

"You rotten liar. Bastard."

He winced and swung his legs over the side of the bed, depositing me on the mattress. "I think I liked it better when you thought I was a ghost. A ghost? Are you out of your mind?"

"I've felt like it at times," I said softly. "You're not dead?" I reached over and pinched his thigh – hard.

"Ouch, dammit. What was that for?"

"You're alive." I reached out again, and this time, he backed away. "Where the hell have you been?"

"I've got a good explanation, if you'll listen."

"I bet it's a doozy." His son's face flashed before my eyes, and my anger ratcheted back up. "I've met Milton—you remember, your son – your son."

"Milton? The little blond kid? Where did you meet him?

"Your wife – Cheryl, in case you've forgotten – introduced us." The pain of that moment came rushing back. Until then, I'd done a good job of keeping all thoughts of Creole's matrimonial status at bay – sort of.

"Cheryl Beaumont?" he asked. I nodded. "I'd never marry her; she's hardly my type. How could you not notice? YOU are my type, and the two of you are nothing alike." He laid his forehead against mine. "She's been an informant for years…and I'd bet good money on her being the reason my cover was blown and my partner is dead."

"Milton?"

"He's not my kid. He doesn't even look like me or anyone in my family."

"He doesn't know a word of French."

Creole cracked a smile. "Milton is Cheryl's sister's kid. His mother and father were killed in a car accident. I thought he lived with his grandparents. I hope nothing happened to them that resulted in him ending up with Cheryl; she's a mess."

"I'd be happy to never see Cheryl again." I wondered how far she would have gone to falsify the paperwork she needed to pull off the scam.

"My head hurts." He gripped it. "Been doing a lot of that lately." He stood up, reaching for his jeans. "Why are all my clothes in a pile on the floor?"

"See the scissors?" I pointed. "I planned to cut them all up, starting with my favorite shirt. I got sidetracked putting it on and started crying." I stood and grabbed his shirt off the end of the bed, putting it on and buttoning one button in the middle.

"Oh, babe." He held out his arms.

I backed up until I bumped into a wall. "Just so you know, Cheryl's suing your estate as your wife and passing off Milton as your son. Claims to have all the pertinent paperwork."

"I don't know what she's done, but none of it's legal. My lawyer is no slouch and will figure it out and send her packing. Besides, as of yesterday, she's in a safe house, which is better than she deserves."

I covered my face with my hands as tears rolled down my cheeks. "You're not dead," I whispered.

He crossed the space between us, boxing me in, his hands on the wall on either side of my head. "You're going to listen to me if I have to tie you to the bed. I'm back, and I will make you understand that I'm not a complete bastard."

"Your death. That woman. Milton, the son that wasn't ours… It's hard to take in." I sniffed. "I'm happy you're not a ghost."

"Yeah, me too." He smiled wolfishly. He wrapped my hand in his, led me to the couch, and pushed me down. "Don't move." He brushed my lips with his. "I'll be right back with coffee, and I'll answer all your questions."

I followed, not wanting to let him out of my sight.

He returned, setting down the mugs on the coffee table. He sat next to me, taking my face in his hands and kissing me like a man in need.

Chapter Twenty-Five

We finished our coffee, and Creole dragged a chair over to the couch and sat facing me, our knees touching. "You can ask me anything you want. I'll answer all your questions, but some work ones may be a little vague due to the ongoing case."

I had told him while he was making coffee that it had been hard to get information but didn't get into any details, other than that even GC hadn't been able to get anything – yet.

Creole had been intrigued by the new guy and wanted to know who it was. "He better be as careful as you say he is. What's he doing isn't legal," he grouched.

"I've missed you. I never dreamed of the possibility of a second chance." I leaned in and kissed him.

"If it had been my decision, you'd have gotten a call the second I woke up. Once the department locks down on a case, though, it's next to impossible to get information of any kind. And files aren't accessible to just anyone who wants to read them." He winced, rotating his shoulder.

"Aren't you still supposed to be under a

doctor's care?" I eyed him suspiciously, knowing that as soon as he got his breath back, he'd tell his doc to take a hike.

"I've got you to take care of me." He tugged on the ends of my hair, brushing my lips with a kiss, a non-answer that could be translated as *yes, I still need to see a doctor, but good luck getting me to go.*

"It could've been me." Creole covered his face with his hands, apparently reliving the final moments of the doomed operation. "When we came around the corner of that warehouse, if our positions had been reversed, I'd be the one who's dead. My partner, Barlow, was dead before he hit the ground, a bullet to the head." He flinched, the pain evident in his words. "We'd had this drug cartel under surveillance for months. Finally got all the evidence we needed to put them away for a long time; some would never see the light of day again. This close." He pinched his thumb and forefinger together. "We were waiting for backup to arrive to arrest the lot of them, including the leader."

I reached for his hand, holding it in mine.

He took a shuddering breath and continued. "One of the suspects appeared out of nowhere on the corner across from us. It was as though he knew right where to find us. I've replayed that moment over and over and wondered how. Without hesitation, he pulled out a semiautomatic handgun and started shooting. I managed to get off several shots before landing face first on the walkway next to my partner."

"You don't have to tell me everything right now," I said.

"Yes, I do. You deserve to know what happened." His eyes burned into mine. "The vest I was wearing saved my life, though the close-range shots caused blunt-force trauma, cracked a few ribs."

I ran my hand lightly down his chest.

"The shot to my pretty mug didn't enter my brain. But this..." He ran a finger over a nasty wound at his hairline. "...will be a permanent reminder." Creole leaned back, lifting his right leg into my lap and pulling up his shorts, showing where a bullet had passed through his right thigh. "At least it didn't shatter a bone." He straightened up, holding out his right arm. "Same with this one." He fingered the angry red scar. "Just a graze."

"When I went down, I took a nasty hit to the head and didn't become fully conscious for several days. Due to some mix-up at the hospital, Barlow's wife got a call informing her that her husband was in surgery. It wasn't until I'd been wheeled back to my room that she discovered the mistake and that Barlow was in the morgue."

I sucked in a breath. My heart went out to this woman I'd never met, who'd faced that heart-wrenching reality.

"Since my name had already been leaked as

the officer dead at the scene, it was decided to put it out that 'Barlow' had died in surgery. The chief feared that if it got out that I was still alive, there'd be a bloodbath trying to locate me. He thought it would be safer for Barlow's family, and since I didn't have one, well… Our cover was blown, but we still had men on the inside and wanted to salvage the operation."

"Any news on how Mrs. Barlow is doing?" I asked.

He shook his head. "I got moved to a private room and had no communication with anyone, except the chief, who stopped by as soon as I was able to receive visitors. I argued with him about contacting you, but he was adamant. He had higher-ups scrutinizing the case and orders of his own to follow." He paused, thinking. "I would've liked to express my condolences to Barlow's wife, reassure her he wasn't in any pain at the end, lie to her that his last words were for her, because I know they would've been had he not died instantly, and most of all to apologize. Could I have done more? I'd like to think not. But contact with her was also off limits.

"I was soon moved to a safe house, where I recuperated." He half-laughed. "Boy, was I a pain in the ass. I constantly badgered the guys that were assigned to babysit me with questions. I got vague or no answers and finally stopped asking, except for one question, which I asked every day: "When can I leave?" I could watch television, walk around the condo, play cards with the other officers, but no interaction with the outside world. I was miserable, and my attitude didn't help the situation any." He pushed back his chair and stood. "Want something to drink?"

"I'll have what you're having," I said to his retreating back, fingers crossed it wasn't beer.

He returned, waters in hand. "You thought I was going to bring back one of those dark brews I enjoy, didn't you?"

I nodded and laughed.

"A change of scenery is in order." He stuck out his hand and pulled me to my feet. One of his arms hooked around me, we headed out to the patio and sat in a chaise.

I settled back against his chest.

"Where was I? The shrink! Not only did the doctor make house calls, so did the psych woman. She harped on survivor's guilt in a tone typically used on a naughty four-year-old. I lost my temper and told her, woman or no, if she didn't get out, I'd kick her out. The next day, I got a letter informing me that I'd have to pass a psych evaluation to come back to the department."

"Maybe we can share the same shrink. I'd go if you were with me." I told him about Mother's newest great idea.

His arms wrapped around me. "I'm going to make this up to you," he growled in my ear.

"And who makes it up to you…your partner…his family?"

"You know the job is dangerous when you sign up, but losing a fellow officer and friend is a tough one. How to change the outcome of that day? Don't know. I probably could use a therapy session or two, but I'll pick out my own damn doctor."

I smiled. "That's what I told Mother."

"I knew when Barlow hit the ground that he'd taken his last breath. Couldn't miss the gaping hole in his forehead, face covered in blood. Thankfully, his eyes were closed. It's a vision that's hard to shake."

He tightened his hold around me. "Ouch." His arms went slack, and he pushed back against the cushion, the pain reminding him that his ribs hadn't completely healed. He looked irritated. One of several reminders that he wasn't one hundred percent. "Feeling the pain makes me feel less guilty." He blew out a breath.

"I'm sorry I was so mean," I said in a low voice.

"Hey." He nibbled on my ear. "Look at us now."

"You're here, so that must mean that the bad guys are dead or in jail."

He took so long to answer, it started to upset my stomach. He downed his water, screwing the cap back on and tossing it on an adjacent chair.

"Not exactly." He sighed. "They're still out

there. I know there's a plan in place to put an end to their reign, but no clue what it is or when it will be executed."

We sat in silence for several minutes.

"You want to hear how I got back to the Cove?" He chuckled.

"I want to hear everything, and if you need to repeat it, I'm here to listen."

"Damn, I missed you. Did I say that already? Well I did, every day." He kissed my neck. "I'd had enough. I waited until the other officer was distracted, and then I walked. Probably don't have a job and not sure that I care. I had plenty of time to think, walking home last night."

"From Miami?" I asked in shock. He nodded. "That's at least sixty miles."

"No money, no phone, nothing but the clothes on my back and, thankfully, a pair of shoes. Sticking to dimly lit residential streets, ready to jump into any bush I could find, I hightailed it out of the area of the safe house. When I hit the commercial district, I hitched the first of two rides. The last one was with a truck driver who I had let me out at the edge of town. I'd have liked to get a little closer, but I didn't want to answer any, 'What's out here?' questions. If you're worried, no one will come knocking; you know this place is not that easy to find."

"Won't the chief be sending someone to beat down your door?"

"The only address on file is an old one that I

moved from a few years back. The title here is held in a trust and not easily traceable. The only two people that know where it is are me and the *new owner.*" He bit down on my neck.

"Ouch." I scooted forward. "I'll take care of you." I stood and reached for his hand. "A shower, a foot rub, and a nap."

Chapter Twenty-Six

We'd lazed the previous day away in bed. Then Creole watched some sports on television while I read. I'd caught him up on the happenings in the Cove while he was gone, relaying the details of Fab's cases. We fell asleep in each other's arms, sleeping until the bright sunshine streaming through the glass woke us up.

"You need more than just Pop Tarts," I said as I opened the cupboard doors.

"Pop Tarts?" He looked excited.

"Just kidding."

"I knew that." In response to my stare: "Really!" He made coffee and picked up the full mugs. "We've got to keep my reappearance secret," he said as he walked out on the patio, setting them down. He pushed two chairs together, and we sat facing one another.

"We'll have to tell Fab and Didier. Hear me out," I said in answer to his scowl. "Without their help, I wouldn't have been able to fend off Mother for as long as I have. Since all eyes are on me right now, I wouldn't be able to see you without attracting attention. I'm not going to be separated from you again." I put my feet on the edge of the cushions, leaning in. "We can trust them."

Creole downed half his coffee before answering. "Under the condition that Fab never picks the lock here," he said firmly.

"I can weasel that promise out of her," I said with confidence, knowing she'd whine a little before giving in. Or maybe a lot. "I thought about it this morning, and I can get a good bargain on a junker car through Crum. That way, you'll have something to drive." He had told me that his truck was parked at police headquarters.

"What about the Porsche?" He smiled, knowing Fab barely let anyone look at it, let alone get behind the wheel.

"Fab finally let me drive it, and it didn't end well." I'd left the Porsche debacle out of the retelling of the Isla story. "Gunz came through and had it repaired." I did my best to downplay how a simple recovery job had resulted in damage to the car, but he saw through my vague story.

Creole's brows knitted together. "What other trouble have you gotten into since… Well…? I'll be checking you over very closely later for injuries. You better not have any."

"Didier has been doing his best to keep Fab and me out of trouble. I think we've about exhausted him. But to his credit, he hasn't given up."

He pulled me into his arms, laying a loud

smoochy kiss on my lips. "Wish I'd broken out and gone on the lame sooner."

"Any chance you'll be arrested?" The thought of that sent a chill up my spine.

"Fired possibly, but not arrested."

"I hope they get this cartel behind bars sooner rather than later. I'm sure you feel the same way. Then you can think about what you want to do without it hanging over your head."

"The head of the cartel—Miguel Santos, a Pablo Escobar wannabe—hadn't been arrested as of yesterday. It would've made headlines, and there weren't any. I hacked into your computer." He winked at me. "Used your phone and called Help. He wasn't all that happy to hear from me, knowing I was in hot water and not wanting any part of it."

Help. I didn't tell Creole that he was the one who'd made the notification of his death.

"Word on the street has it that Santos slipped over the border, heading south. I don't believe that for a second." Creole snorted. "He's too arrogant, thinks he knows it all, and that will trip him up. It almost did once. Getting away has most likely emboldened him and will hopefully make him careless in the future."

"Let's hope he never comes back."

"Don't worry. If he does come back, he won't be getting away."

"The Keys is a great place for you to hide. I can help you keep a low profile. This house has great security. Anyone shows up, you'll know that's the first red flag and disappear down the beach. If need be, I'll find another hideout. I've got connections. Maybe even a boat."

Creole smiled at me, shaking his head. "Sometimes your resources scare me."

I beamed back at him. "And I have a doctor that makes house calls, no questions asked."

Creole stood, pulling me to my feet, scooping me into his arms, and carrying me inside.

* * *

I leaned over the kitchen island, facing Creole, and called Didier's phone. Fab answered. "I'd rather you were pulling into the driveway than calling," she said.

"Since you have me on speakerphone…" I'd noticed the change in tone. "I want to ask the two of you a huge favor that you can never under any circumstances tell anyone about." I also hit the speaker button so Creole could listen in.

Didier's groan came through the phone line.

"Are you in trouble?" Fab asked warily.

Fab and Didier conversed a moment in French.

"I heard a 'oui,' and that means yes," I blurted. "Since I know neither of you talk about bodily functions."

Creole covered his face, and his shoulders shook.

"Cherie, the two of us are going to have a talk," Didier growled.

I laughed. "I look forward to it."

More French talk. Creole listened intently, giving me the thumbs up.

"We're in," Fab said.

"You want to know why?" Didier asked. "Because that was the first light-hearted laugh I've heard out of you in too long. Do I need to pack heat?"

"Pack heat! We've thoroughly corrupted you. No guns necessary."

"You coming home?" Fab asked.

"You're coming to me. I forgot to ask if the two of you have plans for tonight."

"If we did, we'd cancel them. You're important to us," Didier said.

"I placed an order at Bruno's for our favorites, and it needs to be picked up," I told them. "Call me when you get back on the Overseas. Just out of town at the first turnaround sign, exit there, and I'll be waiting. Make sure that no one is following you."

"You sure you're okay?" Didier asked, worry in his voice.

"You'll understand when you get here. This next part is very important. Raise your right pinkie fingers, link them together, and swear your secrecy into eternity."

Creole moved to the couch and leaned back, a stupid smile on his face, shaking his head.

"You're ridiculous," Fab hissed.

"I agree for the both of us to the secrecy," Didier said.

"You two are the best." I disconnected and walked over to the couch.

"I trust them," Creole said, taking the phone out of my hand and setting it on the table, then pulling me into his lap.

I nodded in agreement. "If I'd had any doubt, we would've come up with another plan."

"I like this 'we' business." Creole kissed me.

"Me too," I murmured against his lips.

Chapter Twenty-Seven

Meeting up with Fab and Didier couldn't have been timed better. We rolled up to the turnaround at the same time, Fab behind the wheel of Didier's Mercedes. I powered down my window and motioned for them to follow. A hundred feet on, I turned off onto a gravel road, which appeared to drive straight into the forest but was really the start of the paved road. Curving around, I parked in the driveway of the beach house, leaving room for them to pull in beside me.

"One more promise," I said, standing in front of the wooden fence that was tall enough to block sight of the house from the road.

"For goodness sakes." Fab blew out an exasperated breath. "Yes, okay."

"There will be no picking of the locks on this house – ever. Or any other break-in tricks."

"We going to stand out here all day?" she asked.

"I'll promise for her." Didier returned Fab's glare.

I punched the code in and held the gate open.

"Did I tell you I've got a surprise?"

"You know I don't like surprises." Fab checked out the empty courtyard. "This isn't very inviting. You'll have it filled with flowers in no time."

"Probably not." I half-laughed.

Creole had told me not to plant anything that needed water. That left cactus, and they were a long way from the tropical blooms that were my favorite.

I opened the door and preceded them inside. I took the shopping bag from Didier and set it on the counter, and he set the wine down.

Fab looked around the kitchen, running her hand over the granite countertop. "The Old Lug did a good job."

"Fabiana," Didier chastised.

"It's beautiful," she said, checking out the appliances.

I threw my arms around her in a squeezing hug.

"I think so too." Creole stuck his head around the wall. "Come see the rest."

"What the..." Didier boomed, his mouth dropping open.

Fab jumped. "Is he real? Or is this some weird thing you rigged with our funeral friends?"

Didier took two long strides and pushed at Creole's shoulder. "Nope, he's real." They man-hugged. "You're back from the dead?"

"Long story. I'll tell you over dinner."

"Not so fast, a-hole." Fab drew her gun. "Madison wouldn't shoot your worthless behind, but I will."

Standing next to her, I shoved her arm down before she could think about shooting. "No, please… I just got him back."

"But—"

I cut her off. "He's not married. That woman was a greedy wife wannabe."

Fab turned a skeptical eye on Creole.

Creole threw up his hands. "I never, ever cheated on Madison. And Milton is not my kid. If he were, he'd be living with me, not his scary aunt."

Fab reholstered her gun. "Where the heck have you been? You couldn't call, write, send a pigeon?"

Didier stepped back to the counter, dragging Fab with him. "Let's do this over dinner. Pizza's getting cold." He unloaded the bag.

The mood relaxed immediately. I wanted to hug Didier. "We'll eat outside," I said. "I'll set the table."

"I've got the drinks." Creole took orders. "Lug, uh?" He winked at Fab.

The guys wanted Euro beer, Fab wanted the wine, and I opted for water.

I handed plates to Fab, grabbed silverware and napkins, and led the way.

"Great view." Fab stared off down the beach. "Nice that the neighbors are far enough away not to be a pain."

"I've yet to see anyone on the beach."

"It must be weird." Fab glanced over her shoulder. "Back from the dead?" She wrinkled her nose in disbelief.

"I thought he was a ghost," I whispered. "And I didn't care. If that was all I could get, I wasn't letting go. Then the ghost got a little too lifelike." I chuckled. "I'm going to need your help keeping this a secret. You're about to find out why." I nodded to the guys, Didier coming out of the house in the lead with pizza boxes and a salad, Creole with a tray of drinks in his hands.

Once we'd been made our choices and our plates were full, Didier filled Fab's wine glass. "What shall we toast too? Welcome back?"

I held my glass up. "To ghosts."

Creole laughed and enveloped me in a hard hug.

We all clinked glasses.

Creole took over the conversation, reciting the facts in a dispassionate way, as though he hadn't lived through the situation but was only an observer.

"You need information, we've got Phil's connection," Fab offered.

"Why did everything go south with Phil?" Creole asked.

"You tell him," I said.

Fab and I had never discussed it, but listening to her retelling of everything that went down and the abruptness and sneakiness of the events, it was clear she no longer had any regard for the woman.

"Is this a true-love situation between her and Brad?" Creole asked.

Didier looked uncomfortable; after all, my brother and he were partners.

"More like power couple," I said. "They both aspire to mover-and-shaker status in our little community."

"Back to your situation… The dealer you're after, is he likely to show up at this house?" Didier asked.

"All the pertinent information in my personnel file is outdated and not readily available. The address they have on file is from a few moves ago. The only people with this address are you guys and my lawyer. As for Madison's house, the chief and Help are the only people I work with that know about Madison."

"They're such great friends, neither showed up at your funeral." Fab mumbled something under her breath that had Didier's eyebrows arching.

"Fab," Didier said in exasperation.

"What? It's true. All of it." Fab ignored his scowl. "A half-dozen or so people showed up that Madison didn't know, and not a one of them said a word to any of us. But you were well-covered by the extended Westin family." She pulled her phone out of her pocket, setting it on the table. "I got pictures of everything. Now that you're…ah…not dead, you might want to see who your friends are."

I grinned at Fab. The woman took pictures of everything. I loved that about her.

"A funeral?" Creole questioned. "I'll have to ask the chief. Probably a ruse to reinforce the story that I was dead."

"Cheryl—you know, your wife," I teased, "found me, and that could be a potential problem. At least she didn't show up at the house, but she did summon me to Jake's. How did she know about at least one location where I could be found? You suspect she sold you out; do you think she's hawked my information already?"

Creole looked contemplative and unhappy. "It's hard to know at this point what connection Cheryl had to what happened. I find it interesting that she's in protective custody—that means she's got something worth keeping her alive for." He stared Fab down. "My wife?" He sniffed. "I'm surprised you didn't see through her big, fat, f-ing lie."

"Neither of us were completely sold," I defended us. "But Cheryl was so adamant, and we were both charmed by Milton. I was disappointed when he flunked his French test; I'd have been satisfied with Bon Cheerios as an answer."

Fab laughed, and the guys shook their heads.

"If we were in France, people would not appreciate your humor and would think you're a lunatic." Creole tugged on my hair.

I made a face. "People think that already."

Creole's solemn face returned. "All of us need to keep our eyes peeled. Not that we don't already... Maybe not you, pretty boy," he teased Didier. "We need to be extra careful until Santos is caught. I suspect he and his crew haven't given me a thought, now that they think I'm dead. They're busy figuring out new lucrative ways to push their product, since the old avenues have been shut down."

"Madeline and Brad, you telling them?" Fab asked. When Creole shook his head, she said, "Let's just hope that when Madeline does find out, she's so happy you're alive, she doesn't dwell on being the last to know. Brad will probably be happy to see you alive and well."

They'd both be supremely annoyed with me for keeping them out of the loop, but when I explained it was for Creole's safety, they'd understand – maybe. I wouldn't dwell on it until I had to face the two and surprise myself with how I handled the awkward situation.

"You coming home tomorrow?" Didier asked me.

"Yes," I said quietly, keeping to myself how much I didn't like the idea.

"Call Madeline and make sure she knows you came back a new woman," Didier told me.

"While you've been gone, she's taken to showing up at odd hours, always with Spoon in tow. She probably figures Fab won't tell her she can't come in with her enforcer by her side."

"Well, I have an enforcer of my own." I patted Fab's hand. "Don't I? And my money's on the petite French woman, not the big guy."

"Mine too." Creole chuckled.

Didier groaned.

"I know this is probably a bad idea, but I'd like to take Creole home. If anyone has a way we can work that out, speak up." I turned to Creole. "I'm not going to let you sit out here by yourself and stare at the water."

"Where's your truck?" Fab asked.

"Help told me the police yard."

"You need to make a shopping list for me." I snapped my fingers at Fab. Ignoring her "do it yourself" look, I said, "A disguise – we can hit the party store and come up with something good. Next on the list, a nondescript car that no one would look twice at. Legal title and in running condition both a must." I said to Creole, "That way, you won't feel like a prisoner and can come and go at will."

"Most men would be put off by those kind of connections," Creole said. He and Didier exchanged a smile.

"You're not most men." I gave him a dreamy smile.

Fab stood. "We're having a nice evening here,

let's not get all sickly sweet." She picked up the plates.

"More beer?" I asked Creole before refilling Fab's wine glass and following her into the house.

"Too bad this place isn't bigger; we could all move in here and keep the address secret." Fab deposited the plates in the sink, rinsing them off. "I have a question that I didn't figure was any of my business."

"Please...since when does that stop either of us? Ask away."

"Is Creole setting himself up for big trouble with his bosses? I'm kind of impressed at what he did for love and all—raises my opinion of him. Not that it was ever low. Don't tell him, but I missed him when we thought he was dead."

"Going all romance novel on me," I teased. I wrapped up the leftovers, putting them in the refrigerator. Pizza for breakfast was a family favorite. "You've got to see the bathroom."

Fab looked skeptical.

I tugged on her arm, led her across the room, and pointed to the door.

She barely opened it, poking only her head inside, then pushed it open wide. "I call dibs on the bathtub." She kicked off her shoes and climbed in, leaning back. "I'd sit in here all day." She stared out at the view of the water, running her hands over the sides of the mammoth clawfoot tub.

"Creole hid me here once. The first thing I did was fill it with bubbles, hang a cigar out of my mouth, and sit there reading. One of the most decadent things I've ever done." I held out my hand. "Get a look at the shower. It's for when you're not in the reading mood."

"You could get a crowd in here if you were into that sort of thing." Fab opened the glass door. "Is this why you changed all the shower heads at home to waterfall?"

"Since I'm short on room for the giganto shower and all the jets, changing out the hardware was the next best thing."

She looked out the window. "Private beach, no neighbors…perfect."

"I didn't peg you for the beach hideaway type. I've always pictured you in a fancy condo in South Beach, in the middle of all the action, partying all night."

"For a long time, that would've been my first choice." She walked back to the living room, and I followed. "But now, with Didier…we like it in Tarpon Cove. We need action, we can drive north, spend the night in a 5-star hotel."

I went into the kitchen, retrieving a couple of beers and waters, and joined the others sitting poolside, feet in the water, watching the sunset.

Chapter Twenty- Eight

Creole and I sat out by the pool in each other's arms as the day dawned sunny and bright. Another beautiful day in the Keys.

"I should go and calm Mother down, show her a trip to the looney bin isn't necessary."

"I'm sorry you were that bad off." Creole nibbled on my ear.

"Nonsense." I rolled over in his arms, facing him. "People don't need others butting in and telling them how to grieve. There's no road map—each person is different. It's been two months, not six years; sadness is to be expected. I was still a functioning adult."

He pressed a kiss to my lips. "You coming back later?"

"I'm not going to be able to stay away. Haven't figured out what I'll tell other people. Do you think you can behave while I'm away?"

"There's no fun in that." He smiled. "I'm going to work on my disguise. I'm thinking I can easily become a beach bum. I'll drag a pair of jeans and a shirt through seawater, dirt, and sand; that ought to perfect my look. While you're out, get me a beard, hat, and some big, dark sunglasses."

"Also thinking I'd probably have better luck tracking down an old Chevy or Ford truck. Looks aren't important, but running condition is. You have a driver's license?"

"I don't have jack," he said in exasperation. "My wallet is in my truck."

I laughed. "ID is also obtainable."

"I'll wing it there. If I get pulled over, I'll just have to hope I don't get hauled in. Don't want to compound it by producing phony documents." He scowled at me.

I laughed at him. "At least I offered. You think of anything else, call me."

"Before you go, I need a kiss."

* * *

I peeked into the kitchen before shutting the front door. Fab and Didier sat at the island, their eyes zeroed in on me. I dumped my bag on the entry bench, kicking off my flip-flops.

"Bon martini," I greeted.

Didier rolled his eyes, a smile tugging at his lips.

"About time you got here," Fab grouched. "I think you mean après-midi since the day's half over."

"I worked from home this morning, wanting to hear whatever plan you cooked up firsthand."

Didier snapped the lid of his laptop closed.

"I'm going disguise and truck shopping," I said.

"I'm sure you meant 'we,'" Fab said in her superior tone. "You and I..." She motioned. "...are going to be spending bonding time together."

"Since when do we need that?"

Didier settled back on his stool, amused by our conversation.

"We've got a job tomorrow," Fab said. "All we need to do is get an old lady to—"

"All? Didn't the last *old lady* shoot at us?"

"The last one was dead – natural causes. The shooter was a few cases back."

"That's right," I said, infusing a touch of drama in the story. "I scaled the side of the house and poked my head in the kitchen window, only to get a whiff of dead-body smell."

"You're exaggerating."

"Why, you're probably wondering," I said to Didier. "Why me? Your girlfriend here didn't want to get her shoes dirty."

"They were designer shoes," Fab practically shouted.

"Bought at a discount," I murmured.

"Ladies, ladies, focus. You never did say who the client was," he pointed out.

Fab hesitated so long I groaned and said, "Brick."

"He guaranteed it would be a pickup and

delivery job. Friend of a friend. The woman's been subpoenaed as a witness, and if she doesn't show up, she's going to jail."

"Smells to me," I said.

Didier nodded. "Maybe there's a reason the woman doesn't want to testify. Fear? Could be a whole host of reasons."

"Once we get there, you can handle it any way you want; no complaints from me," Fab said.

"What are you going to be doing? Let me guess...tossing the place while I try to explain your insatiable nosiness."

Didier laughed, closed the space between them, and hugged her.

"I'm surprised he didn't send his butt-kicking receptionist," I said in disgust. "The last job we did for Brick didn't go his way, thanks to us. If this one doesn't end to his satisfaction, he's not going to be happy. Our track record with him has been dismal of late."

"Now that I know this job doesn't include committing felonies, I'm going to take the afternoon off and go see Creole. How's he doing?" Didier asked.

"He's got too much on his mind, that's for sure. Mentioned going for a walk, wants to build his stamina back up."

"I plan to rearrange my schedule so I can spend time down there. Keep him from getting too bored and doing something he shouldn't – like get impatient and chase criminals." Didier didn't look happy at that thought. "He mentioned kayaking, and you've got the perfect spot for it. We'll have to check it out and see if we can make it happen."

"Don't let him overdo it," I said. "I'm going to run upstairs and pack a small suitcase."

"Call your mother." Didier shook his finger at me.

"Talked to her on the way home. Reassured her I was fine and feeling back to my old self. Promised that I'd have lunch with her later in the week."

Fab sniffed. "That's suspicious. Madeline's been unrelenting. Don't be surprised if she pops up without notice."

"I hope you're wrong, but you're probably not. Be ready to go." I pointed at Fab. I ran up the stairs, giving them privacy.

Chapter Twenty-Nine

Fab slowed as she turned the corner to The Cottages. She couldn't pull into the driveway — four cars were parked single file, effectively blocking anyone from coming or going. Across the street, Mac hadn't pulled her truck all the way into the driveway, leaving no room for a second car. Fab circled the block and parked at the corner. We got out and walked up The Cottages driveway.

"What now?" Fab asked in irritation, checking out the cars.

"Let's hope it's not another funeral...unless whoever it is is serving those cool little sandwiches."

"Promise me right now that if it is a funeral, we're leaving. And another thing, no icky funeral food at my send-off — I want an open bar."

"You'll have the best turnout ever once word gets out that there's free liquor."

So far, we hadn't seen anyone. If it weren't for the cars, you'd think we got lucky and everything was quiet. We walked almost the entire length of the property, turning onto the cement area that ran along the outside of the pool area. Here's where the action was taking place, with beach chairs filled with older women. Crum stood behind a table, a cheap plastic pot in one hand and a rusty hand shovel in the other. The only other man, Joseph, sat in the back, appearing to have fallen asleep.

"What the...?" Fab leaned in and whispered.

I squeezed my eyes shut, taking a breath. *This must be the gardening class.*

Judging by the women's clothing—they'd clearly dressed up for Crum's class: dresses, skirts, and one in white pants—they had something more on their mind than getting their hands covered in dirt.

Mac came running up behind us. "The professor is in his element," she whispered. "I warned him he better not be selling sex."

"How much longer is this going to go on? I need to ask him a question."

Mac consulted her watch. "Another five minutes, and then there's refreshments by the pool – watered-down lemonade and cheap cookies."

"You herd the ladies to the pool so I can have a short conversation with Crum, and then we're out of here. Unless—" I frowned at her. "—there are problems I don't know about."

"Your mother's been snooping around, but that's about it. Asking questions that were frankly none of her business. Asked me if I needed help running the place." Mac, who rarely let anything bother her, was clearly aggravated by Mother's suggestion. "Made it clear I didn't need help with my job, that there wasn't anything I couldn't handle. I didn't tell her jack, just gave you a glowing review and told her that you're always here to handle problems anytime I call."

"She's worried about me." I sighed, surprised by Mother's actions. "This is my property; I'm the one who'll decide if you stay or leave, and you're not going anywhere. So if that notion creeps into your brain, broom it out."

"You even think about going anywhere and I'll tie you to your office chair," Fab threatened. "Someone might get the idea I can fill your…" She looked down, confused for a moment. "…saddle shoes." She wrinkled her nose.

The shoes didn't actually go with her outfit of short overalls, but then, they never did.

I poked Fab in the side. "Remind you of your convent school days?"

"I never think about those days."

"Don't give Mother any information," I said to Mac. "Or anyone else. But don't let her guess that she's being stonewalled."

Mac nodded and waved toward the front of the 'class.' "This stupidness is over. I'll corral the women." She moved the group to the pool area, ignoring the complaints of the women, not a one of whom liked being bossed around.

I headed straight to Crum's demonstration table.

"Afternoon, ladies." He curtsied less than gracefully; he'd dressed up in a skirt for the demonstration, shirtless as usual.

I ignored his antics. "I need an older model truck. Today. It needs to run. My second choice would be a nondescript car."

"Do you mind if it's stolen?"

"Heck yes. Since when did you get into that business?"

"I haven't, but that's how unreasonable your request is." He snorted. "Good deals take time to find. I've got a used car dealer I can send you to, but he'll fleece you."

"That the lot where the cops hang out?" It had a reputation as the ideal corner to issue tickets from. "Wouldn't think it would be good for business, but I don't suppose you can say, 'move along' to the cops."

"I've only had one complaint about my special-order car business." At my skeptical look, he added, "There may have been more, but I can't remember. When all you want is to make the most profitable deal possible, you get tagged with the 'crook' title. That's just what a good businessman does."

"You're giving me a headache."

Screams erupted from the pool area, followed by a splash and then another.

Mac scurried over to the pool gate, punching

in the code. "Can you both swim?" she yelled at the two women swatting at each other.

Crum groaned and turned toward his cottage.

"Oh no you don't." Since he didn't have a shirt on and I wasn't about to touch him, I kicked his leg. He stumbled and managed to recover before hitting the ground. "Whatever you've done, you get in there and fix it. Now."

Fab snapped a few pictures of the two drowned rats climbing out of the pool. The other women had grabbed chairs for a ringside seat and were clearly disgruntled that the fun was over so soon.

Mac left Crum to handle the problem, the gate banging closed behind her.

I blew out a long breath and said to Mac, "Let me guess – he's doing them both."

"What's the man to do? Women are hot for him." Mac couldn't hold back her laughter.

"I think I'm going to be sick," Fab said.

"You need to have a talk with him. Gardening classes can continue as long as he can make sure his women are well-behaved. That means no fighting. Good grief, we don't need someone drowning," I said to Mac. "If the police show up, call me." I waved and refrained from running back to the car, even though I wanted to.

Mac returned to the pool area.

"Call Gunz," Fab said. "He can probably solve your car problem."

"He doesn't answer his phone unless he wants

something. I'll call GC." I pulled out my phone and called while walking back to the SUV. I had wanted to call him anyway.

"What's up?" he answered.

Fab slid into the driver's seat while I stood outside, door open so she could listen in. "Creole's shooting was a drug bust gone bad. All I want to know now is what happened to the ringleader, Miguel Santos. Did he leave the country? That's the line right now. Or is he still around? You hear anything about him, I'll pay."

"You need to be careful. The Santos gang is well known for their killings. They enjoy it, the more gruesome the better. Heard you've got to kill someone in front of the group to get initiated."

"Got it. In no way do I want you to put yourself in jeopardy. It's not worth anyone getting hurt. Just wondering if I should be watching my back."

"My best advice: If you two are going to snoop around in other folks' business, you might want to think about living in a more remote place that no one knows about."

"I took steps a year or so back to put my property in a trust. Run a check on me and see what comes up."

GC laughed. "You got a prison record?"

"No, but I've been arrested a few times. No charges were ever filed. And before you ask, that's because I wasn't guilty."

"Anything else?"

"I need an old, nondescript pickup truck. Has to run, legal title, and a good deal would be nice. Oh yeah, and today. Got connections for that?"

"I've got connections for everything. I can do it all," he boasted. "You'll be hearing from me."

I didn't get to say thank you because he hung up.

"New rule," I said, climbing into the SUV. "No more middlemen—it's much more efficient dealing with the Top Dog, and I'm liking it a lot."

"Where to?" Fab gunned the engine and hung a close-call u-turn.

"Party store in the strip mall. They're neighbors with the overpriced grocery store. I want to get this disguise for Creole taken care of so he can feel like he has some control over his life and can come and go as he pleases."

Chapter Thirty

My phone pinged from the coffee table. Creole reached over and grabbed it, handing it to me.

I kissed his cheek.

Since the skies were grey with a smattering of white clouds and the day hadn't made up its mind if it was going to rain, we'd opted to stay inside. I'd been reading, my feet in his lap, while he scanned the internet.

I read the text. "'Truck at Jake's. Keys on desk.' That was fast," I said. "I can drive it here before Fab and I go wherever it is we're going. Local, she said."

"You can drop me off a few blocks away, and I'll have it out of there before anyone notices." He shifted me closer so we were nose-to-nose. "Don't worry so much. Didier told me about this job of yours. Be careful, since Brick's involved."

"Not long ago, Fab casually threw it out that she was thinking about opening her own business. I'm hoping she does it. Hiring others to do the dirty work would force her to take legal assignments, as she wouldn't want the liability for the others."

"Didier would love it if she stopped putting herself on the line."

"I've already signed up for missing-cat cases."

He laughed. "You'll bring them all home." He looked over my head at the clock. "How much time do we have?"

"We'll make time."

* * *

Not wanting to argue with Creole, I reluctantly dropped him off on a side street about a block from Jake's. When he first came out of the bathroom, I'd done a double take. I wouldn't have recognized him in the oversized, wrinkled, once-tan knee-length shorts, now dirty and stained, held up with a rope tied around the waist, and faded blue hoodie over a dirty t-shirt, his feet slipped into a worn pair of tennis shoes. He'd stuck the beard on with adhesive and finished the look off with dark sunglasses.

After a kiss goodbye, I kept watch in the rearview mirror despite being admonished not to hang around. He did a disappearing act reminiscent of his friend Help.

By the time I got to my house, I was in a crabby mood. Instead of getting out of the SUV, I laid on the horn, then climbed over the console.

"You're annoying." Fab slid behind the wheel. "You two can't have gotten in a fight already." She thrust a scrap of paper at me.

"I'm just worried. GC came through with a truck already, and I hated leaving Creole to retrieve it by himself." I input the address in the GPS and got nothing. I fished my phone out of my pocket and texted Mac the address. "How about some caffeine and sugar?"

Fab backed out of the driveway and headed to our favorite coffee drive-thru. The rain finally showed up, drizzling heavily on the windshield. At the same moment Fab was hauling our iced coffees in through the window, Mac texted back the directions.

While I was reading them twice, my phone beeped again. Mac had included a crudely drawn map that had me smiling. "If the turn off is where I think it is..." I glanced at the directions again. "...Ms. Pearl lives just out of town. There's not much out there except a bunch of old trailers that sit on large pieces of property."

"What's your hair telling you?" Fab asked.

The hair on the back of my neck had uncanny perception and had never let me down. "Maybe it'll give me an inkling of what's to come when we get to the property."

"I hope Brick isn't full of it."

"He almost always is." I sighed. "I'm going to do my best to talk this woman into going to court, but I draw the line at strong-arming her. I assume we're waiting for her to finish her testimony and taking her home?"

"Brick said we could leave immediately."

I gave her a puzzled look. "That's weird. How will she get home?"

Fab was silent for a minute. "I asked about that, and he changed the subject. I wished I'd noticed at the time, but all I wanted to do was end the conversation."

"There's no way we're leaving her to fend for herself without verifying she has a return ride."

"Almost forgot: we're not to tell her we're taking her to court."

"And you didn't question that?" I asked.

"Brick texted that part this morning."

"Let me guess," I said in frustration, "we're supposed to sell her a line that two strangers want to take her shopping. As usual, Brick is up to something." I pointed at the road sign, which she hated. "Next exit." Just as I'd expected, it was nothing more than a barren strip along the highway. "Take a left." The directions Mac sent had failed to mention it, but since there was no right turn, it made sense. "Follow the road to the address. Hopefully the property will be marked with numbers."

"There's nothing back in here." Fab checked out both sides of the highway.

"It's deceptive. I've been noticing turn offs that I'm certain are driveways, some with chains and fences across the openings." I lowered the window. "Hang a u-turn; it's that last driveway. We lucked out—the address numbers match and her name is on the mailbox." The properties that ran along the highway were typically occupied by people who wanted their privacy and little to no restrictions on animals, and the houses were set back a considerable distance from the street. What was noticeable first was the livestock grazing in the open fields.

Fab turned onto the gravel strip and drove slowly. "We're not getting out until we're certain there are no dogs."

I released my seat belt and climbed into the back seat. I lifted the lid on a cooler that we kept in the back for snacks and water, which at that moment held only snacks for dogs.

"A bribe." I tossed the bag on the console.

"That was a great idea of mine." Fab shot me a self-satisfied smile.

She pulled up in front of a faded yellow cottage-style house that was showing its age but not crumbling off its elevated foundation. It had an inviting front porch filled with old wicker furniture and faded pillows.

"Cute," I said. "I would've bet on a trailer or some form of manufactured housing." The house had so much character and charm, I pegged it to be fifty-plus years old.

An old, fat German Shepherd came lumbering around the side of the house, a mixed black cat hitching a ride on his back. The dog's rheumy eyes gave us a once-over before it went up the front steps and lay down. The cat jumped to a chair and proceeded to clean itself.

"Not to be cynical, but do you suppose that there are fifty more wherever those two came from?" I asked.

"We are not taking any home," Fab said sternly.

"Oh Mom, can't I have just one?" Twice in one day, it had been suggested I was a cat collector – I had two.

Fab turned away, but I knew she wanted to laugh. "I'll wait here," she said.

I opened the door, slid out, and turned back. "You get out of the car right now. Or else…"

She arched her eyebrow as if to say, *What?*

Instead of an answer, I shut the door and headed to the porch. "Hi doggy," I greeted as I got to the bottom step. Damn, I'd forgotten the treats. So much for that ploy.

He looked at me with total disinterest and closed his eyes.

Just as I got to the top, the front door opened and an older, white-haired woman in military fatigues who appeared to be in great shape filled the space, rifle in the crook of her arm. She smiled grimly.

Great!

Chapter Thirty-One

"Is that any way to greet family?" I said, feeling a tad calmer knowing that Fab had walked up behind me.

"Family!" She snorted. "Not with that hair."

With one hand, I smoothed down my red mess. "Give a girl a break; it's humid out."

"Not a redhead in the family." She slapped the frame of the door. "The cute one behind you isn't kin either—the Pearls are a homely bunch. What do you want?"

"Linda?" I asked.

She nodded, but before I could say anything, an alarm went off inside the house, sounding a lot like one of those state-of-emergency ones. She turned and hurried away, leaving the door wide open.

I turned and grabbed Fab's sleeve, then crossed to the door. "This is probably a bad idea, but I'm going in and you're coming with me. Hopefully, she won't blow us away."

"Not much chance of that happening unless she's got a backup Browning. She leaned the one she had up against the wall before she took off."

I stepped over the threshold and headed inside the dimly lit house. At first glance, the woman was a full-on hoarder…but an organized one, judging by the marked bins. Inside the entry were two rooms on each side of the hallway. Both had had their doors removed, leaving aisles of containers on display. To my relief, I didn't spot a single bug crisscrossing the wall and smelled no foul odors.

The house was immaculate, knick-knacks and houseplants in every room. Three more cats greeted me and wove between my feet in an effort to trip me.

"Linda," I called out, heading down the hallway. I didn't want to scare the woman after having the nerve to barge into her house. I found her in the kitchen, tossing a glass baking dish on the countertop. I flinched, waiting for it to break into pieces, which to my surprise, it did not. "What's that?" The burned mess was hard to identify.

"Brownies." Linda sniffed. "I'm a crappy cook." She crossed to the kitchen sink, leaning over it and raising the window, waving her hand back and forth, ineffectually trying to shoo the smoke out. The smoke alarm had thankfully stopped wailing. She returned to the counter and inspected the dish. "Maybe they're salvageable, dunk them in a little coffee. Want to try?"

Fab peered around my shoulder. "We just ate," she said, saving me from "Oh heck no."

"Stinks in here." Linda motioned for us to follow and led us into a large room I guessed was the living room. More clearly marked containers were stacked up to eye level along one wall. The row closest to me was labeled "food." Another wall held cases of water up to shoulder height; I suspected that was as high as she could lift them.

It was devoid of furniture except for a faded floral sectional with limp cushions, faint overhead lighting, and a large worktable made from scraps of plywood that took up half the room. The top was littered with an assortment of tools, tape, and sharp objects, along with lighters, aerosol cans, and a half-dozen Super Soakers sitting front and center. Also on the table was a gun case holding a military-issue M4 Carbine.

"What are you working on?" I stared down at the assortment of items on her workspace.

"I thought you were from the Society." She looked at me as though I'd asked a stupid question. "It's going to be a flamethrower."

"Those are illegal," Fab said as she casually checked out the woman's unique storage system.

"Except that they work great on dead things." Linda frowned. "Cops?"

"Hardly," Fab said. She'd stopped at the far end of the table, where Linda's laptop lay open. It was playing a step-by-step video on how to make said flame-thrower. "You're preparing for a zombie apocalypse?" she asked, lips quirked.

"Flame-throwers don't work on zombies. You know they're undead, Linda, meaning they don't feel pain like we do. If you set them on fire, they'll still keep coming and be harder to fight if they get close to you."

Linda looked at Fab, clearly disappointed. "Are you certain?"

Fab nodded.

Zombies? *Fab's lost her mind.* How did she know this stuff when I had no clue what they were talking about? This qualified for bumping up our standard rate.

"Let me show you," Fab said and typed into the search box, "Do flamethrowers work on zombies." Several results popped up.

Linda peered over her shoulder. She said through her teeth, "I haven't had any formal training. I've been trying to figure it out on my own." She tapped the screen. "This says I need a bayonet, or I could improvise with a steak knife, tape, and a broom handle. Longer reach means I won't have to get as close to the zombies. Keeping my distance would be important."

This is too weird. I waited impatiently as Linda looked at various comments and threads pertaining to effective zombie killing.

Tired of waiting for Linda to take a break from her research, I circled around the table and interrupted her. "We need to talk," I said and steered her over to the couch.

I sat next to her on the edge of the cushion, the

frame digging into my butt. I sent Fab, who was back to prowling the room, a questioning look, which she ignored.

"I'm not interested in buying anything, and I don't need religion," Linda said, getting up and going back to her worktable. She picked up and tested each lighter. Flick. Flick. They all shot flames. "You're keeping me from important work." She looked up briefly before going back to concentrating on the items in front of her.

I decided anything less than honesty wasn't going to get me anywhere, not with this woman. Besides, I hadn't given serious thought to scamming the woman with the shopping excuse or some other made-up drivel. "Linda—" I got up and crossed to the table, standing next to the woman, hoping to snag her attention. "We're here to escort you to court. In case you forgot, the hearing is today and your testimony is needed."

Linda studied my face. "I'm always being accused of not knowing what I'm talking about, but you're making no sense. Court?" she said, clearly confused. "That's not something I'm likely to forget."

I started to speak, and she cut me off with a wave of her hand.

"Doesn't matter. I don't have a ride, and I'm not taking one from two strangers. No offense, but I don't know who you are; you haven't introduced yourselves. You look nice, but who knows these days? A kid who grew up in the neighborhood was arrested a couple of years ago for murder."

At that point, I figured I'd tell her everything we knew. We had nothing to lose, and neither Fab nor I was going to force her into the car. Out of the corner of my eye, I saw Fab slip out of the room, phone in hand. I filled Linda in on exactly why we'd shown up on her doorstep and the little we were told about the case, making Fab and I out to be benevolent do-gooders.

"Isn't that sweet," she said absently, confirming that she'd only been half listening, if that.

"When do you expect the zombies to show?" I asked Linda as Fab came back.

"Could be tomorrow, the next day. It's just something you have to be prepared for, and if you aren't, you should be getting ready for the apocalypse." The tone of her voice said I should know without having to be told. "You don't want to be the ones running for your life. Get your survival gear together; I got mine." She waved her arm around. "Food, water, and arms." She reached for a Super Soaker and some electrical tape. "You can't wait until the last minute. It's not like there will be an announcement; they'll just show up, and there will be no depending on neighbors and friends," she admonished.

"Do you have a general time frame?" I asked, not knowing what else to say.

"Just got to be prepared."

Fab motioned to me, and I crossed to where she stood in front of a picture window.

"You're not going to like this," she whispered. "Talked to Brick and, uhm…he lied; it's a sanity hearing. Brick only spilled the truth when I told him we were leaving and Linda was staying."

"Sanity?" I covered my face with my hands. "I'm not doing it. I already have a hard time looking at myself in the mirror, hair sticking out every which way."

"Focus." Fab slapped my arm.

"Okay, the apocalypse thing is weird, but it's no different than the end-of-the-world people. Or whatever they are." I brushed my hands together. "Be my guest, haul her away."

To my surprise, Fab walked back over to Linda, who had slid onto a stool and was trying to light the spray of an aerosol can. Unsure, I backed up, prepared to launch myself out the window if necessary.

"That's dangerous." Fab tsked and grabbed the can and lighter from Linda's hands.

I breathed a sigh of relief.

"Ms. Pearl." Fab stood over her. "We were given misinformation," she said, in a patient tone I'd never heard before. "Your court appearance is actually a sanity hearing. I suspect the main question to be answered is are you capable of taking care of yourself? Do you know who wants control over you?"

"My son," she said, not having any doubt.

"Jon thinks I'm too old to be living out in this *hellhole* and wants me to move into a senior home in Lauderdale. He dropped off the brochures in person, trying to sell me on the activities." She studied her fingernails before looking up.

"At today's hearing, your son will have to convince the judge that you aren't able to care for yourself and make decisions." Fab flashed me a look that said she wasn't one hundred percent sure of her assertion. "Most likely, he's wanting power of attorney."

"Did someone come to your door and hand you legal documents?" I asked. When she shook her head, I thought, *none of this is legal*.

Linda buried her head in her hands. "What if I don't go?" she asked in a quiet voice. "Jon can have me arrested? I'll go to jail? Be committed?"

Fab patted her hand. "The judge can order you to be picked up and brought to court. I'm sure only as a last resort."

It won't be by one of us.

"Does your son know that you're readying for the apocalypse?" I asked. I finished checking out the labeled containers, ending up in front of a six-foot painting of a family that appeared ghostly. It sent an unnerving chill up my spine, and I crossed the room, not looking back, but there was no escaping those hollowed-out eyes.

Linda shook her head. "Jon doesn't have an open mind. Told him it was hurricane supplies."

"You need your own lawyer, and not one

appointed by the court," I said, turning away and pulling my phone out of my pocket, my finger flicking through my address book. I needed someone local.

"You call too much," GC said when he answered.

"I need a local lawyer that specializes in competency hearings."

"Someone finally figure out you're crazy?" He laughed.

That was nothing new, but I didn't bother to tell him. "I'm here with your grandmother, and she needs help."

He was silent a moment before finally saying, "I know where my granny is, and it isn't with you."

"I didn't mean yours exactly but in the overall cosmic sense of the word."

"You're lucky I have a soft spot for old ladies. I'll text the info." He hung up.

I'd had enough of my impromptu tour around Linda's house and crossed back to sit next to Fab, who'd taken my place on the couch. As I sat down, Fab asked Linda what she wanted to do.

"My husband, Henry, and I bought this property. He built the garage first, and we lived in it until he finished the house. Our three children were born here. My two daughters agree with their brother and want me to move. Not a one of them asked me what I wanted. I want to stay here and die in the same bed Henry did." Her words were filled with emotion.

I understood, having found a man that I felt that way about. "Maybe they could visit more often."

"My daughter told me I was geographically undesirable. That means I live too far away."

I stood up and moved to stand next to the teary-eyed woman. "I promise you, we're not taking you anywhere against your wishes. But if it is your son that filed the paperwork, which makes sense, he'll likely send someone else to escort you or do it himself. You might want to be prepared."

"I think he does love me," Linda said sadly.

"I'm sure he does." I patted her shoulder awkwardly. *But he's a dick and doesn't want to do his own dirty work.* My phone pinged, and I glanced at the screen. "I just got a referral for a lawyer. Her job will be to put the hearing off so she can familiarize herself with your case. With any luck, she can broker a compromise between you and your son."

"Maybe," Linda murmured, not sounding convinced.

"We'll figure something out." I didn't want to get involved, but hell, I never minded my own business, why start now? I got up and called the number GC had forwarded.

"You've reached the law offices of Ruthie Grace, and she's out. Leave a message. Beep."

I started my message: "I'm going to inform

Ms. Grace how unprofessional her assistant, or whoever this is, is. You *might* have sold that little act if it weren't for the burp after 'law.' And the beep was hardly authentic. Not even close."

An aggravated sigh came through the phone. "Heartburn gets you every time. This is *Counselor* Grace. What do you want?"

"Before I get to the details of the case, do you have the appropriate credentials, all provable?"

"Yes. I. Do. And I'm really good," she blustered.

"Okay, then." I explained Linda Pearl's predicament. She asked where I got her number, and I told her.

"I'll need the court information, and my new client will need to be in my office first thing in the morning."

"You make Ms. Pearl happy and you'll be hearing from me again." After we hung up, I called Mac and asked for her help.

In Fab, Linda had a rapt audience for show and tell. I hustled over and didn't feel bad about interrupting. Fab would get bored and build her own flame-thrower, one that was even bigger and better and shot more flames. I told Linda that Mac Lane would be there in the morning to pick her up and take her to her new lawyer and that she'd wait and make sure she got back home. If she needed anything else, I told her to tell Mac and it would get done.

While Fab helped Linda reorganize her

supplies, she handed me several lighters behind the woman's back and motioned for me to put them in my pocket, whispering, "Don't want her to burn the house down." Then she said to Linda, "Remember to wait until after your court date to pull this stuff out, just in case someone stops by uninvited."

"Like us?" I wanted to say but restrained myself.

Linda walked us to the door. She whistled, and the dog and cat on the porch came inside. The other three had disappeared after the first sniff. We waved good-bye.

Sliding behind the wheel, Fab informed me, "Brick's livid. Yelled the same old things and, before he hung up, announced he wasn't paying the bill."

"Heard that threat before. I only care if you do."

"Don't think I do."

Chapter Thirty-Two

I struggled to be quiet as I tiptoed in through the door of the beach house. When I left, Creole was stretched out on the couch, laptop on his lap. When I saw him, I shoved the door open wider, depositing the canvas bags on the counter. "What do you think you're doing?"

"I'm working out," Creole said, out of breath.

Who knows how many sit-ups he'd done, and no bended knees for him. I stalked over to where he lay on the floor, dressed only in a pair of sweat shorts that clung low on his hips, and stepped over his stomach, straddling his body. "Stop it," I said in my sternest voice. "You look worse than when I left." My eyes zeroed in on his face. The perspiration beaded and dripped down his forehead and cheeks, landing on his chest. His hair was soaked, his face twisted with pain. He was supposed to be taking it easy, not engaging in punishing activity.

He was too busy trying to catch his breath to say anything.

"Are you trying to make your injuries worse?" I put my hands on my hips, glaring at him. "If you're not going to take care of yourself, then I'll do it and drive you over the edge in the process."

He held up his hand. "Come down here, lay beside me, and tell me how much trouble you got into today."

I got down on the floor, lying next to him with his arm around my shoulders. "I could get used to having you around every day." I kissed his fingers. "I learned what items it takes to make a weapon for the coming zombie apocalypse. Not exactly sure how it goes together and I'm leery about experimenting, lest I blow my head off." I made a kaboom sound effect. After he finished laughing, I told him all about our latest client.

"You always have a soft spot for people in need of help." He kissed the top of my head. "Most wouldn't care what her side of the story was or even that she had one; they'd walk away or drag her off to court and not care what happened, just stick their hand out for payment. Does sound like she could use some supervision."

"Except for her fascination with the coming invasion, there's nothing wrong with her. Her desire to stay in the house her husband built tugged at my heartstrings. I totally understood." I sat up.

"Where are you going?" Creole pulled on my shirt.

"To put the fish that I bought in the refrigerator. You're going to cook it later."

* * *

"There's only one person I know that would play on the doorbell. What's she doing here an hour early? I thought we were meeting at the house."

"Knock it off," Creole said into the speaker. "This is the first time anyone's ever rang the bell." He opened the back door and, before stepping out, said, "Didier took the afternoon off. He and I are going for a walk."

A couple minutes later, Fab skipped through the door.

I looked past her shoulder.

"They're out checking out Creole's broken-down ride. Engine sounds good. Going to drive it later." Fab hit her hand on the counter. "Come home. The children miss you. We can figure out a way to hide Creole. I'll have the locks re-keyed today for a start."

"I'm not sure Creole will agree to that – he's worried about safety. What if someone stopped by unannounced?"

"Shoot them?"

I smiled at her. "Maybe we can try it; I'll have to ask. It's hard to be entertaining all the time."

"Don't look at me," Fab said. "How many times has Creole told me, 'You're not the least bit funny'?" She mimicked his growl.

Creole and Didier walked back through the door in time to hear that.

"I haven't said it lately," Creole defended

himself.

"That's because you've been busy being dead," Fab reminded him.

Didier and I groaned.

Creole chuckled. "I've missed you too. No need to walk on eggshells around me; I can take it." He pulled out the coffee maker. "Sit, everyone. The day can always stand another cup of coffee. Before you fly out of here, what are the two of you up to this afternoon? Madison can fill us in on the details."

Everyone passed on coffee and opted for water. Creole directed us out to the patio.

"You going to ask every day?" I asked.

"Get used to it," Fab said. "Didier does it, and then asks again when I get back. I'm thinking he's trying to trip me up – see if the stories match."

"Fabiana," Didier said sternly. "Are you aware of how much work it is to keep up with you? If I don't get updates a couple of times a day, I'll be so far behind, I'll never catch up."

"Well… Didier's no longer outnumbered; that should make it easier for you two." I smiled sweetly. "Cottages, Jake's, that's about it."

"What about Corndog? Bordello?" Didier frowned at Fab.

"We're meeting Corndog later. Not sure what he wants — he said business. I suspect he wants to tell me he's moving out of The Cottages. Personally, I think it's too soon, but I can hardly demand that he stay."

"You stick your nose in everyone's business but draw the line at a grown man who calls himself Corndog?" Fab shook her head.

"I take exception to what you just said. Although true, you could have put it a whole lot nicer." I glared at her.

The guys sat back, arms crossed, grinning.

"Did you have your new friend—GC, is it?—check out Bordello?" Creole looked back and forth between me and Didier. "Are you going to do business with the man?"

"I'm not part of that deal," Didier said. He didn't look happy about that fact.

"I did, and he didn't turn up anything. Apparently, the sons didn't follow in their father's criminal footsteps. Or at least, there's nothing on the record. It's hard to believe that he's not behind the stuff that's happened to Corndog. I mean, who else?" No one had an answer. "I...um..."

"What did you do?" Creole demanded, sitting up.

"I asked GC to run a check on the dealer in your case—did he stay in the area or move on? He knew the man's name well, and his record, and warned me to back off."

"Get anything back yet?"

"Not yet. But you'll be the first to know," I said and sighed inwardly. He took that better than I thought he would.

"Try to arrange the call for when I'm around and can listen in."

"He delivers in writing."

"That's even better." Creole nodded approvingly.

"Let's go." Fab nudged my arm.

"No running." I poked my finger at Creole. "I don't want to hear about bike rides to Key West either. If I get back and you look less than your usual handsome self, I'll put the blame on your French friend here." I scowled at Didier. "And it won't be pretty. I expect you to make sure he takes it easy."

"No worries," Didier reassured me.

"If I forgot to pick up anything for dinner, call me." I stood and kissed Creole's cheek. "Anything at all, call."

Fab kissed Didier and beat me to the door. After she closed it, she said, "Aren't you proud of me? I didn't pick the lock." She opened the gate. "That really is an eyesore." She indicated the faded nineties white Chevy pickup.

"I'm thinking it's a keeper. We're always needing an undercover ride, and here it is." I could tell that she liked the idea.

Chapter Thirty-Three

Fab blew into the driveway of The Cottages, parking in front of the office. We both got out of the SUV.

Kevin waved from the other end of the driveway and headed in my direction. He was dressed in shorts, a pinched look on his face, his day off apparently not going well.

Fab rounded the car and stood next to me. "What does he want?"

"Get rid of the growly dog expression and be nice," I whispered as Kevin rapidly approached.

"In other words, don't open my mouth."

"Hello, officer," I said.

"Can we speak in private?" Kevin sent a look of disgust Fab's way.

"We're a package deal. I'm not in the mood to repeat everything you say. You want privacy, we can go in the office."

At that moment, the door opened, and Mac stood in the doorway. She didn't like being left out either. I'd have sworn she was eavesdropping except there were no windows on this side of the building.

"I could use a soda," Kevin grunted.

Fab grabbed my wrist, leading the way to the office, where she took her reserved spot on the couch. Mac was bent over the refrigerator removing drinks – the consummate hostess unless you made her mad. I sat in front of the desk, and that left the visitor chair for Kevin. One more and they'd have to stand.

"What's up?" I asked Kevin as he popped the top on the can of Coke that Mac handed him. "Skip to the chase. I've got an appointment." I glanced at the clock.

"What do you know about Miss January's boyfriend?" he asked in distaste.

"Young, controlling, snotty attitude. That sums up what I know. Frankly, haven't seen much of him." I turned to Mac.

"Keeps to himself," she said. "He's managed to keep Miss January from venturing out on one of her drunkcapades."

"Why?" I asked Kevin.

"A drunk told me he's wanted but didn't have any other information. It's been bugging me. Every time I see him outside, as soon as I head in his direction, he disappears back inside and doesn't answer the door." Kevin downed his soda, crushed the can under his foot, and sent it flying into the trashcan. "Didn't get a hit off the name Mac gave me."

"So that's what you wanted Nestor's name for," Mac said. "I'll keep an eye out for anything he touches and grab it for you."

Fab opened one eye, staring at her.

"What?" Mac shrugged. "That's what cops do on television."

"I'd like to reassure you that we never get any felons hiding out here at The Cottages, but you know that's not true," I said. "Miss January, is she safe?"

"Drunken snitches aren't always the most reliable. Nestor can't avoid me forever." He cleared his throat. "Those gardening classes of Crum's are embarrassing. I suggest you break it up before someone gets hurt and tell him to hold private classes inside his cottage, blinds and windows closed."

"Crum only has one standard – female and breathing – and he's hardly discreet in his activities. It starts fights. We had another one after the pool incident." Mac stretched a wad of pink bubble gum out of her mouth, shoving it back in.

And here I thought she'd given up the gum chewing.

As if on cue – pop! Mac managed to get all the gum back in her mouth except the piece she was scraping off the corner of her mouth.

Kevin stared, making faces.

"Send out a memo." I kicked the desk to get Mac's attention. "This is a residence, and no business is to be conducted unless all necessary licenses are obtained. Crum will come up with some way around the new rule, so be alert. His

IQ is higher than the four of us put together."

"That doesn't mean he has any sense," Kevin said.

"Meeting over?" I nudged the bottom of Kevin's flip-flop.

"I'll take another Coke." He held out his hand to Mac. "You doing okay?" he asked me.

Until Creole could make his presence known, these moments would be awkward. "One day at a time. Spent a few days on the beach, got some sleep."

The change of topic surprised me, as did that he was going out of his way to be nice. Who knew, maybe one day we'd be friends. I laughed inwardly.

I stood and Fab, who'd appeared to have dozed off, jumped up. I waved and we left.

When the door closed, Fab asked, "Kevin was fishing for something, but what? Shifty look on his face."

"Can you see from under your eye lashes?"

"It's a trick I've perfected." She looked proud of herself.

We crossed the driveway to Corndog's door. I had my hand raised when it opened. "This is my partner in crime," I introduced Fab. "It was Fab's connection that got the information on Bordello."

Corndog lowered his eyes, checking Fab out head to toe, and it was apparent he liked what he saw. He stepped back and ushered us in. Seating options were limited in the small unit. Fab and I sat on the couch, and he claimed the chair across from us. The man clearly wasn't one hundred percent, but he was well on his way, his bruises diminishing in size and color.

"Thank you for everything you've done," he started, seemingly unsure of himself. "I'd like to stay. A short-term lease if possible, but preferably a waterfront unit. I'm not asking for a freebie or discount; I can pay. I did check with Mac, and the rates are fine with me."

"We only do monthly. That way, if you become a problem, we can toss you to the curb faster."

"I won't be a problem," he assured me. "As you're aware, I might bring trouble. If that's an issue, I'll understand."

"I think your idea is a good one," I said, wanting to ease the distress in his eyes. "Although most of the people here have their eccentricities, every one of them would lend a hand if necessary. As you know, we have a cop living here. He likes it quiet and won't hesitate to rein in activities he thinks will become a problem."

Fab drew her Walther from her waistband. "We have another layer of security—Madison doesn't like to shoot people, but I don't share in that sentiment. FYI: we both carry."

"Show off," I mouthed and got the girl-gone-crazy look in return.

He flinched. "Good to know."

"Have you had any more threats, problems of any kind?" I asked.

Corndog shook his head. "That brings me to my next discussion point. Bordello wants my dock-front property to build a shrine to his ego. At some point, he's going to get it. I can feel it in these old bones of mine." He shivered. "I've decided to keep the properties as they are and develop them myself. Also thinking you'd make a good partner/front woman; you've got a good reputation in this town. I'm hoping you're interested."

"Don't you think someone with an extensive real estate background would be a better choice?" I'd recently thrown out the idea of doing a project of my own but certainly not one this large. It was intimidating and, at the same time, exciting.

"You've got the chops, according to what a few of the old timers about town have to say. Good family background – related to a longtime, well-respected local. You took this place, spruced it up, and turned it into a moneymaker. Granted, you've had a few problems, but you've overcome them. You and your ex were also successful in the house-flipping business. I'd say that's a fine resume."

He'd done some checking.

"I think you're a great choice," Fab said enthusiastically.

"I'm honored to even be considered," I said,

and I sincerely meant it. "I'd have to think about it, and I'm sure I'll have a million questions. And after all that, my answer might be no, and I hope you won't be offended."

"Takes more than a no to offend me," Corndog said good-naturedly. "I think this project will interest you. You've got business in your bones." He picked up a leather portfolio off the coffee table and handed it to me. "Here's all the information you'll need. It contains a thorough report, including finances and architect's renderings."

Impressed by the depth of the presentation, I asked, "What is your overall idea for the area?"

"Tarpon Wharf," he said, a big smile on his face. "A destination family experience with restaurants, shops, a few rides, and a boutique hotel."

"Love your idea," I said. "It would attract both tourists and locals. What's the projected timeline for completion?"

"About a year."

I nodded, thinking it was aggressive and everything would have to go off like clockwork. "Do you know if Brad Westin is involved in Bordello's plans?" I asked, not wanting to create an untenable relationship with my brother. If he had any ambitions to work on this project, he hadn't mentioned anything. Mother would've passed it along.

"I've not heard his name bandied about."

Corndog appeared thoughtful. "Bordello's been after the property for a couple of years, and since it's an homage to himself, I highly doubt he'd partner with anyone and share the credit. Unless it was one of his brothers, and then they'd be listed in the legal documents, as they are in other ventures."

"Let's go check out this property," Fab suggested to Corndog. "You could point out exactly which lots are in this deal and give Madison a general idea of the potential layout."

"I've been down there several times, but a mini tour would be great," I said.

Corndog stood, reaching for his cane. Fab was already at the door.

On the way to the car, I said to Fab, "Do you want me to drive now or when we get to the property?" In response to her frigid glare, I said, "You're going to take pictures because you're way better at it than I am. You know what's needed and from what angles. You can drive home, I promise."

Fab slid into the passenger seat, Corndog in the back.

When I got behind the wheel, Fab said, "I suppose this means I'll be rolling down the window."

I laughed, knowing how much she hated it when I did that.

"If you need directions, I'm right here," Fab said.

I rolled out of the driveway and took a side street to the road that ran along the water. "Tighten your seatbelts." I hit the gas and cleared the yellow light before it turned red. Then I took the back way down to the docks. The shortcuts were almost always traffic-free and hadn't been discovered yet by tourists. I passed by the condo building that was owned by a group of family and friends. The landscaping and lighting were finished, enhancing the building nicely. I didn't see any activity and didn't even slow for a look to see if my brother was around.

I turned to the left onto a street that was made up of old historic brick buildings ranging from one to three stories. Some were covered in sheets of plywood, with upper floors missing windows, while others had iron bars across what were once entrances. The potential of the wharf idea leaped out at me.

Fab hung out the window, snapping pictures as we turned the corner.

"I own the entire block on the water side." Corndog pointed. "On this other side, I own the two end parcels, and the rest are owned by individuals that have owned them for a long time and aren't in a hurry to sell."

He told us the hotel would anchor one end of the property, the high-end restaurants the other, with the requisite tourist gift stores and rides in the middle: a ferris wheel, a mini roller coaster, and a train ride that would circle the entire property. The plans were drawn to incorporate all the existing buildings.

"How did you get the senior apartment building from Brick Famosa?" I asked as we drove past the three-story building. I would never forget coming down here for a job and discovering the squalid conditions that the retirees lived in. Fab and I had bullied Brick into doing the right thing – giving them a relocation allowance and a few choices in where they could move.

"Brick's a piece of work. Known him too long." Corndog grinned. "When his plan didn't go according to his timeline, he got bored and sold out. The final blow came when he found out that the code department wasn't going to allow him to bulldoze the building. They're a bunch of old timers that don't cotton to strangers looking to make a fast buck."

"In the interest of full disclosure, I work for the man," Fab said. "Everything you said about him is true. Probably worse things you don't know about."

"I've been backup on most of those jobs," I added. "You have plans for that building?"

"Almost forgot, the architect suggested loft apartments. He says they'd be a money-maker, suggested screw-you rents since they'd be in a chichi area and waterfront always gets top dollar."

"Any water rights for boat slips?" I asked.

"Listen to you," Corn crowed. "I forgot about those. There's a couple of rickety docks that need to be replaced, and I bet more could be added."

"How did you make your money, if you don't mind me asking?" I asked.

"Real estate. Buy cheap, sell cheap, all about volume. Never had an interest in fixing and flipping. I was in it for the quick buck, and it worked out real well for me."

Fab turned and asked, "But this property you held onto. What happened to your formula?"

"I entertained the idea of selling briefly, but I kept putting off making a decision, and now I've come up with a few ideas of my own. When Bordello's nasty personality showed its true self and I got beat up, I put all thoughts of the project on hold. I'd already decided I wasn't selling – not to him, anyway."

"In choosing Madison, you put her at risk," Fab pointed out.

"That's something she'll have to take into consideration," Corndog said. "And for that reason alone, I'd understand if you want no part of the project." He locked eyes with me in the rearview mirror.

In response to Fab's finger-pointing, I pulled over at the end of the block. Getting out and stretching, I looked around. The area had an eerie feel, mostly because it was deserted – a place I would never come at night in its current condition. It wouldn't surprise me if all these buildings housed an assortment of vermin.

Fab snapped pictures as she walked down the street.

"Don't go into any building by yourself," I called after her.

"I feel bad. I hadn't thought too much about the danger I might be putting you in until your friend pointed it out," Corndog said. "Even though I think this is a good idea, please don't have any compunction about telling me 'Hell no.'"

Chapter Thirty-Four

We dropped Corndog off at The Cottages. Mac's truck wasn't in her driveway, so I texted that it was okay for Corndog to change units. Strictly a business deal. We hopped on the Overseas and headed to the beach house.

"All this talk about business plans, I've got a few of my own, made a few notes," Fab said.

I could tell she was impatient for a reaction. "I've got a great location in mind." I motioned for her to make a lane change. "Detour. Get off at the next exit and head towards JS Auto Body."

Spoon owned a business at the opposite end of the dock area from where we had just been. He'd been there for years, and all the nearby businesses sat behind security barbed-wire fencing.

"Why down there?" Fab wrinkled her nose in distaste.

"This property will pass even your finicky standards. I happen to know that the current business is ready to fold and the owner is amenable to a sale. One stipulation – I at least get desk space."

"How do you know this stuff?"

"You know me…standing in a grocery line, minding my own business, and without any invitation, the person behind me tells me about their gall bladder surgery and grandkids. It's what comes from being an interested listener."

"Is that what you call it?" Fab turned up her nose. She slowed going past the auto body shop. "Where now?"

"Four mailboxes up, the gigantic black locking one. Don't pull in the driveway; we'll show up on the security camera."

"Zach's old building?" she asked, surprised.

"Actually two warehouse buildings." I turned toward the window, hoping to catch a peek behind the fencing. "The one on the left was a residence—Zach lived upstairs and parked his cars on the bottom level. The right housed the offices of his security firm. The outside's shabby and appears in need of repair, but that's deceiving. It was left that way to fit in with the neighborhood. The insides have been rehabbed to even your high standards."

Fab hung a u-turn, pulled over to the side, and idled in front of an empty lot. "I was only there once, and the renovations hadn't been finished then." She leaned over the steering wheel. "Too bad we can't see anything except the square roofs."

"This is where you tell me what a super fabulous idea this is."

"Love the buildings and even the location:

seedy, but up-and-coming. The security looks top notch from what I can see."

"I hear a 'but' coming," I said.

"There's only me," she sighed. "I have no idea how or if I can even manage employees."

"You're forgetting me." I frowned. "How about Didier? You know his days using the office space at the condos are about to come to an end, since he and Brad got a signed contract. He'll need a place to go. Since he's staying in the real estate business, he's going to need an office. It's not far from his current location, and I bet he'd love this place."

"We're still partnering on jobs?" Fab asked. "It's thanks to your suggestion that I'm giving this idea serious thought. That and all the crappy cases I seem to be getting lately. I'm tired of jumping out of windows – the last time, the bruises faded quickly, but the pain was so deep, it hung around for weeks, a reminder that it hadn't been one of my best ideas."

"I think once word gets out you're open for business, you'll get more legit jobs and not just ones that skirt the illegal." I kept to myself *and the ones that are flat out illegal.*

"I don't want this to open the door to going our separate ways."

"I'll still be backup," I promised. "I'll just be working on this real estate thing too. It might surprise you, but I understand Bordello wanting to build something to leave behind. Something to say, 'I was here and created something great.' Maybe something to leave the kids that they might be proud of."

"Your aunt made a good choice, leaving her holdings to you; she probably knew you'd build on them. She'd be proud, you know," Fab said.

"I hope so. She changed my life, and I wish I could say thank you to her every day."

Fab pulled back out on the road. "The first thing we should do is find out what kind of deal we can make."

I nodded. "Let's stop at the bakery so I can get a fabulous dessert for tonight."

Chapter Thirty-Five

Waiting until the last minute was never a good idea. I raced home from Creole's to change clothes for lunch with Mother. I didn't know how I would keep Creole's reemergence a secret. All the lying I'd have to do was making me uncomfortable, and I hadn't even started yet.

Over dinner the previous evening, Creole, Fab, Didier and I discussed keeping the secret and how important it was for now. We also kicked around ideas for how to keep it a secret if Creole came and went from the house.

I flew into the driveway, squeezing in next to Fab's Porsche, and ran into the house. Fab waved from the island.

"I don't want to go," I whined and settled on a stool across from her.

"Coward."

"Just go with me. Besides, Mother will wonder why you're a no-show."

"Oh no she won't," Fab said dramatically. "She called to tell me specifically that I was not invited."

I gasped. "She didn't."

"She tried to soften it by going on about

needing alone time with her daughter. I thought she was a bit overdramatic, but I was happy to get off the phone."

"She's up to something."

"That's pretty much what I thought, but you can handle her."

"Please…come with me."

Fab pointed to the hallway. "Go. If you need help picking out something to wear – whistle."

I gave an over-exaggerated eye roll and headed to the stairs, pausing first to scratch the cats sacked out on the daybed.

* * *

Showering and twisting my hair into a messy bun, I made it back downstairs in record time. Fab was still in the same spot, hunched over a notepad. I stood in the doorway and turned, showing her the white, spaghetti-strap, ankle-length linen dress I'd chosen, pairing it with a natural woven belt and matching sandals.

"I like that dress." She gave a thumbs up. "Smile," she scolded. "Have a good time."

"Don't you dare do anything fun while I'm gone." I waved as I went out the door, a forlorn smile on my face as I slipped behind the wheel of the SUV.

As I backed out of the driveway, I went over Mother's call to guilt me into lunch. I had so much to hide, it would be a miracle if she didn't figure it out and weasel every detail out of me. When she eventually found out about Creole being alive and how I'd lied, that would create a drama all its own. I'd stress that it was for his safety, and maybe that would lessen her irritation.

Driving up to the security gate at Mother's complex, I used my counterfeit keycard and the gates opened. I often wondered when it would stop working and was happy that it hadn't happened so far. Even though I had my lockpick stuffed in the side pocket of my purse, I decided to act like a normal guest and call from the lobby. Spoon answered and immediately buzzed the door. When the elevator opened, he was leaning against the doorframe. "This is a first. You usually break in."

"Can't say I'll make a habit of it." I brushed a kiss on his cheek and continued down the hall, kissing Mother.

"How are you feeling?" Mother cooed, checking out my outfit down to my shoes. She ushered me to an overstuffed chair in front of the couch, handing me a glass of iced tea.

"A few days in the sun was just what I needed."

Mother and Spoon exchanged a look that gave me an uneasy feeling. They both took seats across from me.

"Before I forget, do you know the owner of Zach's old building?" I asked Spoon, hoping maybe they were friends. "I'd like to get a contact number if you have it."

"Why?" Mother asked sharply.

That was an odd reaction. From the tight lines around her mouth, one might almost think she wanted the property. "I've got someone who might be interested in the property."

"Brad's putting together a big project for down in that area. I'm not sure whether he's interested in that exact property, but couldn't you give him the first option?"

"First I've heard of that. Seems as though the family is keeping a lot of secrets lately." Myself included. "Fab's the one who is interested. I could stay neutral on this one, let the best bid win." Which I'd do if I knew for certain Bordello wasn't involved in any way.

"Not for an investigation business, I hope," Mother sniffed. "And I suppose you'd be involved, putting yourself in danger every opportunity you get. I don't know why you two can't come up with something else, anything that doesn't require you carrying a gun."

I set my glass down on the table. "You do know that if she's running her own business, she's less likely to be running around, taking every job she can get, and will instead delegate the worst of them."

"Let's all calm down," Spoon said. "I haven't heard a word about the property, whether it's for sale or rent. I think I would've heard if either were the case. I hear something, and I'll let you know."

I flashed him a look that said, *Sure you will.*

He looked away, which told me what I needed to know. I'd have to get the information elsewhere.

"Are we going out to eat?" I asked since I hadn't noticed any to-go boxes on the counter.

"We're staying here. Spoon made us a grilled shrimp salad, and while we were out this morning, we stopped for some freshly baked rolls." She smiled at him, patting his leg. "I thought it would give us more of an opportunity to talk privately."

"About what?" My spine straightened—I didn't care for the seriousness that filled her eyes.

"About your mental health." An older woman I'd never seen before walked into the living room. She wore a lilac woolen suit that hung to mid-calf, her grey hair fashioned into a severe bun. I'd guess her to be Mother's age, but Mother would never be caught dead in that outfit.

"And you are?" I managed to keep my tone pleasant and "hell" out of the question.

"Susan Moore." She thrust out her hand, business card between her fingers.

I took the card, quickly glancing at it. "It's nice that psychotherapists make house calls. Except that I'm certain it must be a breach of ethics if you plan on pushing your services on me when I'm not the one who called you." My phone dinged. I pulled it out of my pocket, checking the screen. A smiley face from Fab. At any other time, I would've laughed.

"Hand that to me. We don't need the distraction." Mother stood and leaned across the coffee table, holding out her hand.

"I'm not a kid. I can deal with my own phone." I sent a quick text: *Get over here NOW!* "I'll put it on vibrate." I shoved it back in my pocket.

"Why don't we all calm down and get to know one another over lunch?" Spoon said before disappearing into the kitchen.

Still standing, Mother said, "Let's move out to the patio — it's a beautiful day."

"Great idea," Susan said with a tight-lipped smile.

Mother ushered us outside, practically pushing me. The patio table had been set for four, a drink cart off to the side offering several beverage choices on ice. I wanted to ask for a shot of tequila, but a voice in my head warned that I'd need my presence of mind for this lunch.

Spoon came through the double doors, a large serving tray in hand — he clearly had everything prepared ahead of time.

My anger at this whole insane situation was about at the breaking point. Mother pointed me to the chair the furthest from the doors and next to the Susan woman. I didn't know how much further Mother would push this grand scheme of hers, which in my opinion had already gone over the line.

I glared at Mother as I sat down. "You are stretching the limits of our relationship."

Spoon offered iced tea, lemonade or water, nothing alcoholic. I'd brought my glass of tea with me and glared in response to his offer to refill it. He put a bowl of salad in the middle of each dinner plate. It really did look delicious with the large grilled shrimp on top, and any other time, I'd be eager to take a bite. Instead, I played with the lettuce, which he'd done a good of job of chopping since I found no signs of the spine.

Ms. Moore took several bites of her salad and then launched into a monologue about the benefits of mental health care.

I tuned her out, tapping my foot under the table. I had to force myself not to pull my phone out and check the time. Mother's house wasn't that far from mine—given Fab's usual driving speed, hopefully she'd be here any minute.

Unfortunately, Mother's focus zeroed in on my eating, or lack thereof. I loaded up my fork, saluted her, and when she looked away, flicked it back in the bowl. Spoon didn't miss a trick and scowled at me. I returned an angry stare that should've exploded his head into flames.

"That looks yummy," Fab said from the doorway. She bent down and kissed Mother's cheek before she could recover from the shock of her sudden appearance. Fab appeared a bit harried, not her impeccable self, her bathing suit top visible under her blouse.

I wanted to jump up and throw my arms around her. Maybe I was overreacting, but it eased my mind to have her pull up a chair and wedge it into the tiny space by my side. "I'll have an iced tea," she said to Spoon.

Spoon growled. "Damn it." He was ready to unleash more but thought better of it and reigned the words back in. He stood, crossed to the cart, and poured her a glass, setting it in front of her with a bang.

"Mother, introduce your…uh…friend." I nodded toward Ms. Moore.

Mother made the introduction.

I handed Fab the woman's business card.

Fab flicked her gaze over it. "One of you go crazy and I'm the last to know?"

I laughed, and it felt damn good.

Mother's eyes narrowed on me. "She's the one you texted," she accused, turning her glare on Fab.

"I did. And you know why? Because I don't trust you," I said, my voice getting louder. "And I've got better things to do than plan my escape from the looney bin."

Ms. Moore sucked in a breath. "I'd never," she said in an affronted voice. "I'm here to help you, my dear, with the grieving process. Your overreaction to a simple lunch is a cry for help."

"What drivel," I said.

"Are you wanting psych services?" Fab asked me.

"I didn't know this was an ambush lunch," I said. "Mother, if I did this to you, you'd be livid."

Fab said, "I'm pretty certain Madison didn't agree to this arrangement. If she needs someone to talk to, she has a best friend. That would be me."

Ms. Moore's eyes narrowed. "You are hardly a professional."

"I told *you* on the phone," Fab said to Mother, "that since she's gotten back from her mini vacation, she's relaxed and happy. If I thought there was a problem, I'd be the first to speak up."

"That's admirable, but have you thought you could be doing more harm than good?" Ms. Moore asked Fab in a condescending tone.

"No, I never gave that a thought." Fab stared her down until she looked away.

I'd had enough and stood, my eyes sweeping the table. "Don't think I'll be forgetting this anytime soon."

"Now—" Ms. Moore reached out to grab my arm, and I wrenched away.

"You listen to me." I wanted to kick the chair back, but it had little room to move. "Don't you ever approach me again. You do, and I've got a lawyer that will make short work of you and your license." I made eye contact with everyone at the table except Fab. "I can't say this has been fun."

Fab grabbed my hand, and we wiggled out from behind the table.

"I'd like to talk later," Mother said.

When I took too long to answer, Spoon crossed his arms and growled.

I leaned down and kissed Mother's cheek. "That would be good."

Fab linked her arm in mine and forced me to walk sedately to the front door when what I wanted to do was kick off my shoes and run.

"I owe you," I told her as we waited for the elevator. "Or I can mark off a few of your IOUs."

Her eyes twinkled. "My pleasure. I like the owing part. You know, that was kind of fun, but let's get the hell out of here."

Chapter Thirty-Six

I'd like to say I followed Fab home from Mother's, but I was doing good to just keep the back of her car in sight. I'd gotten a call from Mac shortly after I got in the SUV—the lawyer had come up with a deal for Linda Pearl. I called Fab and was ready to beg her to come along, but she readily agreed. I told her we'd meet at the house, then go over to the Cottages together.

* * *

We arrived at The Cottages at the same time as a sheriff's deputy. An officer I vaguely remembered seeing about town climbed out of his patrol car and headed down the driveway. Fab backed into Mac's driveway.

Mac charged out of the office in a floral skirt and one of her overly tight t-shirts—this one proclaiming "BACON"—and met us halfway. "Someone kidnapped Svetlana," she announced, out of breath.

"I don't think the cop is going to be sympathetic once he finds out she's rubber," I said.

"Kidnapped might not be the appropriate charge." Mac sniffed. "But he's still going to have to write a report—there's the matter of breaking and entering and theft."

It didn't take long for the cop to come striding back down the driveway, mumbling to himself. He grabbed a notebook out of his car and returned to Joseph's cottage.

I patted Fab on the shoulder. "Why don't you go comfort Joseph?"

Fab snorted and jerked away. "You know perfectly well I'm not the nurturing one."

"I disagree. I think you saved me from being committed. Not sure Mother would go that far, but that's a maybe I wouldn't want to put to the test."

"That sounds like a good story I want to hear later." Mac pouted. "I'll make a note so I don't forget."

"Fab can tell you, since she was 'Star of the Day.'"

"Your mother needs a hobby. I think she doesn't know what to do with herself now that she doesn't have Liam to hover over," Mac said. "As for Joseph, got that covered—I got him a beer. That's why I'm the manager. I manage."

What? I cocked my head.

"I also got a partial license plate for the thief." She buffed her nails on her shirt. "It's either someone local or the car was stolen. Do I pony up the info to the cop or do we organize and nap

Svet back ourselves?"

"Let's move over here." I steered them to the rarely used small patio area at the front of the property. Once upon a time, it had been the barbeque area, but that had been relocated to the pool area, leaving only a large concrete table and benches. Its best feature was that one could sit and observe the entire driveway. The drawback—your butt got sore fast. "I prefer stories that start at the beginning."

"Don't get all excited. I don't know that much. What I do know is I think Svet's endangered." She glared at the bench before smoothing her skirt down and sitting. She hoisted up one leg to retie her tennis shoe, which had some bauble tied to the string.

I eyed it from the corner of my eye, trying to figure out what it was, but didn't ask because I didn't want a lengthy demonstration. If there was a way for Mac to bedazzle her shoes, she was all in.

"Get to it," Fab ordered.

Mac scowled at her. "The urinator next door ran over. He witnessed the whole thing, hanging out his bathroom window, you know, while he was doing his business." She turned up her nose.

"I don't want to think about it," I said.

"What did he actually see?" Fab asked impatiently.

"A drunk drove in erratically, left his pickup running. Neighbor claimed Joseph must have left his door unlocked, because the man went right in and came back out with Svet slung over his shoulder. He swore she only had one arm, and the thief pitched her in the back of the truck bed and backed out, rolling over the planter." Mac pointed across the driveway. "He got a partial, says he has a photographic memory."

"I'll bet," Fab murmured.

"What did he want for all his helpfulness?" I asked. "You know he doesn't like us since we complain about his...hmm...habits."

"That's you he doesn't like," Mac corrected. "Me, he likes just fine. Paid him off. At first he wanted a date with Svet once we got her back. I talked him out of that, and we haggled over cash. Got him down from fifty to twenty and some snacks."

"If this were your case, Ms. PI, how would you handle it?" I asked Fab.

"Run the plate, stage a midnight rescue, impress upon the thief that Svet has friends and he'd better not set foot on this property again. Hopefully, I'd get lucky, he'd be passed out and I wouldn't have to speak to him." Fab shuddered. "Just so you know, I'll be referring any rubber blow-up doll cases FM Investigations gets to our specialist – you."

"Or we might get lucky and, if he's a drunk, he'll trade her for a bottle," I said.

"Either way, we need to get her back," Mac said. "Otherwise, Joseph will never stop his yammering. If need be, I'll handle it."

"You're not to do anything illegal or put yourself in danger," I said. "Got it?"

"Yeppers." Mac nodded.

"In fact, give me that plate number." I took out my phone and sent a text—"Run this plate, please"—entered the tag as Mac read it off, and added a smiley face to irritate GC.

"Here comes the deputy." Fab nodded in his direction.

All three of us watched as he climbed in his car and left.

"What's the update on Linda Pearl?" I asked.

"You got her a good lawyer. I like that Ruthie Grace. She got the family to come together, and they're working on a compromise that keeps Linda in her house and the family happy. Ruthie's got another client who's in strained circumstances, and her thought, since she's a bit younger than Mrs. Pearl, is to hire her as a full-time companion, which would be cheaper than the fancy home."

"Will the zombies be an issue?" I asked.

"Ms. Grace said that it didn't need to be if no one brought it up," Mac said. "She also boasted an impressive win record, which was easily checkable. I went online and read about some of her cases. Since she's local, she's someone you might want on speed dial. Bragged she knew everyone in town, sheriff's department and the like."

"Any news on Miss January's boyfriend?" I asked.

"Nestor's keeping a low profile, and I don't see much of Miss January, but when I do, she appears happy. I hope Kevin's tipster is wrong about him. She likes having a boyfriend, and besides, who knows who she'll bring home next." Mac clearly didn't like that possibility.

"And Crum?" I asked.

"He's going to be fixing the planter that got clobbered. I warned him he'd better not pilfer brick one from any of the neighbors." Mac sighed. "Informed him he had to move the gardening classes inside or disband them. Blamed it all on you." She beamed. "Got to stay one step ahead of him—he'll be cooking up some new hotshot idea; he's addicted to the drama." Mac checked her watch. "I've got to change. Going with the girls to Custer's. There's a handstand kegger tonight. Buy-in's only five dollars for all the beer you can drink."

"And if you fall on your head?" I stood, and the three of us headed across the street.

Mac grimaced. "Let's hope some good-sized men show up."

"Have fun," I said.

Fab and I waved and got into the car.

"I've never done that." Fab wrinkled her nose.

"Neither have I. Guess that means we're not that much fun."

"Didier would disagree," she said smugly.

Chapter Thirty-Seven

Dinner the night before had been cancelled due to a last-minute meeting Didier had to attend. I'd packed up the food and taken it to my house, where tonight, we planned to barbeque and hang out by the pool. We were also testing out Creole's new disguise in the hopes he could come and go from both houses.

"Fab and Didier want us to move back to the house or spend more time there, since there's more room," I said. *"Most of the family get-togethers happen at Mother's now."* Creole seemed to be considering the idea. *"The flaw in that plan is that if someone shows up without notice, you'll have to hide. The bedroom, perhaps — no one ever barges in there. Would you feel safe?"*

"I could come and go out the back. Slither down to the beach like the local repeat criminals and disappear out of sight."

"I'm familiar with that trick." I laughed. *"If you need a demonstration, I'm available."* In response to his raised eyebrow, I said, *"Not that I've done it personally."*

"I've got plenty of practice. Not running from the law either – chasing perps."

Rounding the corner to my house, I did a

double take, not used to seeing a shabby pickup sitting in the neighbor's driveway across the street. Creole had given the engine a thumbs up—he joked it hadn't knocked once and no smoke blew out the tailpipe. I suggested we think about keeping it. At first, he appeared to think I'd lost my mind, but after several moments of hesitation, he nodded.

"I'm home," I said, dumping my bag in the entry and moved into the living room.

Creole—or rather, a scruffier version of the original—stood in the doorway to the patio. "Come over here," he growled, low and deep.

"No one's going to recognize you." I turned up my nose, giving his disguise the once-over. I walked into his outstretched arms, and he hugged me until a tiny grunt escaped my lips. I sniffed his shirt in a couple of different places and tugged lightly on his faux beard. "You don't smell. Although you look like you would." I smiled up at him.

"If that was a compliment, it needs some work." He picked me up and twirled me around, then hissed and set me on my feet, brushing a hand over his ribs.

I stood on tiptoe and kissed him. He pulled me into his arms, deepening the kiss.

The front door slammed with a bang. "Anyone home?" Liam yelled.

I jumped in surprise and tried to wrench away. I didn't get far.

Liam had gone into the kitchen, grabbing a soda, and now stood in the living room, eyes locked on Creole. "Who are you?" His faced pinched as he took in Creole's appearance.

"He's...my...hmm...new boyfriend." I smiled lamely, kicking myself that I didn't have a name ready to go.

"Is this why Grandmother wants to commit you?"

Creole turned me around. "Madeline wants to do what?" he roared.

Liam did a double take and continued to stare. "You got a name?"

Creole ignored the question. "When did this happen?" His voice was still loud.

"Calm down. I... It... Yesterday, and I'm not sure what she had planned." Totally changing the subject, I said, "I'd like you to meet Liam." And to Liam, "This is...Bob."

"Are you sure?" Liam arched his eyebrow.

"Bob?" Creole mouthed. But he returned immediately to the previous subject, saying, "You should've told me." He cupped my chin, his angry eyes staring down into mine. "Let me make this clear — over my dead body will anyone ever have you committed."

Liam glared, arms crossed over his chest. Not having seen him in a while, I was surprised to see that he'd shot up and joined the over-six-foot club. He'd grown up lean and lanky from being on the cross country team. He mimicked his uncle Kevin with the windblown hair.

"Reminds me of Creole a little too much. Family member?" Liam asked. "Now that would be icky." He crossed over to me, grabbing my arm. "Excuse us, we need to have a short talk." He steered me toward the patio door.

"Madison's not going anywhere." Creole hooked his arm around my shoulders. "Icky or not, we're together." He resumed his usual low, deep voice, amusement in his eyes. "Got it, kid?"

Liam bristled. "That depends on Madison."

The door opened again, which saved me from answering when I had no clue what to say, and Fab and Didier walked into the living room.

Fab filled the awkward moment. "Thought you were at school," she said to Liam, hugging him.

"Dropped off a friend for a family birthday party. Stopped by, and I'm glad I did." He shot Creole an "I'm not going anywhere" look.

"You remember Bob," I said lamely.

"I knew it was a 'B' name." Fab grinned. She and Didier had caught on immediately that Liam had no idea he was talking to Creole.

"Why don't we all sit?" Didier suggested.

We'd been standing around, staring at one another. Fab and Didier claimed the couch, Liam one of the chairs, and Creole also sat in a chair, pulling me down on his lap.

"Did you know about Madeline's hare-brained idea?" Creole asked Fab.

Her hands shot to her hips. "You didn't tell Bob how I swooped in and saved your butt?" she demanded.

Liam's eyes shot to Fab.

"Where was that stupid husband of hers?" Creole asked.

"Sitting across from me and the shrink, looking damn uncomfortable." I sighed. "Can we talk about this later?"

"No, we can't," Creole said.

I gave a brief rundown on the cozy lunch. "Mother is getting more controlling, a trait only made worse by Spoon's influence. They both crossed the line with me today, and I won't be eager to go over there by myself for a long while."

"Hey." Didier caught Creole's attention. "If the worst had happened, we'd have sprung Madison."

"That's intense. Surprised Spoon didn't talk some sense into her." Liam leaned back against the chair cushion, shifting his gaze from one person to another.

"We should change into bathing suits and get the barbeque going." I stood, wanting the subject of Mother and her antics to go away.

"Sounds good." Creole stood and said to Didier, "I'll get the barbeque started since you prepped the food." He turned to Liam. "How about I give you a few bucks and you go get yourself a hamburger." The corners of his mouth quirked. "In other words, beat it, kid."

Liam's brown eyes bored through him as though he could see past the disguise. "Not going anywhere unless Madison says. You might want to remember that it's her house and not yours."

Creole leaned forward, an exaggerated frown on his face.

"We'd love for you to stay, wouldn't we?" I reached my hand around and pinched his butt.

"That's settled," Fab said. "Let's go change."

"Behave," I mouthed to Creole.

Creole bent. Arm around my knees, he hauled me up and over his shoulder.

"You're going to hurt yourself," I said as we headed up the stairs.

* * *

It was a warm evening, perfect for sitting out on the patio, the kind we enjoyed. Dinner went well, considering we were keeping the identity of one of the men at the table a secret. Liam interacted with the two men like it was old times. They asked about college, Creole asking several questions, which he answered.

Liam nursed the beer sitting in front of him. When I saw Didier hand him the bottle and Liam take his first sip, I informed him he was spending the night. He laughed at my "overprotectiveness." I responded, "The daybed is all yours."

Now he had Creole under a microscope, so many emotions flitting across his face. I suspected he was putting together a mental puzzle—a few more pieces, and he'd have it together. I hoped he understood the necessity of the deception and didn't stop speaking to me.

Fab waved at Liam and crooked her finger. He stood and left the guys, moving down to where we sat.

"Need you to promise you won't tell your grandmother, or anyone else for that matter, about the dirty one down there." Fab pointed at Creole.

Two pairs of intense blue eyes stared from the opposite end of the table. They had stopped their conversation to listen in.

"Hygiene, Madison." Liam rumpled his nose.

"Look how well he cleans up," I pointed out. Creole looked hot in bathing trunks, except for the ratty beard, which hadn't recovered very well from a couple shots of water.

The three of us laughed.

"Why all the secrecy? Grandmother would be happy to know you found someone. You two get along; he can barely take his eyes off you. He's not a gold-digger, is he?" Liam asked.

"You got money, babe?" Creole interrupted.

I struggled not to roll my eyes, and he smirked in return.

"You can do better," Liam whispered, which

managed to drift to the other end of the table. "Don't do...anything...with him. I can fix you up. We've got a couple of college professors that are available."

I laughed. "How are you going to pull that off? Stick around after class and ask, 'Hey, want to date my aunt? We're not exactly related, but that's a long story.'?"

"The one I'm thinking of is my friend's brother, and he's always complaining about the lack of good women. And here you are." Liam smiled devilishly.

"We should have the professor over for dinner," Fab suggested.

"Thank you, but no. Give it a little time. Bob might grow on you," I said.

"That's what I'm afraid of." Liam shuddered.

"You're so bad." I laughed.

"You can count on me to keep your secrets," Liam reassured me. "Just be careful."

The guys jumped in the pool while Fab and I cleaned off the table.

"Liam's a great kid." Fab patted my shoulder. "He's not going to be upset when he finds out everything."

"This is probably going to be one of those 'no one's going to be happy' situations."

Fab and I went back out to the patio. Creole and Didier had gotten out of the pool, and Didier was busy refilling drinks. The four of us took up two chaises overlooking the pool. Liam dragged an overly large ring into the pool and floated around.

"Got an update on the condos," Didier said. "Brad signed the closing docs on his unit. And as you know, the office unit already sold, and renovations start next week. I thought I'd have more time, but the buyer paid cash. So I've got to get out."

"You and Brad have any new projects scheduled?" I asked.

Didier shook his head. "Brad's going to call an investor meeting and announce everything."

I looked at him expectantly. Creole squeezed my hand—something must be up, and he already knew.

"There is one important item on the agenda. You have to keep it to yourself until the official announcement. Brad and I are dissolving the partnership and going our separate ways."

My mouth dropped open. "You're what?"

"We're leaving the door open to working on future projects," Didier said. "It's all amicable."

"Does this have anything to do with Bordello?" I asked.

"The man has become something of a mentor to Brad, and he now wants to do his own deals. Succeed or fail on his own."

"Why leave you out?" I asked.

"It's not like that," Didier said.

It surprised me that he didn't elaborate. There must be a reason.

"Bordello trash-talked Fab. To her face," Creole said. "Impossible to do business after that."

"Didier—" Fab beamed up at him, "—my hero, told Bordello to shut his mouth or he'd shut it for him."

"Surely it didn't end there," I said.

"Bordello laughed, telling Didier he didn't have the balls or the strength," Fab said. "Too bad we were in a restaurant at the time. Didier upended the man's chair with him in it and told him if he said one more word, he'd kick his teeth down his throat." Fab pulled Didier's head down and kissed him.

"Good thing the owner of the restaurant is a friend of mine." Didier grimaced. "He didn't get the police involved and reassured me that if there were damages, he'd make the a-hole pay."

"There's no graceful way to get back on one's feet from that position." I half-laughed. "Let's hope his ego doesn't feel the need to get even."

"Brad asked me to let it go and ignore the man if I saw him in public. He assured me Bordello would do the same."

"I've got something to share." I detailed the conversation with Corndog. "It's an exciting proposition."

"Sounds like a huge project," Creole said. "Do you want to take it on with someone you basically don't know?"

"That's why, before I make any decisions, I'm

wanting to get stellar advice from someone already established in real estate." I spoke directly to Didier. "You're my first and only choice for such advice because I trust you."

"I'd be honored and thank you for having such confidence in me, chérie. It sounds like an exciting project with a lot of potential."

"I made a copy of the presentation, and once you've read it over, we can have a meeting. How about The Bakery Café until our offices are ready?" I kicked Fab under the table.

"Ouch." She exhaled loudly. "Didier, she kicked me."

"Ohh…" Creole wiped a non-existent tear away.

Everyone laughed.

"I told Didier about Zach's building, and that we're waiting on you to get us inside. You might want to get on it. Not that I'm insinuating that you're dragging your feet," Fab added, clearly leaving the impression that I was doing exactly that.

Whatever Didier whispered, Fab grinned in response.

My eyes narrowed on her. "I'm on it."

Liam climbed out of the pool, wrapped a towel around his middle, and dragged a chair over, sitting down in front of us. "Business talk over?"

"Maybe when you graduate, you'll want to join the family business," I teased.

"Odd family, in that none of us are related. But I like it. Well…" He glanced sideways at Creole, *except for him* left unsaid.

Creole knuckle-rubbed his head.

Liam jerked away. "Keep your hands to yourself, dude. I can take you. You're in crappy shape."

I bit back my laugh but couldn't hide my smile. Creole's eyes filled with amusement. He was enjoying the back and forth. He'd make everything right with Liam. No worries there.

I stood. "There's dessert. When isn't there?" I chuckled.

Creole stood and grabbed my hand, heading for the fence. "We're going for a walk."

"I'll chaperone," Liam said.

"We're going to make out," I said.

"Eww…"

Chapter Thirty-Eight

The next morning, coffee downed, the guys filed out the door, each going off in his own direction. Before Didier left, I handed him the portfolio that Corndog had given me. I'd made a copy because I knew I'd want to review it again.

Liam wrapped his arms around me, hugging me tight. "I'll keep your secrets," he whispered in my ear. "*All* of them."

"You're welcome any time, you remember that. No matter what we're doing."

He winked and kissed my cheek, then stalked down the driveway to his Jeep, parked across the street.

I waved as he drove away. *He knows.*

My phone started ringing as soon as I crossed the threshold into the house.

Fab picked it up off the island and handed it to me, but not before checking to see who was calling. It surprised me when Corndog's picture popped up.

I barely got a greeting out before he interrupted. "Fire down on the docks. In the old residential hotel," he relayed breathlessly. "Cops say looks like a homeless person started a fire, either to keep warm or heat up their dinner."

"Keep warm? In this weather?" I hit the speaker button. "Since when do the homeless hole up in a boarded-up building? It's been warm enough to sleep on the beach." Not to mention the homeless problem was a minimal one in Tarpon Cove.

Fab flashed me a questioning look, and I mouthed "What?"

"Good news: Fire department got it put out in short order. The brick exterior survived, but the inside is a burned-out rubble. The question is whether it's still structurally sound, and I'm thinking it might be."

"Fire," I mused.

"The reason I'm calling is I want to hire you to go check out the place. Nose around, see what you can find out."

"Do you want Fab and me to pick you up so you can check it out for yourself? Or we can come by after."

"I'm fine staying out of it," he said, sounding relieved to be doing so.

"We'll drop by The Cottages after we've taken a look."

"Be careful and don't take any unnecessary chances."

We disconnected.

"My guess – arson." Fab picked up the keys and jingled them in front of my face. "Ready?"

"I'll drive." I made a fake attempt to grab the

keys out of her hand.

"Gee thanks...but *no!*" She headed to the door, slowing to grab both our bags.

We tried to shove our way out the door at the same time, banging hips. Advantage Fab. I followed her to the car.

Fab squealed out of the driveway, rocketed to the corner, and stopped long enough to turn and laugh at my look of disgust.

In retaliation, I leaned sideways and made a retching noise.

"That better be phony barf," Fab yelled.

I leaned my head back against the seat, sighing in contentment. Pranking Fab was always so much fun.

Fab zigzagged across town, taking an unexpected turn or two, and pulled up near the docks—once again, another record arrival time. She peered around the corner, noting the sole fire truck and couple of police cars, and parked at the corner for a clean getaway, if necessary.

She rested her head on her hands, still wrapped around the steering wheel. "Takes a lot of work to get boards off windows, not to mention the necessary tools. I've yet to see a homeless guy carting around a tool bag."

"Even so, I'm hoping that the fire department's working theory is correct. My other thought...incentive to sell. Burning down a building is a poor idea, though; it could have burned out the entire dock area." I perused the outside of the building. Corndog was right; it had held up well. The window openings were blackened from the fire, but none of the outside was soot-stained.

"Except…" Fab paused. "They're historical. Hence no tearing them down. But if they burn down, that's where the code becomes less restrictive. Haul away the mess and build what you want."

"Look at you." I reached over and flicked her hair. "Ms. Businesswoman spouting building codes. I'm impressed."

"I listen to everything Didier says," she said, wrinkling her nose, "even if I find it boring. First Corndog gets beat up, now arson on one of his properties… This isn't looking good. Let's hope no one ends up dead."

"Kevin's here." I slid out of the car, catching up with Fab, who had gotten out and was already on the sidewalk.

Fab pasted an insincere smile on her face. "Do I look friendly?"

I laughed. "I love that you try."

Kevin walked in our direction, and when he got close, said, "What are you two doing here?"

"This is Corndog's property, and he wanted us to stop by and make sure no one died or anything," I said dramatically.

"Arson," he declared. "No one hurt. I'll have some questions for Corndog. At least I know where to find him."

"You sticking to the homeless story for the public?" I asked.

"That was never an official story," he answered in disgust. "I'm not even going to ask where you heard that."

"How long before the building can be secured again?" I watched as firefighters hauled their equipment out the front door.

"I'll check with the fire department and let you know."

"Got any suspects?" Fab asked, not trying to hide the fact that she was taking pictures of everything.

"Unless either of you want to confess, the answer is no." Kevin arched an eyebrow. "You know something I don't, something that would make my job easier?" He started to walk away and turned back. "You can't go inside until the building's been released, and that won't be for a few hours."

Another officer yelled Kevin's name and motioned to him. With a wave, he walked quickly down the street.

Fab and I got back in the car, and I called Corndog.

"Nothing to see," I told him when he answered. I told him about my conversation with Kevin. "I've got a guy who can clean up the debris and board the place up again."

"Call me after you see inside, and I'll make up my mind based on your observations."

"You once boasted to me that you knew everyone in town. You sticking with that story?" I asked.

Corndog laughed. "Yes, missy. What do you want?"

"Heard through the grapevine that Zach Lazarro's old waterfront building might be for sale, and I want it. Can you facilitate an introduction to the owner?"

"Hmm… Can you do a fast sale?"

"You talking cash?" I asked, my mind wrapping around how much and whether it could be pulled off.

"I'm certain you could seal the deal with cash."

Fab nodded wildly.

"Make it happen, then. Fab and I will owe you."

"Nonsense, girlie. It will be my pleasure."

"I'll give you a call tomorrow," I said.

We ended the call.

"We're going to get that building," Fab said gleefully. "We need to keep the deal top secret until we have the keys in hand."

"Oh yes."

* * *

My phone rang, and Mac's picture smiled back at me.

"I got Svetlana back," she crowed happily

when I answered.

I blew out a sigh of relief. "No problems?" I pushed the speakerphone button. I'd forwarded the information about the thief's vehicle as soon as I got it and told her to offer cash.

"Butcher seems like a nice guy. Seemed surprised Joseph called the cops."

"A nice guy that steals?" I asked.

"Joseph owed him money and had been dancing him around about repayment. He thought kidnapping Svetlana would speed up the process. He went back to talk to Joseph, and the cop car was in the driveway, so he left."

"So Svetlana is back, Joseph has calmed down, and Butcher has been banned from the property?" I asked.

"Pretty much. I did pay the two hundred Joseph owed, and now he owes us. He can make payments," Mac said.

"Another job well done. Fab and I thank you, don't we?" I looked over at her.

"Yeah," Fab grunted.

"Could you schedule a couple days' reprieve from any drama?" I asked.

"I'll work on it."

I disconnected. "You're so rude," I said to Fab.

"I know and don't care," she said, trotting out her snooty voice.

"You disappointed that we weren't the ones to stage the rescue?"

"Probably a good thing. I'd have wanted to

shoot the locks off, nap Svet, and run." Fab looked pleased with herself. "Saves us from jail." She beamed.

"And I'm the crazy one."

Chapter Thirty-Nine

Creole texted, "Meet me at the beach house."

It had been a week since we'd spent any time there. When I arrived, he had a bathing suit and wrap skirt lying on the bed. I changed quickly, and we headed down to the beach. After splashing through the water, we walked up to the shore and sat facing the Gulf, watching the tame waves lap the shore.

"Miguel Santos is back," Creole said, matter-of-fact.

I *knew* he had something on his mind. I inwardly groaned, guessing it had been too much to hope Santos would drop out of sight and stay there.

"Bold as brass, making his presence known, and yet managing to elude the police. He won't be able to do it for long. Chief's not the lead on this, FBI and DEA are."

"How did you find out?"

"I contacted Help. He updated me. Didn't try to talk me into coming back. Informed me the higher ups weren't all that happy with me."

"Is there an APB out on you?" I asked.

"They're pissed, but they've got bigger fish to fry and I haven't been stupid. I've maintained a low profile and haven't tried to interfere in the case. I was right about one thing—they had someone check out your house. They didn't send Help, figuring since we were friends, he'd cover for me."

"Should I be wary of knocks on the door? Will I get hauled in and your whereabouts tortured out of me? Telling you now, I'd cave. Sorry, babe."

"You're not funny." He frowned. "I'd never allow that to happen. Besides, torture is illegal."

"Shoo," I sighed. "That's good to know."

Creole wasn't in the mood to be teased. "Called the chief because we're friends, least I thought so. It was a short and chilly conversation. He told me to give thought to my future and act accordingly."

"In other words, if you want to keep your job, start playing by the rules." I leaned my head against his shoulder. "Until you've decided, you need to be careful."

"I've taken a page out of Fab's book, getting off at different exits and looping back, eye in the rearview mirror. Didier and I had a good laugh about Fab coaching him on how to be evasive behind the wheel."

"He wouldn't admit this, but he's enjoyed some of the sneaking around. I think it even surprises him. Keeps his mind off not having a another project ready to go, which makes him a bit melancholy."

"I think in the beginning," Creole said. "But I got him to open up, stressing he didn't need to keep everything inside."

"You're a good friend." I snuggled closer. "Is there a plan to catch Santos?"

"Word has it he's planning to receive a large shipment of cocaine and heroine. The guys are ready to take out him, his guards and lieutenants. He'll be buried under a slew of charges, and he'll never see the light of day again."

My head spun with the new information. What happened to Santos disappearing into South America, never to be heard from again, and our letting the police down there deal with him? "Are you going to be part of the operation?" His hesitation had me worried. "*Creole*, you've got to tell me."

"Depends on the timing. I can't share any details. I've already told you more than I should," he said with some sympathy. "I thought about not telling you at all, thinking that was the best thing I could do for you. I changed my mind and hope it wasn't the wrong decision. You're going to have to trust me."

"What am I supposed to do? Wait around for you to die for real this time?" I wanted to be supportive, but it was hard. And hard for him, looking over his shoulder, not being in the middle of the action. My irritation faded as fast as it came on.

"What I'm asking is that you do everything I ask of you when I ask and don't argue. Our lives may depend on it. There always has to be a leader, and that's me. When Santos is behind bars, you can tell me what an unfair bastard I am."

Intellectually, I got what he was saying, but I wondered how Fab would take that speech. I smiled at her imagined reaction. "Maybe if you went back to work, they'd put you back on the case." Hopefully, they'd want a physical, which he wouldn't pass as he wasn't a hundred percent yet. "In the meantime, I'm yours to boss around."

"Chief made it clear that until I jumped through a bunch of hoops, I'd be holed up in a safe house and not part of any team. He also threw out that if one of Santos's men spotted me, Santos would get away, and there might not be another shot at him."

I didn't have anything sympathetic to say, as his not being reassigned to the case was fine with me.

"My only job is to keep you and our friends safe. Let's hope that none of Santos's men come south." He grabbed a file off the table. "I want you to know what Santos looks like." He pulled out several 8x10 color close-ups, and others taken from a distance, of a tall man with short-cropped hair dark as midnight wearing what appeared to be expensive suit pants and a crisp button-down shirt. The knuckles on both hands were tattooed with letters that made no sense, and a design disappeared up inside his sleeve. If you didn't see the tattoos, he could easily pass for a businessman, as opposed to the drug-dealing killer he was, but his hands demonstrated he was capable of committing the act himself.

Creole was impressively calm in the face of danger.

"You know how much I love you." He held out his arms. "When this is all over, we're going to become a very boring couple."

Chapter Forty

A few weeks later, during which everything had been quiet, the four of us decided on a night out. We drove down to Marathon with the plan to order our food from a seafood bar on the beach, take it to an isolated section on the sand, and eat picnic style. But the place was closed for repairs. Didier suggested we continue on to Big Pine Key, where a friend had opened a new restaurant, the Key Grill.

During dinner, a few of Didier's friends showed up and joined us, and we ended up out on the deck, having a good time under the moonlight. We closed the place and briefly discussed staying overnight, but Fab, who hadn't had a drink, assured us that she was fine to drive.

About fifteen miles outside of Big Pine Key, Fab announced without taking her eyes off the rearview mirror, "Um, guys…we got company."

Creole's eyes flew open. He spun around in the back seat and squinted through the rear window. "You sure? Which vehicle?"

Beside him, I opened my eyes and yawned. "What's going on?" I asked.

"The metallic-silver SUV," Fab said. "They've been back there for a while. Where they got on the highway, I'm not exactly sure. Every time I slow down, so do they—they've consistently stayed a short distance back in the other lane."

I turned in my seat. The SUV in question had tinted windows, wide tires, and a custom grill that shone in the moonlight. It looked brand new.

While we talked, the vehicle had come up behind us fast, but once again slowed and dropped back to follow at a discreet distance. Fab pressed down on the gas pedal, and the speedometer of the Hummer eased up to and beyond the speed limit. At midnight, other traffic was sparse to nonexistent, and except for the occasional delivery truck going south for overnight deliveries, the Overseas Highway looked lonely and desolate.

The silver SUV stayed close, increasing its speed to match the Hummer but still keeping its distance.

One eye glued to the rearview mirror, Fab said, "It's a Mercedes. I recognize the shape and make of the car."

My heart thumped hard in my chest. If this turned into a game of cat and mouse, which looked likely, could my SUV outrun the Mercedes? It wasn't a question I'd asked when purchasing the Hummer. Fab pressed down on the gas, taking the speed way past the posted limit, and the Mercedes hung on like an unshakable, elongated shadow.

From beside me, Creole's voice sounded cold and hard, like he had resigned himself to something inevitable. "We're about to find out if we're overreacting or not. Slow down, speed up, try to lose them—we'll watch their reaction," he said, removing the .45 from his shoulder holster and checking the clip.

Since Creole had found out that Santos was back, he'd ordered us all not to go anywhere without a loaded weapon, reminding us to be careful and pay attention to our surroundings. He didn't have any reason to believe Santos would show up in the Cove but wanted us on alert just in case.

"We'll go with your instincts on this," Didier replied. He too took an automatic pistol from his shoulder holster and double-checked to make sure it was fully loaded. To Fab, he said, "How far to Tarpon Cove?"

"An hour, tops," Fab said, and then added, "There's nowhere to hide out here. We're sitting ducks."

Creole took his eyes off the Mercedes and glanced quickly left and right. He cursed under his breath. "My instincts tell me that is no coincidence."

There was nothing but water stretching off into the darkness; water and the reflection of a ghostly moon shimmering upon the deceptively gentle ripples of the Atlantic Ocean. The two-lane Overseas Highway was probably the only stretch of road in the entire US that was flanked by water on both sides for over a hundred miles. There were no turn-offs, no detours, no alternative routes. No way to ditch the tail, and nowhere to hole up until we were better prepared to face an enemy.

With a guttural, internal grunt, Creole asked, regretfully, "Have I let us fall into a trap?"

I wanted to reassure him that he hadn't, and I certainly hoped it wouldn't turn out that way.

"Tarpon Cove is our only chance," Creole thought out loud. "The only way to get there is by traveling the Overseas. Am I right, Fab?"

"The only place I could possible lose the SUV would be closer to Tarpon. I don't know of any options out here," Fab said.

Was this a trap? If so, and it was Santos, then he'd chosen the moment well. The only thing left was to defend ourselves. Hopefully not to the death.

Creole turned to me. "Babe, I need you to trade places," he said softly. Over his shoulder, he called, "Didier, in the back, buddy."

I waited until Didier squeezed awkwardly into the back within the tight confines of the Hummer before moving to the front. Creole waited until I had buckled myself safely into the front passenger seat, then said, "Fab, you ready?"

I reached down and pulled my Glock out of my purse. I didn't check the clip, as I'd loaded it before leaving home.

"Ready as I'll ever be," Fab replied and swallowed hard. She had removed her Walther and had it lying between her legs. Her hands gripped the steering wheel in a white-knuckle grip.

Creole let a heartbeat skip past, then said, "Go!"

Fab rammed her foot all the way down on the gas pedal. The Hummer's engine yelped in protest, and the SUV leaped forward with a violent lurch. Instantly, the trailing Mercedes picked up speed, the driver switching its headlights to full beam, impaling the Hummer in a harsh corridor of accusing light. Within seconds, the gap between the two vehicles had closed to less than thirty feet.

Before sliding down in the seat, I flipped up the visor. Now, eye level with the side mirror, my stomach turned to stone as I watched two swarthy figures squeeze their upper bodies through the Mercedes's rear passenger windows and point something at the Hummer, their hair flapping wildly in the wind, their body language determined.

"It's Santos," Creole said. "He's found me. I suppose it was only a matter of time."

"I guess this is it, huh?" Didier said.

Fab increased her speed. Temporarily boxed in, the Mercedes weaved around a truck and fell in behind it, changing lanes, sticking close to the bumper. Fab slowed down deliberately, then suddenly accelerated. The Mercedes shot forward with a burst of speed. A truck turned in front of the Mercedes, which twisted sharply and squeaked past the truck with just inches to spare.

"Fab, get close so I can get a good shot," Creole directed. "Stay down, Madison."

Didier got into position. "I've got them in my sights."

"Damn!" Fab yelled a second later, swerving harshly away from the Mercedes, provoking an angry beep from the vehicle next to her. "Hang on! What's wrong with you two? Why didn't you shoot? They've got Uzis." She began to gently nudge the steering wheel first left, then right. The Hummer started to weave from side to side in a heaving, chassis-groaning, tire-squealing zigzag.

I covered my mouth to keep back a scream.

The first salvo of machine gun bullets missed completely. The second volley destroyed the Hummer's rear window in an enormous explosion that sent shards of safety glass flying through the interior.

Didier swore and wiped his brow.

Creole took aim and fired off three shots at the driver of the Mercedes. The windshield shattered. The Mercedes swerved for an instant, just long enough for me to catch a glimpse of the angry, twisted expression of the man in the passenger seat; then it kept on coming.

Another hail of bullets swiped the rear of the

Hummer. Two pierced the bodywork, blasting through the back seat between Creole and Didier to lodge themselves in the dashboard, the Hummer's radio disintegrating in a cloud of metal and plastic. The car filled with the biting stench of smokeless powder.

"Be careful," I yelled, on the verge of freaking out.

"A little more…little more…" Creole instructed. He fired two more rounds at the driver's side.

How long had Creole worked the Santos case? And he now had the thieving, murdering drug dealer in his sights.

"There's no way Santos is getting away this time."

I peered around the seat. Creole had the look of a man who figured his time had run out. Outmanned, outgunned, and without a chance in hell of outrunning the Mercedes, we needed to do something Santos would never expect.

Crouching down as low as he could get, Creole shouted, "Madison, hand your gun to Didier. He's out of bullets."

I passed it between the seats to Didier.

Didier nodded and exchanged his firearm for my Glock.

Barreling down the tight two-lane highway, both SUVs weaved around the occasional car.

"It's time to end this," Creole barked. He discarded his half-empty clip on the backseat and produced a full one from his back pocket. He slid it into place with a satisfying click and cocked the weapon. "On your mark, Didier," he said, giving his friend a weird, almost insane, grin.

Aiming as well as he could, Creole took a shot at the tires.

I heard a voice yell, "The cop! Get the cop— he's in the back!"

"Hold on," Fab muttered, slowing a little so the other car would come up alongside and make it easier for the guys to get off a clear shot.

"No, no, what are you doing?" Creole demanded. "Move up!"

Fab mashed on the gas, pulling ahead again. Another salvo of bullets rang out, but her zigzag tactics were paying off. Firing from a vehicle at speed and actually hitting your target was no mean feat. Especially when that target was lurching crazily from one side of the road to the other. But it worked both ways. To get a good shot at Santos, we needed to be close, very close, and damn near stationary.

"Fab!" Creole called out. "I need you to stop."

"What the hell?" she replied, shaking her head in disbelief.

"When I tell you, hit the brakes. As hard as you can. Ready?"

"No way, Creole!" Fab was screaming now, screaming and fighting to keep the Hummer on its swerving, weaving course, sweat trickling down her face and wild panic in her eyes.

"Do it, Fab!" Creole screamed back at her. "Do it now!"

Fab let out one more scream, louder and even more primeval, then took her foot off the gas and stomped on the brake pedal. Unable to brake in time, the Mercedes shot past.

"Move up!" Creole yelled.

Snorting, Fab did as she was told, now side by side with the Mercedes and trying to sneak a look at the driver's face.

Behind her, Creole let off two shots, shattering the passenger window on the Mercedes.

Fortunately, Fab was smart enough to have her own window down, avoiding any damage. Santos turned his head, gun in hand, but Fab was one step ahead of him.

"Hold on!" She slammed on the brakes again. We stopped while the Mercedes kept going, giving Didier a perfect shot at the back window.

"Come on…come on…" Creole muttered, hanging halfway out of the car to fire three shots in rapid succession. Two ricocheted off the exhaust pipe, while the last one hit the back of the Mercedes, tearing a small, clean hole in the exterior. The driver of the Mercedes goosed the gas, and the vehicle leapt forward. "Move up a little, Fab, so I can hit them."

It didn't take long for the three of us to realize that whoever was riding in the SUV with Santos was no slouch. As soon as we got close enough, shots flew from a semiautomatic, forcing us all to duck.

"Fab!" Didier shouted, checking to see if she'd been hit.

"I'm good, get them!" she yelled. "Creole? Madison?"

"Uh huh. Pull up next to them," Creole said, his weapon at the ready. As soon as Fab got us close, he took a shot. Meanwhile, Santos was clearly still trying to at least take out Fab, if he couldn't get to Creole. In all the shouting, it was hard to make out what Santos was yelling to his accomplices. I could only hope that the Mercedes was close to running out of ammunition.

Fab brought the Hummer up alongside the Mercedes and deliberately sideswiped it. Getting into position, Creole took another shot at the SUV.

Tires exploded, first one and then another, before the Mercedes swerved violently, smashed nose-first into the steel barrier, and flipped.

Fab careened across the road, narrowly missing a car, and embedded the Hummer in the railing, bringing the SUV to a stop.

Chapter Forty-One

"Let's hope this is the last car chase we're ever in," Fab groaned, rubbing her arm. "It's a good thing I don't race cars for a living." She looked around the car, taking a head count. "Is everyone all right?" she asked, sinking back against her seat.

"Yeah, Didier and I are fine," Creole said. "Need to call 911." He jumped out of the SUV, Didier on his heels.

Both men ran in the direction of the Mercedes. Creole motioned Didier back and dropped to the ground, checking out the interior, sticking his arm inside. He stood, went around to the other side, and dropped out of sight momentarily. When he stood up, he shook his head.

"Dead. That's good," Fab sighed.

I sat up, shoving my butt back against the seat, and fished my cell phone out of the pocket of my skirt.

"You okay?" Fab asked.

I nodded and said, "At least I didn't throw up."

"There was a time or two I thought…

maybe...I would."

Creole appeared in the driver's side window. "I'll make that call." He held out his hand for my phone, which I handed to him. He pushed the buttons and, after a pause, said, "There's been an incident on the Overseas, northbound between Big Pine and Marathon." He answered a couple more questions and hung up. He flicked through my phone log and made another call, turning and walking a couple feet away.

Fab grabbed some Kleenex out of the console, slid out from behind the wheel, and walked into Didier's outstretched arms. After a long hug, she dabbed at his forehead, which had bled a little but appeared to have stopped.

Since my door wouldn't open, I climbed gingerly over the console, having banged my head a good one on the dashboard a time or three. I settled sideways in the driver's seat, feet on the ledge. A few cars had come to a halt to avoid a pileup and were now inching slowly by the scene, occupants gawking out the open windows.

Creole pocketed my phone and motioned to Didier.

Fab walked around the Hummer, checking the damage, and came back to lean against the frame of the back door. "Judging by the coolant dripping from the radiator, we're going to need a tow truck. My educated guess is that the insurance company will total it out—broken windows, bullet holes, the entire passenger side wiped out."

"I'll be lucky to have insurance once they find out the Hummer was damaged in a shootout. I don't really give a damn. We're alive and unhurt, and that's all that matters to me."

For being in such a deserted spot, it didn't take long for the first police car to respond to the scene. Of course, our insane driving had probably been reported long before we called 911. Sirens could be heard in the distance.

Normally, Fab would be across the street with the guys, but the newest arrival curtailed her plans. She would want to steer away from the police investigation.

Creole met the officer as he got out of the car. After exchanging a few words, they shook hands.

"Have your identification handy. The cops may or may not ask," Fab said, reaching into her purse and extracting hers. "I don't suppose the chief is going to come to our rescue."

"The chief isn't very happy with Creole right now. Not sure how he'll feel once he hears what went down here tonight. In our defense, Santos shot first."

Two more officers showed up, along with two unmarked police cars—at least, I assumed they were, since they parked next to the patrol cars. One man got out of a truck reminiscent of Creole's, except it was blue. He must have been top dog because he shot out a few orders and the men responded.

He and one of the uniformed officers directed Creole off to one side. It made me happy that Fab and I were close enough to hear.

After introductions, it turned out he was the Chief of the Marathon police department. He asked, "What happened?"

"We were driving north on the Overseas. Fab—" he pointed, and the chief looked over and inclined his head, "—was driving. Some men pulled up next to us in a silver Mercedes and began shooting. In fear for our lives, I drew my department-issue pistol, and Didier and I fired to stop the threat and get to safety. Their car crashed."

"I'll need to confiscate all the weapons," the chief said. "I spoke briefly to your boss, and after we take everyone's statements, you're free to go home and rest. I'm asking that you come to my office voluntarily to give a detailed statement and answer questions."

"Name the time," Creole said.

"I'll most likely have questions for all of you, and we can schedule those interviews for tomorrow."

Emergency services arrived on the scene and checked everyone over, giving us all the green light.

Creole and the chief continued to talk, motioning for Didier to join them.

An Expedition rolled up. Help got out.

"Nice ride," I said, an incredulous look on my face.

"What did you expect?" he asked.

"A Dodge Dart with the windows broken out."

He laughed. "I heard you needed a ride home."

After an officer had taken Fab's and my statement, we left the guys at the scene. It was a quiet ride back to my house.

Chapter Forty-Two

As soon as Didier and Creole got home, he and I returned to the beach house in the old truck. The Hummer had been hauled to the police impound lot, where it would sit until the investigators were done with their reports. We slept in, getting up and going for a walk on the beach and coming back for lunch and a swim. It was quiet poolside without Fab and Didier, but they also needed alone time.

I stood in the kitchen, stretching my body, and wondered if the others were feeling as achy as me. I wouldn't ask, not wanting to sound whiney. I brought a cold beer and bottle of water back out to the pool, handing Creole his over his shoulder before moving around him and sitting on the chaise between his legs, facing him.

He snapped the lid of my laptop closed, leaned forward, and kissed me.

"The 'accident' made the news," Creole said with a frown. "It's big when the Overseas is closed for a few hours. After what happened, with Santos's death now making headlines, I'm mostly certain that the department will spin it as a random traffic accident. They won't want to jeopardize the rest of the case."

"I'll need to tell Mother before she reads about it online or someone tells her. It would be better coming from me. Especially the part that you're alive."

"I'll go along with however you want to handle it."

"It's better if she finds out you're alive before she sees you, so it doesn't come as a shock. But I'm afraid if I go to her condo to break the news, she'll have me carted away." I grimaced. "I'll arrange to meet her at The Crab Shack. Westins are well-behaved in public. For the most part."

"Except when a certain sassy redhead tips a few back and wants to climb on the furniture."

"So ungentlemanly of you to bring that up. I've done that, what, once? Well, maybe a few times."

He tapped the end of my nose and smiled, a second later turning serious. "Talked to Chief Harder this morning. I've been given a one-day reprieve before reporting to his office tomorrow promptly at nine. There will be agents from other agencies in attendance, and he told me that he expected me to stay after for a one-on-one with him. He ended with, 'Do not be late.'"

"He's going to want to know what your plans are. Have you decided?"

"From the tone of his voice, it won't surprise me if he sacks me on the spot. It's hard to know what to do when you don't want to either stay or go. It's not like I've got something waiting in the wings. That would make it easier."

"It's not like you can go right back to work anyway—you've yet to get a medical release. That will buy you more time."

"And a psych evaluation." Creole made a face.

"Didier is the only one in our group that no one's suggested see a shrink."

"Did you see Didier in action last night? I was impressed. He was cool and calm and deadly under pressure. So much for the pretty-boy jokes."

It rankled that I'd been the only one with nothing to contribute to last night's showdown.

"You okay?"

I leaned forward and brushed a kiss against his lips. I didn't know how the man did it, but he picked up on my every mood shift. I reached over and grabbed my phone off the side table. "While I have you here for added courage, I'm going to call Mother."

Mother answered on the second ring and said hesitantly, "Madison, how are you?"

I hit the speaker button so Creole could listen in. "Good. I'm calling to ask you to an early dinner – if you can make it, meet at The Crab Shack? I have a few things I want to catch you up on."

"A better idea would be for you to come here. I can order takeout, and we'll have privacy."

"My idea is better. I don't feel comfortable coming to your house by myself, and I'd like it to be just the two of us."

"I admit," she said, clearly hurt, "trying to force therapy on you wasn't one of my best ideas. I'm just worried about you. It won't happen again."

"I think getting together will allay a lot of your worries. Will you meet me? I'm thinking four-ish—it will be before the dinner rush and quiet at that time."

"Fine." She disconnected.

"Mother took that well, all things considered. At least I refrained from telling her 'you brought it on yourself' when I refused to come over."

Creole took my phone out of my hand, putting it back on the table, and wrapped me in his arms, hugging me. "Maybe before I slip into the restaurant undercover, I'll text you and see if it's safe to come inside. In the meantime, I'll hang out in the bar. She'll never recognize me in that beard you bought me.

I laughed. "Fab picked it out."

* * *

When I drove into The Crab Shack's parking lot, my heart beating rapidly, I saw Mother's car right off. I had hoped to beat her to the restaurant to secure a table. As usual, she was even earlier, and I knew I'd find her in her favorite spot on the outside deck. Since the dinner crowd hadn't started to filter in yet, she'd have her choice.

I'd taken care with my appearance. Fab had given my belted black tent dress and wedge sandals a thumbs up. The humidity demanded that I secure my hair in a clip.

I spotted Mother first, waving when she caught sight of me, and walked through the bar to the table. She stood, and we hugged and kissed each other on the cheek.

"You look good," she said, checking me over.

"So do you." I smiled. "As always." She had on a simple black A-line dress with low heels.

We both sat. Mother had ordered her signature Jack Daniels on the rocks. A minute later, the bartender came over, setting down a margarita in front of me. We clinked glasses.

"To getting back on track," Mother toasted.

"I have a lot to tell you."

"That's what you said. Before I left the house, the news showed the remnants of a drag race. The surviving car looked like your Hummer— not many of those in the Keys. Since I'd talked to you, I wasn't worried." Mother scrutinized my face. "I hope that you're not here to tell me you were caught up in the middle of that mess."

"Well…you're correct that it was my car." Or what's left of it. "I assure you, there was no drag racing involved."

"Another job with Fab?" Mother snapped. "Are you two waiting until you're both dead to get out of the business?"

"Fab's taking her business in a new direction. She should be the one to tell you." I sighed. "We'd been out to dinner. On the way home, we certainly didn't think we'd get in the middle of what turned out to be a chase—mostly us trying to get away from them—but it happened."

"Us? Didier, I assume? I'm surprised he went back to Fab after complaining about her lifestyle. He could find someone a little less exciting without a lot of effort."

I did my best not to roll my eyes. "Nobody thought you and Spoon were a good couple, and look how that's turned out."

Mother humphed. "The rest of the story." She downed her drink.

I was ready to follow suit but restrained myself and just took a large gulp. "We're all fine, by the way," I said in exasperation.

Mother frowned and waved her glass at the server.

"Sometimes you can't control life's events." I took a few more sips of liquid courage. "There's something I need to tell you that's rather shocking. I want you to stay calm and hear me out." The words "Creole's alive" stuck in my throat.

"Just spit it out," Mother ordered, her exasperation matching mine. "I'm tough, I can take whatever it is."

"I love you."

"This must be a doozy."

I grasped her hand, holding on. "Creole's alive," I said. "He was severely hurt, and after coming to in the hospital, he was taken into protective custody. It was decided, for the safety of the officers still undercover, to keep it secret."

"He's what?" The server had just set a new glass in front of her. She picked it up and drained half of it, ordering another before he could leave the table.

I tapped the top of my glass and smiled at the server. I'd take a cab home.

"Have you actually seen him?" Mother asked in disbelief. At my nod, she asked, "How long have you known?" Anger tinged her words.

I started with Creole's reappearance, stressing the need for secrecy, and ended with the accident, omitting any part about drug dealers and bullets from that part, since she didn't seem to know. Thankfully, the local news had left that out of the story and made no mention that our lives had been on the line.

Mother slammed her glass down on the table. "So Creole waltzes back into your life, knowing full well you could end up dead. And I thought he loved you."

My eyes filled with tears. "He does," I whispered. "And I love him."

"Was this dead driver a disgruntled client of Fab's or some felon acquaintance of Creole's who wanted to get even?"

"We'll find out everything once we read the police report."

Mother knew a dodge when she heard one and jumped to her own conclusions. "Now what?" she demanded. "Everything goes along swimmingly until the next criminal shows up at your door?"

"I thought you'd be happy to know Creole's alive."

"I am, but not at your expense."

My phone pinged, and instead of looking at the screen, I scanned the bar area. Partially hidden by a pole holding up the tiki bar sat Creole, sans disguise. I waved him over.

Mother turned. She watched as Creole crossed the room with his long-legged stride, an incredulous look on her face despite what I'd told her. She stood, and he scooped her into his arms in a long hug, kissing her on the cheek.

"It's good to see you," Mother said. "You look good for a man who's been what you've been through." Her tone relayed that she wasn't clear exactly what that was.

Creole picked up immediately on the tension. He sat down between Mother and me and relayed the events in broad strokes, starting from when he was shot. He answered her questions. Not a mention of last night, as he didn't know that she knew.

The menus sat on the table, ignored. No one seemed to have an appetite.

"You know you could've trusted me," Mother said. "I suppose Fab and Didier were in on everything from the beginning. And Brad?"

"Brad doesn't know. You can tell him." I smiled weakly, not addressing the issue of Fab and Didier and who knew what when. This get-together was already filled with enough half-truths that might come back to trip me up. Not to mention the mental energy it would take to keep my stories straight.

"The family needs to know so they won't be blindsided if they should run into you somewhere. The sooner the better." Mother paused to give her plotting some thought. "I'm going to throw a dinner party, and we'll celebrate your return."

"I'm sorry this couldn't have been handled better. There was no easy way to tell you," I said.

Creole reached across the table and covered my hand with his.

"The time to tell me was in the beginning," she snapped.

I nodded, not wanting to argue. Mother was entitled to her hurt feelings.

Mother had Creole and I leave the restaurant before Spoon arrived so she could be the one to update him. I thought we should wait, but Mother had other plans. Creole put his arm across my shoulders, leading me out of the restaurant.

Chapter Forty-Three

It had been almost forty-eight hours since I'd talked to Mother and I wasn't anxious to make the call myself, but I wanted to know what she was planning to mark Creole's return. I tried tricks and pleading with Fab to get her to call, but she ignored me, taking a book out by the pool.

Creole's meeting with the higher-ups had been delayed by two days with no explanation offered. But today was the day. Didier had left the house that morning with Creole, driving with him to Miami so Creole could bring his own truck home.

I hung over the kitchen sink, looking out the garden window. I wanted to know the minute Creole arrived. So far, it had been boring, with almost non-existent traffic, but I continued my watch.

When Fab came up behind me, I jumped and squealed.

"Creole's not going to arrive any faster just because you stand guard," she said. She ignored my annoyance and asked, "What's for dinner?"

"Let's hope you're not cooking."

"That was mean."

I flashed a devilish smile. "Made me feel a little better." I inclined my head toward the patio. "You need to get the boyfriend in here to cook us something edible...or there's always takeout."

"I assume you're talking about me." Didier appeared in the kitchen, having just come down the stairs. He strode over and tugged me away from the window, pulling out a stool. "Sit. Relax." He smiled. "I ordered pizza—it'll be here shortly."

"Where's Creole?" I asked in a whiny tone. "I had no idea his meeting would take all day, and I bet he didn't either."

"He just pulled up across the street." Didier had taken my place, keeping an eye on the window.

Fab's and Didier's cars were in the driveway. I'd contacted my insurance company about the Hummer, and they'd be letting me know the verdict once their adjustor filed his paperwork.

I jumped off the stool and raced to the front door, opening it as Creole came up the driveway. I planned to sedately meet him halfway...until he opened his arms. I ran and launched myself at him, and he held on tight, stopping us from tipping over.

"How was your day, honey?" I asked.

"It blew."

I clasped his hand in mine. "Let's go inside." I

led the way. "I'll get you something to drink. Dinner's on the way. And then a swim."

We walked into the kitchen, and Didier handed him a cold beer. "How did it go with the chief?" he asked.

I helped myself to a bottle of water and stood next to Fab.

"Ice-cold for the most part. Thawed a tad by the time I left." Creole took a long swig off his bottle. "I'm officially still on medical leave. To come back, I have to get signed off by a medical doctor and a psychiatrist."

"You decided to stay on the force?" I asked, more than a bit surprised.

"What do you think of the idea?" Creole asked, looking at each of us.

I spoke up first. "I want you to do what makes you happy." I wasn't thrilled because of the danger, but I knew about that when I got involved. It was his decision to make, and I'd support it.

"If it's what you want, go for it," Fab said.

Didier clapped him on the back.

"It isn't set in stone. By the time I hop through all the required hoops, I'll know if it's the right decision."

The doorbell rang. Didier headed for the door.

Creole quirked an eyebrow in question.

"Pizza delivery."

He gave me a thumbs up.

* * *

Once we'd finished dinner and cleared the table, we dragged the deck chairs poolside to enjoy the cool evening air.

Didier refilled my and Fab's wine glasses while Creole grabbed two cold beers.

"Most of Santos's crew is dead," Creole said, looking relieved. He handed off a beer to Didier. "No worries about any more episodes like the other night. As far as the media is concerned, it was nothing more than a traffic accident caused by a speeding driver."

"What happens to your case?" Didier asked.

"It's over. There were times I thought we'd never bring down Miguel Santos and shut down his drug distribution network. He'd proven extremely elusive in the past. Made an art of disappearing into thin air, leaving others headed to jail. And they never took a deal, knowing their lives would be over and it wouldn't be pretty. Now that the case has concluded, I hate having to hear about it second- and third-hand and read the reports." Creole let out a long sigh.

I put my arms around his shoulders and enveloped him in an awkward hug. I, for one, was happy he was home safe, but I didn't think voicing that opinion would make him feel better.

"Santos's untimely death moved up the timetable, and they changed the date of the raid, figuring if they waited, the body count would only get worse. The struggle for power began immediately and was coming to a bloody crescendo. A few of his lieutenants thought the best way to decide who would hold the power was to shoot anyone they saw as a threat."

"Who's left? Anyone with any interest in you?" Fab asked.

Didier's eyebrows shot up.

"What? We didn't go through all this not to find out how it all shook out. I know you want to know; I certainly do," Fab said.

"Me too," I said in a quiet voice.

We sat in silence, studying our drinks.

Chapter Forty-Four

"Your mother put together this dinner in record time," Fab grumbled.

Mother really had organized it quicker than usual...my guess, by strong-arming the invitees, like she did Fab. You'd think a dead man's reappearance would be incentive enough—that didn't happen every day. Fab had ignored Mother's call, but that didn't slow her; immediately after not getting an answer, she'd called Didier's phone, which really irritated Fab.

"I'm sure your family dropped any previous plans to get a look at the not-so-dead guy," Creole said humorlessly. He and I were in the back seat, his head in my lap.

Fab hustled through the security gate behind another car and pulled up in front of Mother's building. We got out and filed over to the entrance.

Instead of picking the lock, Fab entered the code. When Spoon answered, she yelled, "Open up!"

Didier nudged her, but I noticed he was smiling. He held the door for us and punched the button for the elevator. When we arrived at the top, Liam was lounging in the doorway.

"Nobody brought a lockpick?" He laughed, headed straight over to Creole, and they hugged. Liam slapped him on the back. "You okay, dude?"

"Good to see you too."

"I'm happy for you and Madison. I get why you had to keep it secret." Liam gave him a once-over. "You know, you remind me of Madison's replacement boyfriend – Bob."

"Heard old Bob wasn't big on hygiene." Creole and Liam traded smirks.

Once inside the entry, I shoved Fab in front of me, forcing her to lead the parade to where Mother and Spoon waited in the living room.

We were the first to arrive.

Spoon man-hugged Creole, making a joke that had them both laughing.

I slowed and kissed Mother's cheek on the way to a cart of non-alcoholic beverages that sat next to the wall, thinking a clear head would be better than getting sloshed, which was my first inclination.

Fab came up behind me, sticking her head over my shoulder. "Soda with lime? Boring," she said in my ear.

"Tonight's not the night to get our drunk on, although we could dominate the conversation by making asses of ourselves."

"I have never —"

"I know." I patted Fab's cheek and laughed.

Fab gave me a huge smile. "Well… maybe…once."

The front door opened, interrupting our conversation as the entry filled with voices that made their way into the living room.

I turned, expecting to see Brad and possibly Phil, but behind the two of them were James Bordello and a woman I'd never seen before. I tightened my jaw to keep it from hanging open.

"What the heck?" Fab said from behind me. She stepped up next to me. "I thought this was family only," she said, loud enough that the room went silent.

Mother appeared flustered as she greeted the newcomers, Spoon by her side. Brad clapped Creole on the shoulder, and Bordello and Didier joined them. Introductions made, they traded laughs. Their dates weren't amused.

I leaned towards Fab and asked, "Now that Brad is partnering with Bordello, we have to look at him across the dinner table?"

"Didier said you're getting better at faking sick. Now would be a good time to trot out that obnoxious noise so we can go home."

I quietly made a puking noise in her ear, and she jumped.

"What the…" she started and burst out laughing.

"Stop that." I finger-wagged. "Before we have to explain what's so funny."

Fab looped her arm in mine. "Put your friendly face on." She dragged me over to where Bordello's date sat ignored in a chair.

I introduced Fab and myself.

She responded in a soft voice, "Kat."

Fab stuck out her hand. "You ever need help getting away from Bordello—" She motioned with her shoulder. "—call one of us; we'll help."

"Aren't you two cute?" a deep male voice said behind us. "Heard my name, had to step over and see if it was anything remotely nice. You don't disappoint." He shot daggers at Fab.

Creole and Didier interrupted, Didier maneuvering Fab away before she could respond. Creole took drink orders from Bordello and Kat, hooked his arm around me, and we went back to the cart that now held two varieties of wine.

"Bordello's a little slick for my liking," Creole said. "He seemed a little too interested in digging into my background, asked too many questions, all of which I ignored."

Timers started going off in the kitchen, and Spoon snagged Creole and Didier to help him get dinner to the table. Mother had configured several small tables into one large one outside on the patio. Walking outside alone, I refrained from moving the centerpieces around. Her table setting preference was uniformity, everything matching. I'd gotten my love of mismatched things from my aunt.

Mother had opted for place cards, something she didn't usually do. We had a tendency to claim the same places at a table, no matter whose house we were at. In tonight's seating arrangement, Creole and I were seated together at one end of the table, far enough away from Bordello so I wouldn't have to engage in small talk.

Fab appeared at my side. "Seating arrangements?" She turned up her nose.

I turned to see if anyone was looking. "Hand me Liam's card." I pointed, snatching up Bordello's and trading with Fab to put the businessman across from Mother and move Liam down closer to me, where he'd have much more fun.

"If your Mother asks, I don't know anything. I'm going to go find Didier before you get me into more trouble." Fab disappeared as quickly as she'd appeared.

It would be too late by the time Mother discovered what I'd done. It was my hope that with a couple of possible people to blame, she wouldn't choose me outright. I slipped down the patio and went in a different door in time to join the others being shepherded outside to find their seats.

Creole came out of the kitchen, giving me a scrutinizing look before he strode over and pulled me into a hug. "What have you been up to?" He bit my earlobe.

"Me?" I squeaked.

"You've got that look—ha, ha I did something, good luck figuring it out. Am I wrong?"

"You're so suspicious."

He nipped at my neck in my favorite place. "You'll tell me later."

When we got to the patio doors, Didier handed Creole a wine bottle and motioned for him to fill glasses. He disappeared back into the kitchen, only to reappear a moment later, setting plates down in front of each person.

Once everyone was served and Spoon and Didier seated, Mother smiled, looking around the table and thanking everyone for coming. Her eyes stopped briefly on Liam, and she appeared confused but recovered, one eye focused on checking out the seating arrangements.

I avoided making eye contact and leaned towards Fab. "Pretend you're interested in what I'm saying," I said. "It's good practice for when you need you to do it again."

"Whatever you're talking about, I'll be collecting later." She faked a smile.

At the opposite end of the table, Spoon stood and toasted: "Welcome, family and friends."

Brad stood and raised his glass to Creole. "You owe me. I saved the day at that weird funeral of yours and managed to come up with a few nice words."

Everyone at the table laughed, which lessened some of the awkwardness.

Creole tipped his glass. "We should plan a bike ride. You two look out of shape."

That brought more laughter. Brad and Didier were relentless when it came to working out.

The dinner of stuffed salmon, asparagus, and red potatoes went off without a hitch—no fight-starting conversations and the food was excellent. Spoon, it turned out, was great in the kitchen and had cooked the meal by himself. Mother and I had stopped cooking when we moved to Florida, fine with leaving it to the guys or takeout.

I felt sorry for Kat. Bordello ignored her, and she somehow managed to make herself barely noticeable. Even Phil, who sat across from her, didn't include her in any conversation. I missed get-togethers at my house and decided I would throw a pool party soon, minus Bordello.

With dinner over, Spoon mentioned dessert and was met with 'no thank you's'. He made it about halfway down the table before dropping the question. He never made it to our end of the table.

I spoke up and said, "I'll take mine home with me."

Mother frowned.

"What? You'll have to share it with someone. Who better than your favorite daughter?" I said. Apparently not finding me amusing, she looked away without a word.

Spoon cleared his throat, and heads turned his

way. "I have a surprise for my lovely wife." He stood, reached for an envelope on a side table, and handed it to her, not breaking eye contact while she opened it. "All this family drama, she deserves a break."

Mother opened it and withdrew a card. "Ohhh," she squealed breathlessly. "We're flying to Antiqua and then will cruise the surrounding Caribbean islands." She leaned over and kissed him. "I only have two days to pack?" It was clear she'd already mentally started organizing her wardrobe. She kissed Spoon again. "You spoil me."

"Guess he's getting laid tonight," Creole whispered.

"Stop." I made a face. "We've both been so well-behaved."

"The night's not over." He leered.

Brad pushed his chair back and stood, glass in hand. "I have an announcement to make. James and I are partnering on a new project." He lifted his glass. "You'll be seeing a lot of him, since we'll be working together." He stared at Fab and me.

Fab smirked, and I looked away. Everyone congratulated the two men, but Fab and I were silent.

"Did you get the office building you wanted?" Mother asked Brad.

Phil answered for him. "No, another investor came in at the last minute." She turned her head, looking directly at me. "I can't imagine how that happened."

"Maybe it's because one of your clients is a bastard and no one wants to have any dealings with him." Heads jerked my way as my words went down the table. Mother and Spoon glared.

"Do you know who the new owner is?" Fab asked.

"A corporation," Phil snapped.

"Enough of the business talk," Mother said.

"Just one more question," I said. "You get the dock deal?" I asked Bordello, a smirk on my face.

His only show of emotion was the white-knuckle grip on the stem of the wine glass.

Phil answered for him. "Your friend, Corn, reneged on the deal."

"It's *Corndog*, and there was never a deal to renege *on*." Turning my attention to Bordello, I said, "Besides, arson and attempted murder killed any thoughts of deal-making."

Creole stood. "I have a toast." He raised his glass. "Besides the fact that I'm alive." Didier and Brad laughed. "It's good to see all of you again."

He garnered a few more laughs, but he accomplished what he wanted, steering the conversation into more neutral territory.

Individual conversations started up. Didier asked Liam about college, and he launched into a couple of entertaining stories. Everyone stopped talking to listen, and it had them all smiling, except Bordello, who shot hate stares my and

Fab's way. Kat was still off in her own world.

Spoon asked about my Hummer and offered to help me find a new one.

"A nice sedan," Mother suggested.

"I haven't heard from the insurance company." I squeezed Creole's hand under the table. He kissed my cheek and, for the second time, derailed a conversation.

I'd already gotten the name and number of a vehicle repair "artiste" in case the Hummer was salvageable. Sedan? I almost snorted. Even Mother drove a SUV.

Mother suggested that we move inside.

I leaned in to Creole and whispered, "I want to go home."

"We can't eat and run."

"Dinner has been over for a while. And I got gypped out of dessert."

"What are you going to do if we have children that are anti-sugar?"

"Take them back to the hospital because clearly there was a mix-up."

He laughed. "When I was recovering, I thought a lot about your laugh. And damn it, I missed it."

He kissed me chastely on the lips.

When we went back inside, Fab approached us, Didier at her side. "How are we getting out of here?"

"I'm going to go tell Mother that Creole's ribs are hurting." I looked up at him. "So muster up a pitiful face." I walked away, pretending I didn't hear the playacting going on behind me.

"You okay, pal?" Didier asked, putting an arm across Creole's shoulders and turning him slightly.

Spoon saw and quirked an eyebrow.

"My ribs are really killing me," Creole said, lowering his voice. "I don't want Madison to hear that I worked out more than I should. She stalks me when she thinks I'm overdoing it."

I walked over to Mother and told her the same story. "Can I take my dessert home?"

"I'll need it for those not leaving early," Mother said.

"Let's talk tomorrow, before you leave on your trip. You're going to have a fun time," I said sincerely, kissing her cheek.

"When I get back, we'll do a girl lunch," Mother suggested.

"That's always fun."

I walked over to my brother. "We're leaving. Creole overdid it again today. Really, I can't let him out of my sight. And I don't want to."

"I'm really happy for you."

"And I'm happy for you. Congrats on your new deal. Lunch soon – just the two of us," I said.

"Sounds good."

I looked at him skeptically.

"I really mean it." He laughed.

I turned and hugged Liam, who'd joined us. "Stay out of trouble."

"You too."

On the way to the door, I paused in front of Bordello. "If anything happens to my brother, I'll make sure the pieces of you that float up are too small to identify." I smiled sweetly. "Capeesh?"

"How dare you!" Bordello hissed.

"She dares a lot." Creole laughed, not amused. "Let's just agree that you ignore us and we'll do the same. Okay, pal? Great." He dragged me out the front door. "You got connections for that pieces thing?"

"You'd be surprised what you can get in exchange for a twelve-pack."

Chapter Forty-Five

Fab opened the front door and bellowed, "Car's here. Get a move on." She smirked at Creole. "No fighting about who's driving this time. The reason is obvious." Over her shoulder, I could see a suited gentleman standing next to the pristine black limousine parked in the driveway, sunshine glittering off the windshield. "More importantly, you don't know where we're going," she told him.

We had agreed that it would be fun to go away for a few days of R&R. Before many ideas could be thrown out, Fab insisted on taking over the planning, saying she didn't want to do anything cheesy after Creole mentioned Disney World. She kept the plans to herself, managing to plan the "coolest trip ever" in a couple of days. She did let it slip that she used the services of a trip planner out of Miami who owed her a favor. We were each presented with an itinerary that showed only departure and return times, "Be ready — latecomers will be left behind" in bold at the bottom. I knew she added that for Creole's benefit, as he'd threatened her with that once.

Also at the bottom were packing suggestions: tropical and casual.

Creole put his arm around me. "I understand Fab better than I used to, and that scares me a little."

The limo driver strolled through the open door like he lived there. Everyone except Fab stared in confusion. She didn't draw her Walther, so he must have been following her instructions. I'd already informed Fab that my firearms were locked up. If I needed a gun for a vacation, I didn't want to go. The man grabbed up several pieces of luggage and disappeared back outside.

Didier peered over Creole's shoulder. "Nice." He smiled at Fab.

I grabbed my purse and pushed Creole out the door. "Are you driving?" I teased Fab.

She pointedly ignored me. "Get in. We've got champagne on ice for a little toast."

"It's morning," I groaned, once again ignored.

"Wait…" Creole said. "What if this trip sucks, and we want to come home early?"

"You've got two of these." She held up her thumb. "It only takes one to snag a ride."

Didier laughed and helped her into the car, then held out his hand to me.

Low-key interior, leather benches on each side against the windows, a bar at the far end, and a large-screen television—not bad.

Creole double-checked the front door and stopped to talk to the driver on the way back to the limo. He shook his head, climbing in.

"I told him sucky tip for him if he gave out where we're headed," Fab said, immensely pleased with herself. "Trust me, this is going to be fun."

The driver headed out to the Overseas Highway, turning south. No one said a word about the last time we traveled this way.

I stretched out and laid my head in Creole's lap. Rubbing my fingers together, I said, "Five bucks on Key West."

Didier turned, looking out the window. Only water ran along both sides of the highway. "I'm in for five," he said. "Sunset Key. It's just off Key West, and there's a resort offshore that she likes."

"Yeah, yeah. It won't be that easy, will it, Miss Fabbie?" Creole eyed her. "My five is on nowheresville."

"You can't start the trip being a growly curmudgeon. You know *Fabbie* – it'll be first class all the way." I smiled up at Creole.

"Thank you." Fab sniffed. "Enough with the cutesy name. I can't shoot you now because I left my gun at home." She tossed Didier an *I told you I'd need it* look. "But I'll remember when we get home and do it then."

Didier pulled her into his arms, whispering French in her ear.

Creole covered my ears.

"Just great. Some sexy stuff and I'm missing it," I said.

Creole leaned down and whispered French in my ear.

"I don't have a clue what you just said, but it sounded hot."

"He said—"

Didier clapped his hand over Fab's mouth.

Her look of frustration had us laughing.

* * *

I checked my watch twice. It registered the same time both times I looked at it, the downside of never setting it. My phone sat at the bottom of my purse, turned off.

"Well over an hour," Creole said in my ear as the driver turned off the highway. Several turns later, he pulled onto an airstrip and stopped not far from a helicopter with its door open and steps down.

We got out, and Fab separated from us and walked over to talk to the pilot. She waved us over and climbed the steps, settling into a seat next to the window.

The rest of us followed.

Halfway up the steps, I asked the pilot, "What about our luggage?"

"It's going over by boat." He motioned to a van pulled up behind the limo, the back doors open and our luggage being loaded.

"I hope when it's our turn to plan a vacation, we don't have to outdo this," Creole said.

"You know we'll be held to the same high standard," I said in an amused tone. "No camping. Or, heaven forbid, a cheap motel, the kind where you stick in a quarter and the bed jiggles."

His mouth twitched in reluctant amusement.

As soon as we got on board, the door closed behind us. A minute later, the pilot fired up the engines, and we lifted off and flew out over the water. Several small islands could be seen below, appearing green and lush against the blue-green waters of the Gulf. A short ride later, we landed. There was nothing but an airstrip, private by my guess, as there wasn't a single sign indicating where we were. This time, a golf cart awaited us.

The man driving the cart spoke with Fab and nodded to us as we climbed in. He drove down a paved path that weaved through trees, a flourishing green landscape, and a variety of blooming tropical flowers. Coming out into the open, the road continued along a white sandy beach. Tied to the dock were a speedboat, jet skis, a catamaran, several kayaks, and my favorite, water bicycles. My guess was the small building not more than a few hundred feet away held lots more fun toys.

The ride continued past the pool and tennis courts, and a three-story oval house came into view. The driver parked at the front door, and another man—dressed in white shorts, a tropical shirt, and deck shoes—came down the wide stairs.

"Milano," he introduced himself. "I'm here to make sure you enjoy your stay." He smiled sincerely.

Catching me looking around, Fab said, "We have the whole island to ourselves. Except for the staff to spoil us."

Milano directed us through the open-air patio that wrapped around the first floor and over to the elevator, which we rode to the second floor. The doors opened into an unbelievably large living room that took up almost the entire floor, a tropical oasis decorated in soft shades of green, the furniture oversized and comfortable-looking, and from every window, water as far as the eye could see. Three sets of double doors opened out onto the veranda, which ran the length of the second level.

"I'll show you to your rooms. Your luggage will be here shortly," Milano said, directing us toward the stairs that went up to the third floor. "Unless you'd prefer the elevator." He pointed to an ornate wood door.

Fab answered for us by starting up the stairs.

Another man in similar tropical attire met us at the top of the stairs. He motioned for Fab and Didier to follow him while Creole and I followed Milano to our room, a master bedroom suite with all the traditional island details in greens and reds. The massive king-size bed overlooked a private balcony with a view of the water. From here, we could sit in one of the comfortable chairs and watch the waves lap the beach. The en-suite was almost as large as the bedroom, with a six-person tiled shower stall and oversized jetted tub.

Creole tried to tip the man, but he waved it off and left.

"This is amazing," I said. "Looks like you won the bet."

"Fab's never going to admit I won." He laughed. "I'll take Didier's money, but from you... I want something else."

"Yeah?" I taunted, putting my hands on my hips and shaking them.

* * *

Didier had informed Creole that he would see us at dinner, so after Creole and I took a nap, we changed into bathing suits, grabbed two bicycles, and explored the islands, then came back and showered.

When we came out of our room, Milano came up the stairs, directed us to the elevator, and pressed the button for the roof. To my relief, it was a smooth ride.

The doors opened to a breathtaking view on all sides. Torches were lit, and intimate seating for four had been set up on benches with upholstered backs, although the entire area could hold fifty. A full bar and kitchen occupied one side of the rooftop terrace. In the middle were four long couches that wrapped around an outdoor fire pit.

Fab was curled up on one of the couches, martini in hand, looking quite smug.

Didier had taken over bartending duties—he set a margarita down in front of me and held out a couple of bottles of beer for Creole's inspection.

"You outdid yourself," I said to Fab, sitting down across from her.

"I'd like to take all the credit." Her lips curved. "But…I had to trade a few IOUs to pull this one off. I specifically asked for a private island where we could entertain ourselves, doing whatever the heck we wanted with no chance of unwanted visitors."

"Great idea," Creole said. "We explored a little earlier but can't wait to do more."

"We have a lot to celebrate." Didier saluted with his bottle. "We survived to laugh about the car chase one day."

"I promise not to complain about your driving in the future. Or to try anyway," I said to Fab.

The guys laughed.

"Damn fine job." Creole stuck out his knuckles, which Fab ignored, but she smiled despite trying to maintain her cool.

I leaned into Creole, who'd sat down next to me, and brushed his cheek with my lips.

Fab sipped her martini. "Do you think Bordello knows that we bested him on not one but two real estate deals?"

Milano set a large tray of seafood appetizers down on the table in front of us, each one more delicious looking than the next. Another man put down china plates, napkins, and silverware.

We each chose something to try.

"I sensed a high level of frustration in Bordello when the deal was mentioned, but I think if he knew he'd have retaliated already. He's definitely a get-even guy. Phil suspects, but if she had solid proof, she'd have announced it at Mother's dinner. Brad's probably the only one who knows nothing of our involvement. If he did, he'd have confronted me."

After Didier and I had talked, he'd indicated that he was excited by Corndog's plans and wanted to be part of the project. I suggested that we present ourselves as a package deal. We met with Corndog the day before Mother's dinner. Didier had lots of questions, and I'd had a few of my own, all of them answered to our satisfaction. Then Didier and I presented our proposal, which Corndog readily agreed to, relieved to have someone like Didier, with experience in real estate development, involved. It had been a while since I'd been in the business, but I was a fast learner and excited about the Tarpon Wharf plans.

"Your acquiring Zach's old building will rankle the most," Creole said. "I overheard Madeline consoling Brad over losing the deal. He shook his head, not appearing happy—in fact, irritated it got away. The news upset her, judging by her tone of voice."

"There's no hurry to break the news," I said. "Maybe by the time Brad finds out, he'll have found another building."

"I think it was a great idea to make it the headquarters for our two businesses, FM Associates and the real estate offices," Didier said, nodding his approval. "Since there's currently no signage, I vote to keep it that way."

No one objected.

"Do I get an office?" Creole asked in a joking tone. "I'm not sure what I'd need it for."

"Yesterday, I scribbled your name on a piece of paper and taped it to one of the doors." I winked at him.

"Until I go back on the force, if any of you need help, backup, I'm available," Creole said.

"I'm going to need you around, pal," Didier said. "These two are a handful."

"We're just two women. It's not like we get in trouble *all* the time," I said.

Fab and I exchanged an amused glance, then burst out laughing.

"We should celebrate new beginnings," Creole suggested, pulling me into his arms.

Next to Fab, Didier hugged her tightly. "To friendship." He tipped his wine glass.

"Friendship." I smiled at Fab.

"Friendship." Fab smiled back.

"And love." Creole kissed the top of my head.

PARADISE SERIES NOVELS

Crazy in Paradise
Deception in Paradise
Trouble in Paradise
Murder in Paradise
Greed in Paradise
Revenge in Paradise
Kidnapped in Paradise
Swindled in Paradise
Executed in Paradise
Hurricane in Paradise
Lottery in Paradise
Ambushed in Paradise
Christmas in Paradise
Blownup in Paradise
Psycho in Paradise
Overdose in Paradise
Initiation in Paradise
Jealous in Paradise
Wronged in Paradise
Vanished in Paradise
Naive in Paradise

Deborah's books are available on Amazon
amazon.com/Deborah-Brown/e/B0059MAIKQ

About the Author

Deborah Brown is an Amazon bestselling author of the Paradise series. She lives on the Gulf of Mexico, with her ungrateful animals, where Mother Nature takes out her bad attitude in the form of hurricanes.

Remember to sign up for her newsletter to keep up-to-date with new releases and special promotions:
www.deborahbrownbooks.com

Follow on FaceBook:
facebook.com/DeborahBrownAuthor

You can contact her at Wildcurls@hotmail.com

Deborah's books are available on Amazon
amazon.com/Deborah-Brown/e/B0059MAIKQ

Made in the USA
Las Vegas, NV
24 June 2024

91420071R00216